X

D1192295

WALKING TOWARD HOME

By the Author

Child to the Waters
Our Fathers' Fields
Poems from Scorched Earth
A Carolina Dutch Fork Calendar
Fireside Tales
Poetry and the Practical

WALKING TOWARD HOME

James Everett Kibler

PELICAN PUBLISHING COMPANY
Gretna 2004

Copyright © 2004
By James Everett Kibler
All rights reserved

Library of Congress Cataloging-in-Publication Data

Kibler, James E.
 Walking toward home / James Everett Kibler.
      p. cm.
 Includes bibliographical references.
  ISBN 1-58980-226-8 (hardcover : alk. paper)
1. Southern States--Fiction. 2. General stores--
Fiction. 3. Country life--Fiction. I. Title.
PS3611. I26W35 2004
813'. 54--dc22   2004002206

This is a work of fiction. Any resemblance to actual
people or events is coincidental.

Printed in the United States of America
Published by Pelican Publishing Company, Inc.
1000 Burmaster Street, Gretna, Louisiana 70053

To all those who in all times have sought truth and told it honestly and bravely despite the displeasure of Mammon. To all who have called the good, good, and the light, light.

As we walk our own ground, on foot or in mind, we need to be able to recite stories about hills and trees and animals. . . . The sounds we make, the patterns we draw, the plots we trace may be as native to the land as deer trails or bird songs. . . We cannot create myth from scratch, but we can recover or fashion our stories that will help us to see where we are.
— Scott Russell Sanders

And the end of all our exploring
Will be to arrive where we started.
— T. S. Eliot

Contents

I	Chauncey	11
II	All Saints Eve	27
III	The Hindquarters of Bad Luck	35
IV	Rome	46
V	Kildee's Store	60
VI	Our Green Island Home	68
VII	Shot-Face's Veil	77
VIII	Nails	83
IX	Triggerfoot and Flop-Eye	97
X	Our'n	108
XI	Triggerfoot Strikes Back	117
XII	Mad as a Hornet	127
XIII	Accent Reduction	135
XIV	When Shall the Swan	154
XV	Chauncey Cuts Loose	161
XVI	One Lost Sheep	166

XVII   The Day D-HEC Made Kildee
        Take the Flypaper Down 174
XVIII   Houses on Wheels 181
XIX   The Road 194
XX   Miss Sparta Mae 201
XXI   September Gale 213
XXII   United We Stand 223
XXIII   The Eighth Circle 234
XXIV   Gilead's Balm 243
XXV   Chauncey's Christmas Dream 253
XXVI   A Mid-Winter's Tale 271

        Envoi 286

        Notes 287

WALKING TOWARD HOME

I

Chauncey

~⌾~

Chauncey Doolittle lived by himself in a big old house that the builder had tucked into the side of a hill rather than on top, thus honoring the contours of the place, so that he had both hill and home. Chauncey appreciated that.

Some folks laughed and said Chauncey lived so far back in the woods that he had to pump daylight in to make morning. But this didn't bother him at all. His was a quiet place, where being solitary did not mean being alone.

He still tried to farm, but couldn't do much at it. It wasn't a good time for farmers like him, and hadn't been for years. He didn't like machines or chemicals. He didn't want to mortgage everything to buy more land, thinking it risky, and unwise and selfish to eliminate his farm neighbours in that way. That's right, as you may have concluded, he didn't go in for agribusiness—or what the big ones had now rightly called agri-industry. Chauncey was just not cut out to be a CEO.

But then Chauncey exercised forbearance and didn't

need, or want, a lot of things. In that, the world had just passed him by. Good thing it had. For greenbacks around his farm were scarcer than kangaroos. To him the dollar was like an idol, requiring faith in the worthless unseen. For many, it took the place of God, and he wanted none of that scene.

Chauncey was ever mindful of not preferring comfort to joy. Comfort could be bought, but joy couldn't. When some of the neighbours put in central heat and air, he didn't. As he said, in their gentle climate, real winter was only a matter of some weeks, and even then there were warm days—enough to give you relief and a thaw, enough to make you appreciate the warmth when it came, and that in itself came close to bringing joy.

He was outdoors working dawn to dusk anyway. And he liked the discipline and ritual of a fireplace fire. Cutting wood gave him physical and mental pleasure. The act of laying logs at the hearth linked him with all who had done so before in the old house and in similar old houses in the neighbourhood—like a procession down the years. At times these early ones seemed to be there with him making him question in his drowse who were the living, and who the dead. He felt their hands shadow his as he lifted and lowered a log. There was something about keeping the home fires burning that did his soul good.

The thermostat and electric switch were just not his way. He said to his friend Kildee about the latter: "Instant gratification, I reckon. That's what everybody nowadays requires. Out of nowhere into nothing, they go, like flicking a switch." The light switch was for him the main symbol of the times.

As for AC, the sturdy old house, with its many tall windows and high ceilings, was built for the Carolina heat. During the hot days when the temp reached into the 90s, he simply slowed down. Sometimes he slept through the hottest hours of the afternoon. It stayed daylight enough to work till after nine, so he could make up the time. With early rising besides, he'd learned to do just fine. Folks who knew him said that if ever a man's last name didn't quite fit, it was his; but they joked that they'd never heard tell of a Doolot round these parts. Old farmer Lyman liked to say that Chauncey was busy as a bee in a molasses barrel. Unknown to Lyman, Thomas Jefferson on his own farm once had used that very same expression to describe himself. Knowing this, Chauncey would have approved. He tried to be independent, not be beholding to any system or great economy, subservient to none. And time was not money to him. It was a more precious thing.

Anyone casually acquainted with him knew that Chauncey was not enslaved to labor-saving devices. He was once heard to say, "You know, this new slavery to the machine has improved on the old by making slaves who don't even know that they are."

As for Chauncey, he'd rather do on his own. Often the gadgets didn't really save time anyway. Gas had to be bought or electric cords run. The machines didn't always crank and it sometimes took hours to get them going, longer than it would have taken to do the job. If they did finally crank, they were smelly and noisy and disturbed the peace of the place in ways Chauncey didn't approve. Machines broke, wore out, and had to be replaced. If they broke, they were the hay to fix, that is, if you could. Frustration was the usual result. But some made a life of gadgets, gadgets for the sake of gadgets. Labor-saving indeed. Chauncey said to his friend, "You know, Kildee, in the long run, in the big picture of things, machines are really less about saving labor than doing away with laborers. Men ain't cost-effective, you see."

And he'd rather deal with the devil himself than a world that denied him, and had only faith in technology. Yes, give him the devil any day and a world where Satan walked, rather than one operated by IBM, Monsanto, and genetics labs with cloning machines. DuPont and GE had nothing for him. And these *'ologists* pushing their *'isms,* and forgetting man's pitiful nature, denied the plain, simple facts of the world. They were missing the point, Chauncey felt—to him as clear as the nose on his face, missing it clean. For all their science lab reality, their world was not real, for they'd built it on the key superstition that there was nothing beyond the here and the now and what the eye could see. He had taken of late to praying a prayer learned from a friend: "Lord have mercy on dumb-ass man. Pity us, and save us from ourselves." That about summed up his attitude toward the world.

"The world seems to be gone machine and thing crazy," Chauncey would mutter, "And will spend itself within two-whoops-and-a-holler of the poorhouse." In one way or another, even some of the neighbours had taken that route too, would even buy things on time and would often wear out the thing before they'd paid up the bill. This didn't make sense to him at all. He couldn't figure why the world hadn't caught on. He reckoned the scam was now so deep and widespread so as not to be seen. As for himself, he never bought things he couldn't pay for up front. If he didn't have the money, he'd wait or do without. As to mortgaging his land, he had one saying, "Mortgaging land means losing it."

It was rare around these parts for anyone to lend money, and none borrowed. To do so depended on an abstract-based economy few of them liked. It was an un-Christian thing. Chauncey had a little under-the-breath rhyme about these matters he'd picked up from his reading several years ago. He'd gone so far as to make a little tune for it too. The words went this way:

> *With usura hath no man a house of good stone*
> *Usura is a murrain*
> *Usura blunteth the needle in the maid's hand*
> *Usura rusteth the chisel*
> *It rusteth the craft and the craftsman*
> *Contra naturam is usura.*

He always smiled as he sang his made-up song. It was

a kind of talisman that he used when he got to hankering after buying this thing or that.

In truth, Chauncey had learned to reduce his desires for the things of this world. He replaced these cravings with a relish for all manner of home desires: cured ham from the smokehouse, blackberries in summer, strawberries in spring, sweet potatoes dug from the patch in the fall, the growing flock of wild turkeys that crossed his grassy meadow, a meadow he wouldn't cut when it seeded, so they could feed their fill. Winter would be coming and they were putting on fat. The coveys of bob-whites, he loved, and served the same way, planting yellow partridge-pea and lespedeza for them, rooting out the fire ants that might take their young. He left his harvested fields unploughed in the fall for the wild things that fed there. There was plenty enough time in the spring to plough.

He could well remember the morning that he heard the first crystal cry of the bob white on his place, the hen calling in her young. He would have marked it down as a red-letter day on his calendar, if he did that sort of thing. Joe-Ed Kleckley, a wise old neighbour versed in the land, told him quite rightly that having bob-whites was a good sign, that their return to his farm was best signal of all, a token that the place was in health, back to a balance between beast and man, and that as a real farmer, he was doing better than a responsible passing-fair job. Chauncey wore that declaration more proudly than any medal of war.

When he happened upon his first covey there, their

clamorous takeoff startled him. He stood frozen stiff with amazement and his heart cut a pigeon-wing. Yes, he'd leave some extra ears in his cornfield when he harvested this fall. He'd not miss it, and he'd like to live and let live.

In fact, all the birds were wonders to him, and he had more than his share in number and variety from songbirds and warblers to owls and hawks. For the benefit of the wild creatures of the place, he multiplied the margins, giving fringes of brushy cover between pasture and deep wood. A place of contingencies, it was here that life went on best, a cradle of richness like the teeming place in the coastal marsh downstate where fresh water mingles with brine in the comings and goings of tides. Chauncey said he was just as satisfied with bob whites and a good crop of field peas or corn as the angels must be in glory.

Chauncey had this habit of girdling a tall pine in his hardwood forest, then leaving it standing to rot down and fall. This gave the pileateds, and redheads, and downies quite the good time. Some of his friends thought him strange—to waste money like that—for they counted the pines in the number of cords times the current rate a cord would bring. Chill binomials, these. It sometimes seemed to Chauncey that they had pocket calculators for eyes.

But unlike these so-called "pine tree-farmers," Chauncey loved the hardwoods, as the old Upcountry forest had been before the pine plantations had killed most of them off. "God don't plant in rows," he'd remembered an old neighbour saying long ago, and he was now in the habit of repeating that truth himself. "No, God don't plant in rows," he would affirm. While some of the more old-fashioned agreed, others of the new tree-farming sort in private shook their heads. "What would he be up to next!" they declared.

Despite his disdain for pines, Chauncey was an indefatigable planter of trees. This activity was another of the little things that he loved. He got pleasure in seeing them grow. They would struggle to send their roots down, through droughts and what would seem to be impossible clay. They would for a time mainly just sit, unless there was an unusually wet year. But then suddenly, unpredictably, they would just jump and grow several feet at a time. As Chauncey explained it, they'd found they were home, had found moisture and sustenance below the variable and shifting thin surface of earth, and knew that here they'd stay.

Chauncey had done the same and knew the same. As he became older and more thoughtful, he was coming to terms with the place and the people around. He was edging his way down. Shifting surfaces that more often than not had to do with motion were less and less in his mind. Little things, yes. When blackberries were plenty, he'd be picking, you could be sure. And plums, and the figs on his place, the apples and pears, scuppernongs sweeter than any grape known. He loved the tasselling corn and fat beans on the vine, tomatoes red and shining under the bright July sun. Nature's bounty amazed him, and the partnership of nature with man. It was second-nature instinctive for him to celebrate this in each passing day, and he did so with most every breath that he drew. Some days the rhythm of his thoughts amounted to near constant prayer. At these times the trees seemed to have a mind to him and the gentian and fringed orchid spoke.

Chauncey lived so quietly, that the cry of the pileated was the loudest sound that would be heard on his place. The streak of deer with startling white scut or raucous dancing of crows on his lawn were probably, besides him, the most motion you'd see, discounting the wind's swaying of trees.

When he had to be away, coming home always impressed him with two things he sometimes took for granted. The first was silence. Cities, even at three in the morning when they were quietest, still gave off a constant, irritating hum.

Chauncey said they were like plants dug up from the good earth and put in pots. They might grow for awhile with chemical fertilizers, and blossom to amaze the eye, but would soon wither and die, taken from the continuous soil.

The second thing to impress was the blackness of the sky that let the stars appear glorious in full majesty. In the cities, he could see the Big Dipper, but the sky around it was not black, only a muddy and sickly yellow grey. As for the Pleiades, forget it. You'd not even need bother to look. At that diminishment, Chauncey would sometimes get angry and think what man in his wilfulness had robbed himself of—what a foul-up he, in his arrogance, had made of the world. It was good to have spirit, but he was coming to understand that there was a fine line between that and wilfulness sometimes, a line that Chauncey had learned you better be extra careful with. He'd finally come to the conclusion that the first product of knowledge was humility.

For drama, in his quiet realm, Chauncey didn't need movies or the theatre. Instead, he liked the simple planting of a seed, liked seeing its tender, pale tendril break through the crust of the soil in a burst that no coiled spring of man could outdo. When he planted, he always had the Parable of the Sower in mind. He hoped for fertile soil. Then to watch the new young plant stand there stoically, in heat and drought, with cutworms and beetles around, to grow up to feed him and his, a drama enacted in silence without any fanfare, any applause. Each seed was God's primal brave gift of hope to mankind. It never ceased to be a miracle to him to feed himself from the soil, and he often declared it to those closest to him, those who'd understand what he meant.

Chauncey had become something of a philosopher in living this simple way. He didn't need books to point out the old truths. And as far as he could see, there weren't any new truths worth calling that name. He had heard from a friend at a university that some of the high-flying presidents of colleges spoke of their schools creating new knowledge, producing it as if on the conveyor belt of a fast assembly line. About this, he was flatly amused. He'd like to go about their offices and see where and how this new created knowledge would be kept, how it would be stored. Maybe in boxes? Or lead-lined cylinders? Or just a bucket under the desk?

New knowledge indeed. At least Chauncey had learned enough to know this quite well: there wasn't any new knowledge that man really would need, when the genuine old that had got him to here, was forgotten in a mad rush for the questionable new. The more the world changed and the older he grew, he was sure there was really nothing new under the sun. Even this very piece of knowledge was certainly not new—new for him perhaps, but certainly not new. He couldn't rightly claim it as his. Chauncey smiled at the thought of new knowledge as he remembered the stately old lines that had been with him now for so long: *The thing that hath been, it is that which shall be; and that which is done is that which shall be done: and there is no new thing under the sun. Is there anything whereof it may be said, See, this is new? I have seen all the works that are done under the sun; and, behold, all is vanity and vexation of spirit.*

He was sometimes truly dismayed. A mad world it was, vanity of vanities, a silly dog chasing its tail, gone further insane, with its gadgets and things and new knowledge of chemical poisons and petroleum fertilizers and nuclear waste. BETTER LIVING THROUGH CHEMISTRY! or PROGRESS IS OUR MOST IMPORTANT PRODUCT! the ads used to proclaim. It seemed to him that the ancient old enemy and lord of misrule was truly in control. The root of his name after all was "lie," and the world seemed to have swallowed it in one big gulp, hook, line, sinker, bobbing cork, and all.

Nuclear waste—a product of some more of that new knowledge, he'd suppose. And "waste" was the operative word. As it seemed to him, everything in this new time was planned to be discarded soon after purchase and then bought again new. No one could fix a thing anymore if it broke. Indeed, just buy another one new. This was the way of the industrial machine, the "industrial devourer," as Chauncey dubbed it, and which he foreswore. It had a way of eating up people as well as the earth. And as for Chauncey himself, he'd not waste a thing. A chicken or beef bone left on the edge of the wood, like an offering of old, would be gone the next morning, or at least severely chewed, and then most certainly gone the next. A dead squirrel or rodent would get recycled in quiet by a mysterious and unknown one deep in the night. No, nothing wasted on his acres, and he liked it that way. When carrion disappeared in the secret of night, he didn't ask questions of the space that the dead thing had left.

A long rainy day after a drought, the sound of the runnels coming from the roof, the gentle patter of acorns on tin in the fall, the great flash of summer lightning, electrifying the dark of the sky, the sighing of leaves and branches in a storm, daybreaks and sunsets, the play of the light as it changed hour to hour, day to day, the giant round-crested white oak on the hill that glowed burnished gold when all the world beneath it was dark, the robins that flocked there to its crown by the hundreds, their sunset-coloured plump breasts facing last rays of the sun, these were the things of his day. The chicadee's cry, mockingbird's song in the night from the rooftop, the nervous scolding and flutter of wren, cooing of dove, the diligent phoebe, the red-birds gashing the overripe figs, turkeys flocking in fields, possums in the 'simmon tree, red-tailed hawks and undulating lines of cranes and V's of geese on the wing. The nightly drama of the waning and waxing of moon, like a silent companion moving about the windows, kept him company inside, the tilted silver slipper of moon pouring, predicting a rain—all these he relished, and they never grew old or were felt two times the same. "If a man in good physical health can't love life," Chauncey's friend Kildee Henderson would say, "he's a damn sorry man, and sure to be pitied by me." And Chauncey agreed: "Such a man lived on the real edge of the world, the farthest side from joy."

Chauncey never could quite see how anyone could be bored, or how living could be deemed a burden by so many of those living today. Things had gotten bad twisted for these, he would conclude. In his mind, he conjured up images from his reading late into the previous night. It was of the Harpies, those strange avenging birds out of Dante's imagination, feeding on the living trees enclosing the shades of suicides—those who had commited violence against themselves, who will not resume their bodies at the Resurrection. "For man may not have what he takes from himself," the inspired author had said. Chauncey prayed never to be brought so low. For those who were, he had great pity; but mainly such total despair just mystified him.

Mystery—yes, for Chauncey another operative word. The stars were enough, of a clear winter night. An egg pipping to life, and the big knotty black snake at the edge to take off a few. Cyclings and recyclings, the drama as old as the land. All things unquantifiable, without the tidiness of pinning down, or easy equations, all these he loved best and consciously sought in his world. Without his doing a thing, mysteries seemed to multiply at his very feet. They were as many as the bluets, the tiny Easter flowers, that on one late winter morning would spring up overnight from the bare ground to surprise him at his feet. Sunrise and the rising of his spirit born again with it each morn were the most joyous mysteries of all, the sunlight gently increasing, bird sounds mounting, things moving, easing him awake, and to joy. How could this be? There was never a wearing out here.

Maybe it was because he woke slowly to rhythms, with no alarm clock to startle him awake. "Alarm" after all was built into the word for this particular machine. No wonder so many dreaded its sound and dreaded to rise. If doing things with such a jolt and in so precise a time-frame required the shock of alarm, and such frantic motion, he'd question his life.

Mystery. In his desultory reading last evening, he had

run across a passage from a writer newly discovered, one James Agee, dead now half a century, whose slim volume of poems spoke a language Chauncey could understand. Of the Creator, he wrote: *Not one of us has seen You, nor shall in our living time. We fumble all blind in the dark. Our very faith, the only way to truth, deludes us and ever will, into false visions and wrong attributions. Little as we know beyond the sill of death do we know God's nature, and the best of our knowledge is but a faith, the shade and shape of a dream.*

Yes, mystery, indeed, and the great unknowable. Chauncey wrote out this passage on a scrap of paper—dearer than gold this find was to him—and pinned it among others to a wall of the alcove where he kept his books and the big overstuffed wingchair in which he read.

More and more these days, Chauncey was constantly impressed by the fact that he would be in the scheme of this world only an eyeblink or two. He had taken to quoting the words of a local old wise man, now himself gone in an eyeblink from the scene. "No, you always wear out life before you exhaust the possibilities of living," the old man had said. And truly, Chauncey thought, you would. That was the supreme saddness of it all. Chauncey'd buried a family, he'd buried good many a neighbour and friend. He'd buried his furry companions, mules and horses, setters and pointers and beagles and spaniels and hounds, and was not at all ready to join them on that other dark side. Chauncey slept the sound, untroubled sleep of the guiltless, a sweet sleep unburdened by desires for more things, and made sweeter by the physical draw and pull of his muscles for most of the live-long full day.

The spring breeze of a night rustling in the curtains seemed to say, "Sleep, Chauncey, sleep. You've deserved it. Rest your tired bones." And that he did. Then the sounds of the birds rising at dawn never failed to greet him hopefully, and led him stalwartly on into yet another new day.

II

All Saints Eve

~ ∾ ~

Who shall ascend into the hill of the Lord?— Psalm 24

But for all his content, Chauncey sometimes walked in the shadow of grief. He had not always lived by himself in the old farmhouse. Here, he'd taken his new young bride near three decades ago. Her name was Hoyalene, and he'd known her from childhood on. To him, she was the beauty of her time; and the others around had also deemed her fair. It was her gentle nature that further gilded her beauty. From the day they were married in the church of their fathers a piece down the road, she wore a small golden locket on a delicate gold chain. In it she'd put a tiny picture of him that she'd cut from a crude Kodak print. That locket she wore till her death six years after her marriage to him. Now he wore her locket, albeit on a heavier chain. He had cut her face from another snapshot and placed it on top of his. He reckoned he'd wear that same locket till his own earthly day here was through. He took it off only to swim in the river and bathe.

He'd put the grief behind him now, mostly that is. The

27

rest he could centre into that tiny gold picture that hung at his chest.

She was a small person, delicate and frail. From his earliest recollections, he'd remembered her that way. She lost their first baby, prematurely born. The doctor felt it some unwise to try to have more, but this she decided against. "A matter of priorities," she said in her gentle, life-loving way. She doted on all the children around, went to them like a magnet to steel, and so it was natural to want babes of her own.

She miscarried their second child early in the pregnancy before, as the old folks said, her apron rode high, and seemed to get weaker each day. The headaches began and the doctor found cancer spread too far to cure. Now they knew it was that which had caused all the trouble with the babies. Chauncey felt the treatments were worse than the disease. She lost all her hair; and the usual indignities happened to her. It was painful for Hoyalene at the last, and Chauncey wept in the night. He sometimes woke himself crying out loud, "No. No. No." In the daytime he kept it all in and saw her through tubes. This all took its toll. Now the locket he could feel at his chest was what he had left; that and a simple granite marker in the old plot, canning jars lined on neat pantry shelves, and a closet of print dresses, breezy and summery, neat gingham and flowered, simple and pretty as she was in life. She was a flower herself, blasted by frost. He left closet alone as it was when she lived. All stayed the same.

But Chauncey had come out of that deep grief. For several years the world seemed to stop, but his friends and neighbours and kin, all of whom were kind, drew him out like from a deep, deep well, gradually, slowly, at his pace, giving him time, not intruding, waiting for some bitterness to heal.

Then one spring morning, with the smell of burning broom sage in the fields and the scent of new-turned earth in the breeze, he went back to his plough. The land reasserted its powerful hold on him. "You know, your father always loved to follow a mule," his mother had said. And so, he was learning, did he. It was one of the balancing acts, the gentling, easy-gaited, reassuring motions of life that tied him continuous in time.

Yes, he loved to stir earth; it was in his blood, like his father's and grandfather's before. The food Hoyalene had put up in the bright rows of the pantry had gone. He'd fill it again and move on. He had much catching up, cleaning up, much work on the place. Bushes had grown, weeds and brambles crept in. His fields were a fright.

He hit the ground running and had everything straight in less than a year. The neighbours were pleased to have back one of their own. Then one of them died, and again he grieved. The memory came back almost like it had just happened and that he'd lost her only the day before.

His circle got narrower but stronger throughout all of this. He was sorting things out, what mattered, what didn't, what he could do, and what he could not, what he should try to accomplish, and what leave alone. It was at this time he began to define success as the *how,* not *how much* he'd achieve. It would be measured in *being,* not *having,* as Hoyalene had always declared, remembering a saying her daddy had taught her before he had died. She was guiding him in the path of the Beatitudes, the humble blessed, the meek, the pure in heart. Before she had died, she was already with Him on the hill, which she imaged as her favorite tree-covered rise in view of her kitchen window to the east where she washed the dishes from their meals. Now she beckoned Chauncey along.

He began deeply to read, in his Bible, in the ancients, in the good thinkers who wrote from the soil. These he read by the word, not the page, and pondered their sense, and in time they became welcome dwellers with him in his old house. "The only contemporaries I want to have close just now, and that matter the most," he told old farmer Lyman down the road, "are Homer and Virgil of old." Farmer Lyman knew Homers and Virgils in other communities and in Clay Bank, the county seat town, but had to express to our Chauncey that he didn't know them particular two. He didn't know the fellow Dante either, but was acquainted with several Donnies around. To that, Chauncey smiled in the wry curious way he was developing of late, and told Lyman that maybe one day he'd have to introduce them all, if ever Homer and Virgil or Dante drove their pickups this way.

Fads affected Chauncey none. He may have been a

provincial of place, but no matter, he was never a provincial of time. The past, deep and near, lived on in the now and led to the future in the healthiest way. Hoyalene had herself been much of that mind, and he'd started to move well in her direction before she had died. She had not wanted the life supports and tubes. But that, it was beyond his will to deny, at least at that time. Today, he still wouldn't be sure. For himself, maybe, he might refuse, but for her, it would be too hard to say.

Land had a way of healing its own way. "If it don't claim you completely six feet under, and make you entirely its own, you can get in its rhythm and walk in its pace," he'd say, "leading home mostly like after a hard day in the field and no water or tea left in the jar in the shade at the end of a hard row."

He'd made it through, squeezed sweetness from little overlooked things, like the oozings from the cheesecloth strainings of fermenting scuppernongs in fall, or the strangely winey sweet puckery taste of rich handfuls of clusters of pomegranate seeds.

Pomegranate red was a red of its own, a purple-red redder than blood, and his mother had planted several trees she'd grown up from seed. A pair grew at his back door, and he remembered how well the two trees bore the month that he and Hoyalene wed, and how she ate of them her fill, hoping like people of old that her babes would be as numerous as the seeds, now for Chauncey so bitter a thought. The trees bore that same bumper crop the month that she died, and one of her last clear-minded requests at the hospital was for him to bring her a fruit still attached to its yellow branch. With his help in breaking out the sponge-cushioned red clusters, and taking the seeds to her lips, she savored their taste and their fecundity, fed from his cupped hand. How rich a pomegranate seemed, like the sun, like life itself on a deep and warm Southern soil.

Now each passing year, he celebrated the ancients' own pomegranate seed alone, a communion too much and far deeper for his finite mortal mind to fully comprehend. But celebrate it he did.

Today, it was the last day of October again, All Saints Eve, and the pomegranate trees at his door were full burgeoned with fruit. It was in days-long-since-past that the wise ancients felt that on this holy day the line between living and dead was weakened and often sometimes removed, yes, completely erased. It was then that the dead could walk unabashedly next to the living.

From the arch of a golden willowy branch, Chauncey picked him the largest ripe globe. Its color was of roseate orange, with burnished yellows and browns in patches on the sides. It had all the colors of fall. He'd seen them complete like this, only on the wings of a red-tailed hawk high above, burnished golden by a still living, albeit setting, sun, while the world was fallen into darkness below. The pomegranate's fluted puckered crinolations, where the fruit formed, looked for the world like a crown or a ruby red pursed mouth, Hoyalene's own. He looked long as he sat on the steps in the afternoon sun and turned the fruit in his hand. It was lobed in sixes and fives. He could see the faint swollen lobings that reminded him most of the shape of a perfect sand dollar he and Hoyalene had found on their single trip to the sea. The symmetrical pattern was faint, but unmistakably there, evenly, satisfyingly complete. It looked like the jewelled orbs held in the hands of ancient kings. The rosey blush on the rind was the color of Hoyalene's cheeks on the day they were wed, smiling at him beneath the intertwined rosebuds and orange blossoms of her fresh bridal wreath gracing her raven black hair. Even now, the recollection of the flowers' fragrance was realer than the rays of the sun on his skin.

Too much, too much. It was all coming back. He sank his thumb deep in the fruit. Some of the winey rich juice trickled out and spattered beside him on the steps. The bone-dry weathered wood soaked up the drops with a thirst, leaving dark spots on the grey. He took a firm grip and broke the fruit clean open in half. It tore with a sound like the rending of silk, and he buried his lips in the spongy white pulp and rich clusters of seeds. No doubt Pomona and gods of the harvest looked down on the scene.

The strange, winey taste was exactly what he needed to refresh him, revive him to life. He had it only one time of the year and could mark with its tart taste the close season—day and time. As he sat long on the steps, touching the locket through his open shirt, Hoyalene was beside him, and the sun glowed on their skin, while he prayed for the harvest, for the fellowship of those gone before, his neighbours and kin, the fertility of another year's soil, and the grace of another new day. In this vision of fullness, he found himself asking, *Who are the living, who the dead?*

He continued to sit there as he watched the sun set. It was colored with saffron, orange, and the wine dark of pomegranate seed. He thought to himself, how gloriously beautiful the sunset, forever old and new at the same time, always and never the same. And he was once again at peace with the world.

III

The Hindquarters of Bad Luck

~∿~

This fine autumn morning found two of Chauncey's neighbours from just down the road stopped at his gate. They were the main local passers on of news, and were the collectors too of the same. Very little, in this way, ever got by anymore, or never got told or heard.

Mattie Lou DeWalt and Goldie Oxner were old friends and distant cousins on their mothers' sides. They'd grown up together, had seen a lot of life, and were mostly inseparable, through six decades of raven, starve-acre days. They and their families had farmed on good land and bad, and in bad times and worse. "Some of the fields we worked," declared Goldie, "was so poor you'd have to sit on a bag of fertilizer to raise up an umbrella. And even then it would be hard." In the midst of raising a passel of younguns, she took in washing from white folks in town. The brightest clean clothes still always hung on her lines. They carried within their creases and folds the fresh smells of newly ploughed fields and old mossy forests after a rain. Passing by, the traveller would always see these clothes hanging there. Like familiar landmarks, they were—saying out to the world that Goldie was well, and so was it too.

Goldie's favorite expression was fairly common with women in these parts, "The Lord willin' and the clothes line don't fall down." With her, it took on a most literal meaning, and she got a kick out of that. "Yes, I'll be there," she'd say, "Lord willin' and the clothes line don't fall down."

Mattie Lou, close to seventy, her ten children all raised and gone, was resident hauler of sick and infirm, gatherer of groceries for those without cars, greeter of shut-ins, carrier of news and messages and tales.

The community far and wide knew both of them 'round. And as was their habit, the two women were now stopped at Chauncey's gate to carry some bit of the news and to bring him a blackberry cobbler our Goldie had made. They knew that Chauncey was still learning to fend for himself in the kitchen, and, as usual, joked with him about the latest mess that he'd made. They gave him this credit though—he cooked with imagination, and if he didn't like the result, he just covered it with cream gravy and ate it anyway. The talk bubbled on in the usual friendly, meandering way.

But today Chauncey noticed Goldie had her arm in a cast in a sling. It seems that she and Mattie Lou, in the dry deep of the summer they'd just had, had taken to fishing, just fishing every day of the week. Without rain, there wasn't much in the garden that could be done, and very little extra to can. So they'd been catching all kinds, so many, in fact, that they'd given away messes of fish for so long that the air of the neighbourhood hung heavy in the summer twilight with a faint blue haze and the smell of the cornmeal-and-flour batter of deep-fried and crispy perch, catfish, and bream. Yes, fish fries abounded from the supple cane poles of Goldie and Mattie Lou. And they didn't waste a one.

Now fully old enough to be eligible, they'd got what they called "The Paper," issued by the state as a fishing license for life—a paper that stood up quite legal before game wardens and such. This they had managed to maneuver, but they had not mastered God's sometimes onerous nature quite as smooth.

So Goldie's tale of her arm in the sling was spun out to Chauncey from Mattie Lou's little grey truck at the gate.

Our Goldie had walked to the banks of the river and had nearly stepped flat on the coils of the biggest thick, brown-patterned copperhead snake. She'd run out of her hat, her minnow bucket, and pole, and never looked back. "I could never stop till my broke arm stopped me," she exclaimed. And it did stop her cold.

She fell head over heel, and hard; but before, her great bulk had moved agilely fast in her flight, like a boat with full sails.

Mattie Lou saw it all, and she heard; for how could she not? Goldie's high mellow-voiced screams were blurred in the air, as she, bless her heart, ran so fast it stretched out the words.

"Jesus! Sweet Jesus, deliver!" she cried, time after time, moving fast for a big woman in the acre of petticoats and indigo skirts.

And now, not daunted a bit, she was fishing again this fall, her good hand on a pole, the other to steady it firm. One eye out for snakes.

Mattie Lou had a way with the news. She was a skilfull purveyor of tales. As she admitted, she'd not have to ask for the gossip, just maneuver the story her way, encouraging the flow. She could extract the tale from the teller quicker than a dentist a tooth, without having to tug and pry. In this she was expert indeed. Albeit rarely, if her skill in this way didn't work, as she said, she'd then flat-out, straightforward ask. No, not often she'd have to resort to this desperate measure to know. "I'd hate to be called just a gossip," she said. "And I'd no need to hear all the tale; fill in at the pauses, it don't all have to be said for me then to know." As the long-ago folks had told her ofttimes as she said: "Don't need the whole cow to know I've had piece of beef."

So the story of Goldie's encounter with the snake reminded Mattie Lou of another fishing tale. Like all of their stories in this part of the world, the tales she chose to tell, told you who the teller was, told you more of her values and view of the world than about those in the tale. The stories were more often than not jokes on the tellers themselves, about themselves in an awkward predicament or comic tight place. That was a part of a learned humility. Nobody liked a puffed up braggart or blow-hard, always making himself the hero of the piece.

Mattie Lou began, "Lord, back then, I could get around. I could cross a fence without getting barbed as easy as a fine lady descending a mahogany stair. It was one nice spring day on the river, when fish were biting up a blue streak, that a couple of us was down on the banks of the Tyger to get us a mess of fresh fish for a Saturday fry.

"I was a young married but already with three younguns to feed, and Eison and me were having a struggle to make it along. There was just too much to pay out, not enough coming in; and the taxes had been due and overdue on our pitiful few-acre farm. We'd had license tag to pay on our broken down truck; and the taxman had sent us a letter two times. As all of y'all know, Eison and me weren't the welfare, food-stamping kind. Some of our kin and neighbours were; but we didn't approve. Many at our Seekwell Church made a regular business of filling out forms to get this or that; but not Eison and me. This we couldn't abide. Eison and me, we'd rather work. We'd been taught a different way. Never been afeared to sweat honest sweat, or sleep tired at night.

"That day, after another tax dun in the mail, and the old truck once again just broken down, I'd about clean had enough. I told Eison I've a mind to just go fishing. So the four of us, Eison and me, Goldie and her Dan, we was getting away for an unmolested break on the banks, bank fishing with long cane poles of Eison's own cut and make. We each fished two, their ends held still on the bank by a rock. This way we got eight in the water, and one was always getting a bite. The day was perfectly quiet, not a whisper of breeze, so the sun shone silver on water as slick as glass. We all kept peace of the quiet in glow of the joy of the place and the company and the day. It didn't much matter whether or not any of us caught a fish or even got a bite.

"I'd even forgotten the bills and the threats, in the restful depth of the calm.

"We'd pulled out several big catfishes, a dozen large perch, and a passel of red-spotted bream.

"Goldie and Dan were in lull between talks, and all was right with the world. The red and white plastic corks bobbed as happy as bubbles at play. Each made rings that played ever out and crossed mingled with the circles from others nearby, like the lives of our neighbours and kin.

"Far across the river on a low hillside, we could see cows against the green of the hills, a picture still and quiet at peace. Not even their lowing could reach us across. In the sun, we were all in a state 'bout to doze.

"Into this quiet, from far off came a whine. It grew louder and harsher by graduals to our ears as it neared.

"It was one of those little putterboat gasoline motors to disturb all our days and make wakes that would wash in our lines. No mind for us there on the bank, the power of motors a prideful rebuke to those without means to have one, looking down on us four who were walkers, not riders, bank fishers with canes and without rod and reels.

"I could soon make him out—a short man in blue with a bright shiny badge, the game warden from town. He had a face that would've soured milk, a look that would've stopped an eight-day clock. For all the world, he just looked the hindquarters of bad luck. He was the law walking around on two legs and making sure we'd know, checking each fisherman for licenses as he prowled down the bank.

"I don't know what got into us gals, 'specially me, but as he got close I pretended to see him for the first time, and jumping up as fast as Goldie moved when she saw that snake, I left my poles and broke into a run. Goldie picking up on what I was doing, screamed out in her high voice, 'Quick! Mattie Lou, run! Quick! Mattie Lou, run!' You could have heard her three fields off. 'Lord God,' I screamed, 'I got to go.'

"The motor growled and grated louder and faster as it raced to crash into shore. The warden jabbed the boat's prow into our soft riverbank mud, like some deadly spear, splashed out, two-footed, wetting the pants just over his boots, and went after me fast on the run. He knew he'd caught him a law-breaker for sure. No license and thus a juicey fat fine. We fished for the fish, and, as I reckoned, he fished for us and the fines.

"It wasn't like the pair of us would take more than was seemly or flaunt nature, so the scene 'peared to us as downright mean. When the law is a badge and not kept inside in the heart, something has gone foul wrong.

"I was agile them days and having had a few minutes head start, I ran him a long merry chase. Too, all them bills back home poured the energy on. I just cut loose and set my feet free, taking all my frustrations out on making them go. And go they did. Over stumps and field rocks, through blackberry briars where rabbits wouldn't even go, through bushes and scrub-oak thickets, under barbed-wire fences, and tearing through tangles of brambroo catbriars and honeysuckle vines, I led him a merry chase for a quarter of a mile, a right far piece as it was, but through them conditions, it was more like a mile.

"Yessir, Mr. Chauncey, I gave it all I had; but he caught me at the third fence, and both of us clean out of breath. His hat was gone, taken away by a limb. One pants leg was in tatters, the victim of briars, and it looking like he'd stepped on a grenade. His shirt was soaked with sweat, as was mine; but he was in far worse condition than me. He'd a steady and fat government job often at a desk, where I worked in the fields, raised our younguns, and did most of our chores top of that. Fit as could be. But he was shingle-butted, and with no power to run. Too much desk, not enough plough.

"His curled-down thin lips uttered the words: 'License! Now!'

"I played him a pause, like a fish on a line, taking my time.

"'Your license, and now!' he said, sweat-faced between pants for his breath.

"I tried to look pitifully captured and scared, saying not a word.

"He repeated demands, sounding all the world like those duns today in the mail. Good gracious, if it didn't make my blood run hot and cold!

"'Oh, is this what you want?' I finally answered, unfolding the paper I had pinned in my blouse.

"His face was already red from labouring up the hill with a sloshing half water-filled boot; but it turned even redder then. With the sight of my license, I could see him explode from within and I was glad I'd some distance between.

"He peered at the paper for a date so close it looked like he needed a microscope or a magnifying glass, squinting his eyes and running it over and over. Then I put an end to the show. Making like to start heisting the back of my dress tail, I said, 'Mister, turn your head. I just got to go. I caint wait no more.'

"That was it for my mister in blue, chasing long after a poor modest woman who'd only been trying to answer nature's call. That bright shiney badge was just tin after all and coated with brass. The closer it got, the cheaper it showed. And the wearer was human behind his disguise. I could almost pity his red, sweating face and hard breathing—so shallow his lungs—and felt a mite sorry for his poor shingle-butted behind.

"He turned with a lurch as if a snake had bit him, and crashed through brush, bush, and briars. After awhile, I heard the furious rip of his cord starting up the little ill-tempered engine that set him back on his city-bound way, to sit at his mahogany desk, turn in reports, and fill out papers in threes and fours. For such is the way of shingle-butted men in brass badges that shine bright—from away off yonder at a distance—in the sun. All vines and no taters—just a show, but mighty dangerous just the same.

"When I got back to my poles, they were crooked askew, the corks washed to shore; and Goldie was shaking her big self with laughter. So were our menfolks too. They'd seen quite a to-do, a reg'lar dumb-show. Good gracious-a-mighty! Who needed TV, or a circus or comedy play?

"After the settling of ripples and stilling of wake from his boat, and the shaking of laughter from several retellings of the scene, the warden's skim of blue oil on the water remained. So did the foul smell of exhaust from his motor linger behind."

Goldie also remembered all this quite clearly from decades before as if it were just yesterday, and adjusted the sling on her cast-heavy arm. Mattie Lou had it just right, she said, precisely the way that she told it had been, vouching for the truth of every small detail in her tale. She capped off the story with what wisdom she could conclude from the scene.

Yes, to her, the little ill-tempered motorized man was a snake of a different hue, complete with a brass badge of power that was fake at the core, but as perilous, as deadly dangerous, as fangs, and not so easily escaped or outrun as nature's honest own. A fall broke an arm, but a fall from that type could take more than a month or a sling thus to heal.

"I reckon nowadays his type is a cross we just have to bear," Goldie concluded as she summed up melancholy observations on the same. Adjusting her sling, she remarked, "Lord willin', I'll never get in a tight where I'll see snakes again, whether of the no- or two-legged kind."

"To be safe, we just all better stay contrary," Mattie Lou replied. "Throw me in the river, and I'll float upstream." She spoke in her usual cheery, musical voice that lightened the surface of the scene, but had a deep undertow.

Yes, with these and like sage conclusions, the pair of neighbours took their leave. Wise observations all, and which Chauncey duly noted and then mulled over from time to time. To his way of thinking, there was much he could learn from these two, for they'd been there before.

IV

Rome

~⚬~

Chauncey's friend and cousin, Kildee Henderson, ran the country store some few miles away. Today, he was in his element, and in his usual pose, which meant he was standing by the big roaring pot-bellied stove, which Kildee cut the wood for himself, thinning out some of the forest around. The stove was double-cylindered and man-tall. It threw off a powerful amount of heat. A neat stack of hickory, cherry, and oak conveniently stood at the shed at the back door. Today, half a dozen gallused farmer neighbours and friends sat around the stove in straightback split-oak rockers that fanned out from the circle of warmth. The stove and its rockers were the store's centre, rather than a cash register. Kildee didn't have one of these machines. He decided against the jingle and slam of a money drawer as a sound too harsh, final, and abrupt.

"Come on in and light, sittin's a whole lot cheaper than standin'," he'd say. His "light" either signified lighten the load on your feet or stop buzzin' round like a blue-bottle fly, or both. As usual, his faithful blue-tick, walker, and red-bone hounds sat or lay in turn at his feet, and sometimes on them. If you stood for a time, one of his dogs was more likely than not to sit or put a big paw on your foot to anchor you in place.

Kildee's store was a jumble of about everything you'd need. Well-stocked shelves crowded with their motley array of general merchandise, farm necessities, and curiosities—*notions,* as they were called in earlier days. Galvanized tin pans, pails, foot tubs, and buckets hung from nails on the rafters. Split-oak baskets were hanging or tucked in to shelves. These were made down the way by old Uncle Pete, who cut and seasoned the white oak with his granddaddy's drawing knife, then shaped them into baskets of varying sizes for varying needs. Folks still called for them, though the cheaper mass-produced plastic pails of the Wal-Mart variety had seriously diminished demand. A big tin RED ROCK COLA sign showed prominently above the shelves. Sardines and saltines and pop-top cans of vienna sausage were neatly marshalled in rows; and the fragrant fresh hoop cheese sat on its stand under its glass bell, its knife ready beside. Out of the shadows projected the fourteen-point rack of a buck he and his sons had killed many years ago, the dust of time upon it; and beyond it dangled strips of molasses-coated flypaper, still there from the summer before.

They moved as they caught the slightest draft. With the shifting shadows in the store, created by a single naked light bulb over the counter, they had a ghostly effect.

Kildee's ten-year-old grandson was sweeping the floor,

doing a good job of it, pushing the broom along gently so as not to raise dust, as his grandpa had taught him. But he soon got distracted by Kildee's big black and white cat, which after a dash and circular flash around the room, allowed him to take it in his arms. There they both now sat on a stool.

On the wall over them hung a hand-lettered poster titled in big black script: 500 DOLLARS REWARD—followed by the description of a lost favorite dog:

> *Missing right front leg*
> *Blind in the left eye*
> *All teeth gone*
> *Recently castrated*
> *Answers to name of Lucky*

It was a joke poster whose humor often passed by the gullible from cities and towns as being just true. The 500 dollars had temporarily short-circuited their brains. "I'd like to find that dog and get that 500-dollar reward," they'd sometimes say. At that Chauncey and Kildee would want to smile, but kept their face muscles straight.

The old pine floor, polished by several generations now, creaked every time someone entered. Its sound was better than one of those citified PUSH TO ENTER buttons that would buzz you in with the squawk of its unfriendly noise. Far from door buttons to mash, the store didn't even have screens. Its door was always open, with no buttons or buzzers or even screen door between Kildee and the world. This also gave the dogs and children free run of the place; and that, Kildee particularly enjoyed.

This fall day had been leisurely enough with a few deer and turkey hunters in their camo stopping in to buy tobacco and tins of this and that for their trails and their stands. Some days there were so many hunters in camo in the store that it looked like the great mottled brown and green forest had come inside. But this day was slow. Russell Davis was the only hunter who had lingered long enough to tell a brief anecdote. It was about his first hunt, when he was so green, nervous, and so poor a shot that he declared, "Ding me to indignation if that day I could hit the side of a barn if the door was swinging," an old phrase they all understood. But Russell had soon left, so Kildee had time to spin out his yarn.

The presence of hunting dogs outside led to talk of the three good hounds at his feet, what they'd most recently gotten into at home with the wife and her broom. The hounds seemed to know they were being talked about, and would like to've known why. But Kildee launched then onto the subject of his dog Rome, one large, bright black lab, dead now of old age some years ago.

As a puppy, he already showed a particular eagerness for life, unusually strong even for the ever present passel of young dogs about the place. He would eat twice as much as those in the litter. Not that he'd root the other pups out of the pail, but that he'd stay longest, eating more than his fill.

And that is how he almost came to be named Stuff-Gut. But Kildee held off naming him this out of respect for that something in the pup he already saw.

Still Kildee could joke that he was going to wear out his snout rooting in the bowl to get the last smidgen there. He thought that he might soon even need a Band-Aid for a raw nose. After he fed, he'd lie flat on his back, his feet straight up in the air, and his puppy belly round like a blown-up balloon.

Then after awhile, off he'd roam. He just got into everything as a pup, far and wide, roaming here, roaming there, and learning as he went. He might get his nose bit, scratched, or burned on his perambulations; but he learned. Kildee could hardly keep him at home, not that he really tried. For "Live and let live" was Kildee's motto, and things around there, beast and man, as a result took a free ease. So roam the dog did; and that is how he eventually got the name that stuck. Roam it became, that is, when Rome was a pup.

Cousin Kildee had always been a lover of dogs; and this one in particular stood out as more than a friend. The two became inseparable like brothers, like twins. The makeshift plywood deck liner of his old pickup truck was worn concave and smooth where the dog rode whenever the wheels turned—this for near twelve years.

So through this devotion and friendship, Kildee altered the spelling of his name, when he'd had occasion to spell. *Roam* became *Rome* because the dog now in truth didn't roam, but was always with him. And, well, the dog was large and had grown into a dignity that matched the new spelling of his name.

Kildee remembered a series of things that Rome recalled to his memory. One time, strange dogs got loose onto a neighbour's pasture, where they were near about to cause a stampede. Rome hunted down the calves, and tackled them, and put his great weight on all fours to pin each down in its turn, till our Kildee and neighbours could run the troublesome dogs away.

But Rome's chief gift showed him true to his blood and his breed. He could retrieve. Could he ever retrieve! His ma could before him, and her pup got all of her talent, and more, it seemed. Rome's very life was lived to please— to answer his master's command to retrieve. Still even better than that, he obeyed the letter of command to stay. And despite his great eager and passionate Labrador's good-natured heart, he would never retrieve until told. He would sit on his haunches eager to fetch for an hour, but awaiting command so intense that he trembled from nose to his toes. Kildee always said that you could really teach a dog just about anything if the dog's nature was wanting to please his master's whim. And sure, it was true.

Kildee felt how wonderful it was that Rome was able to do what Rome was good at. He had the complete freedom to be himself, and he often wished that blessing for all women and men. "Pure joy," Kildee would say as he watched Rome do his thing.

This day, Kildee turned to one particular story of Rome that had played out right here at the store. With his shadowy shelves as backdrop, he stood at the stove, his back to the fire, with hands crossed behind to the warmth, striking unselfconsciously an orator's pose, as he faced his assembled audience in their circle of chairs.

He spoke in his usual unhurried, deadpan way, his rich voice a mellifluous monotone base that somehow magically never resulted in the slightest hint of tedium. In this way and in this familiar and homey setting, he raveled out his tale to the assembly, who gave him their more or less undivided attention.

It was a leisurely narration, full of digressions and asides. As all acquainted with Kildee could tell you, he didn't know the meaning of the word haste, and no one around the stove had any pressing business to attend to today or anywhere in particular to go. So the unraveling was easy and slow.

Both Kildee and Rome were in their prime at about the same time when this story occurred. It happened during what might have been called Kildee's good old days 'round the store. There were gas pumps here then. The shed porch covering the front door had always a visitor's car. Now the gas pumps were gone, and other than the neighbours, customers were few. Kildee laughed and called his place and community a regular hotbed of tranquility.

The place almost lost its post office about the very same time that Kildee's pumps pumped their last. The other little store down the road was still running then, though ready to give up the fight, as it finally had now some time ago.

Even then in the good times, Kildee had to make up the slack in his revenues by working on cars and trucks, out there under the porch at the front door. At the back of the store, just by the bread and tins of sardines, were black rows of gaskets and radiator hose, fanbelts and tubes, all factory-numbered with white labels for size. As a mechanic, Kildee had quite a knack, fixing what other and brighter city establishments could not. And, as in all things, Rome attended him close by his side at every step and wrench-turn of the way.

As now, so then, Cousin Kildee loved his innocent pranks and his practical jokes. His existence was full and easy and happy in life in its prime, and his spirit was generous and light. He could always find time and a reason to smile a good-natured broad smile.

Seems a man from Illinois, the Land of Lincoln, you know, was just passing near and had engine trouble. This brought him to Dee. Dee worked away right earnest on this job that wasn't all that easy or small. The traveller wasn't unfriendly, but looked around a little uneasy, even some distrustful, observing what he must have felt to be a foreign land. The hamlet was small and exotic and strange to the man; and truth to tell, as we've said, the place was a bit shabby run-down. The stranger was more comfortable on concrete and more at home shadowed by office towers, rather than trees. No doubt he'd been raised (*reared,* he would say) on Hollywood's negative notions of the South. And he was indeed far, far from home in more ways than one, and of the kilometer the least. It didn't help that he was stuck here with no way to get home—quite a fix he had gotten himself into. He looked quite as nervous as a black cat crossing a great interstate, or the proverbial cat in a room full of rockers, you might even say.

So it didn't take Kildee much time to figure all this out, and much more. He'd a built-in barometer, special at gauging the attitudes of men, tuned sharp from a score of years running this small country store, and dealing with folks and their ways day to day. "Human nature," he would say, "is more amazin' than the seasons, that's one thing for sure." And this interest led him to know.

Thus, Kildee thought he'd have him a little bit of fun, not harming or hurting, but getting in his licks just the same. A certain type of greenhorn city-folk was always fair game.

So in private Kildee made pact with his Rome. They had understanding that worked as smooth as hot-bladed ice skates on Illinois ice.

Attended by Rome (of course), Dee went to the rear of the store to the long wall of gaskets, fanbelts, and such, all mounted proper in order on nails and factory-numbered with big labels thereon. There on the floor he made a neat stack of four items he'd need. At his elbow, Rome watched every move. The top item was a new radiator hose labeled with factory number 533. The next down the stack was a large red 489 wrench. Here Dee had put a split rubber hose on the shank of the handle for Rome to retrieve. The third was a blue wrench, even larger than the red. The last, on the bottom, was a radiator hose bearing the number 553.

Rome saw before him a veritable feast of items to bring, and trembled all over at the prospect to grab and retrieve. But our Dee as was usual had given the proper orders to stay and await his commands. And Rome, as was always his way, obeyed to the letter of law.

"This here dog Rome is a miracle, you might say, a downright wonder of nature," Kildee slowly intoned in his resonant casual drawl. "He's the natural best helper any mechanic could have. He can work with me in the ways no mortal has ever been able to do. I've had to let three human boys go, who could never come up to old Rome."

All this was said casually to the visitor as Cousin Dee was thumbing for numbers intently in his thick auto parts catalogue.

Land of Lincoln made no comments to that, but looked on with suspicion, not knowing exactly what to make of Dee's comments or what to believe.

The stranger's ailing auto car was now pulled under the porch at the front of the store; and Kildee was under it on his back on the little rolling dolley he used to slide in and out. Now his voice came magnified through metal to the audience outside.

Rome sat quivering at attention by the bright red Coke chest that sat outside the front door and which hummed its assent.

Kildee had taken the parts catalogue with him under

the car; and thumbing its pages, he called, "Rome, go to the back wall and bring me a radiator hose, number 553."

Rome exploded to life and was off through the front door and to the back of the store. The floor creaked its music as he went, complete with the click and patter of toenails and paws. In a second, he had the top item of the pile firmly in his mouth and retrieved it to his master's right hand. The bright 533 shined prominently. But Kildee made no mention of the discrepancy in the numbers, as if he didn't see. Rome returned promptly then beside the Coke box, awaiting next call. He was careful not to knock over the tin, where customers put in their quarters for Cokes, any time of the night or the day, for the chest was outside.

"Rome," Kildee quietly, off-handedly called, "Bring me that red 489 wrench, if you please."

Off Rome exploded again and was back in a wink, as sure as you breathe, with the red 489. Then back to attention, beside the coin can, looking as proud as a dog with two tails, and awaiting next call.

Land of Lincoln's mouth this time fell seriously ajar.

"Sorry, old Rome," called our Kildee from under the car, "the wrench is too small. Bring the big blue 589."

In a second, Rome selected the wrench, the third of the stack, which of course was now on top of the pile, and took it straightway to our Dee.

"Rome, don't know what I'm going to do with you. You missed the number on the radiator hose. I need 553, not 533. Bring me, if you please, the 553."

Rome brought it forthwith, this time correct number 553 on the label in plain view.

Lincoln's eyes grew wide and wider with each call. With this last, he absented himself from the scene of a dog who could understand talk and could cypher and read. He just needed a moment and some fresher air to get his head straight and process the marvel he'd seen. And to figure it out, he then went to the wall at the back of the store to see where old Rome had a tangled forest of numbers on gaskets and hoses and belts to pick from between. The sight bewildered him further and did his brain nothing to soothe.

When the stranger returned to the front, Rome sat at attention, awaiting what he'd hoped was another command to fetch all the world to his dear master's hand.

"Rome sure is a solid marvel," Cousin Kildee casually intoned as our Lincoln paid up for the job.

No answer at all.

"But he never could hold a candle to his famous old sire, Buford," Kildee completed his tale, like turning a wrench one final time on a nut, or the screw-driver's last turn of a screw.

No word.

"But Rome is still young. Give him some years and some patience and real training, and he might measure up to his dad. I'm thinking of sending him off to Winnsboro to obedience school."

In truth, this about did the trick. Obedience school! But through all, to his credit, Land of Lincoln spoke not a word, and Cousin Dee kept a straight face, deadpan as deadpan could be. And Lincoln got on his way without hitch, engine purring again just like it was new.

As he left, there stood Kildee at the front open door, stroking a big grey cat he had crooked in his arm. Looking from Dee, Lincoln then gave one last earnest glance at Rome, who was still quietly seated outside by the door in the last rays of an autumn's afternoon sun, his tongue out his mouth to the side in a pant, watching the traveller go, and no doubt waiting Kildee's command to fetch, or go ride in the truck, save the cows, or whatever adventure this sweet golden day of our Lord might unfold.

From Land of Lincoln, still not a word.

But you may be sure Rome was talked of afar in lands neither our Kildee nor old Rome would ever see. The miraculous smart dog of a line of crack canine helpers of mechanics was a wonder to those who'd hear and believe. And in his zeal to convince his skeptical listeners, our Lincoln stated his case ever stronger and louder as he went. Truth to tell, some of his co-workers and companions, even his boss and best friend, counselled therapy, even a session with shrink. Heads shook around the coffeemaker and watercooler at the office, at the golf club, and even in a staff meeting or two. At one such solemn conclave, the words "leave of absence," "stress," "burn out," and "termination" were heard. Poor Land of Lincoln. His chill, deadly serious culture had caught up with him.

When Rome, with his big, gentle heart and great,

passionate zeal for his master's command, breathed his last, our Kildee shed many a hot and unashamed tear. Now himself getting on up in age, he recalled Rome today by the man-tall, red-glowing pot-bellied stove with that distant far look he'd been taken to showing of late these dwindling down years.

V

Kildee's Store

For the process of well over a century now, the three wooden steps that led to the front door of Kildee's store had been worn concave in the middle of each rung a good two inches deep, worn by the motion of feet, scraped and hardened by rough boots in winter, and polished to the sheen of old silver by summer's bare feet.

Like the old store itself, the steps were of heart pine. They and the store had once pre-existed in times long past as a lofty stand of virgin longleaf pine. The wood that came from the entire tree was as straight as a plumb line, and all as hard and durable as heartwood. The structure was built carefully, constructed with pains to last, and had lasted indeed.

The wood, though unpainted, had never turned ugly or dull, not lifeless and dry as bone as the wood made from today's quickly grown soft tree-farming pines would appear after only a short time, and would rot before it had time to weather silver grey. The old building gave off the feeling that, barring catastrophe, it was going to be some time yet before this well-made geometry of pine would return to the good rich native soil from whence it grew.

Although in this place, such a return might seem appropriate enough to the cycle of things, the store in no way showed much hurry to oblige. Effortlessly, and with the grace of all things genuine and true, it was holding out, holding on. An air of unmistakable dignity surrounded its honest, grey-weathered walls. Of it, Kildee rightly always proclaimed in his jaunty way, his bright blue eyes giving you a wink, "What you see is what you get." And get it, the neighbourhood did. Here the community gathered to catch up on and share the news, swap a few stories, reaffirm their more or less common purpose, and draw strength from the whole.

The rhythms of the seasons and generations of feet falling and lifting across this threshold, going into and out of this familiar place, had worn their impress into its marrow and core. The shoddy is fleeting, the well-made remains. The people who came inside were looking for more than plough shares and hardware and notions. As Chauncey had come to realize, in their own modest way, they were seeking out the permanent things.

In the flush old times half a dozen decades ago, just let it rain or get rough weather outside, and in through the door would come a flocking crew. Just wait for a busy day at the cotton gin across the road, with cotton stacked to the sky, and there'd be so many overalled and shuffling farmers and towheaded children that sometimes it would be the dickens just to move around. So many men would be sitting, rocking, propping, or hunkering down on bent knees that even the children or resident hounds and cats wouldn't have much place to move through in their play. The farmers would settle up, buy overalls and a new pair of shoes, maybe a box of shotgun shells or a bag of coffee, before heading back home as happy as larks.

Among the men, there wouldn't be a one who couldn't spin out a rattling good yarn. Fewer came in recent years. The cotton gin, with the collapse of the cotton market, had long since shut down, but the men and children of the neighbourhood still came, yes, diminished in number, but they still told tales that rang out true, and Kildee and Chauncey and a more or less dependable crew of lads were among those who told and continued to tell.

Yes, life was easy around the store. Like his daddy, granddaddy, and great-granddaddy before him, Kildee had only two rules. First, cussing maybe, but no profane swearing at all. Second, leave the mules and horses outside. And that was all—the sum total of prohibitions there. Free and easy and friendly, their days jog-trotted along with the gait of one behind a plough. Yes, life went on more or less smoothly to the rhythm of rockers and the pat of bare feet to banjo and fiddle on summer porches at dusk just as the screech owl calls.

Every Saturday, old Joe-Blair Graham took up his post at the store. This was the only day his children or grandchildren could get him there, for they now commuted to jobs in the town, and he lived several miles away. He no longer could drive and was in failing health. Mr. Joe-Blair was in his eighties, only half a dozen years younger than the oldest man who came there, so he had an honored station among the men.

Even at his age, and despite his heart condition that had already occasioned a mild stroke, he was as hard as a lightered stump, harder than the heart pine's core. Years of farmwork had made him that way. He had a place in the store there that he preferred, and this Kildee just set aside as Mr. Joe-Blair's own. It was a tall stool in the dark corner of the building, out of the way and undisturbed, where he could perch and do what he was known for in these parts.

That was to make handles out of hickory and oak, handles of all kinds for venerable, old tools whose handles had broken, or new ones he'd select from among the hardware in the store.

Everyone who came in would pay him a word of respect, speak a gentle bit of news, passing the time of day. He would nod pleasantly and answer slowly the wisdom of the old in his soft countryman's drawl. Like all the other things of value—land, home, name, church, and faith—the community had inherited Joe-Blair Graham from their grandparents. On this particular Saturday afternoon, as on every Saturday, he was a still point in the cluttered store, quiet and wise, patiently working a piece of hickory cut from Kildee's woods by Joe-Blair's own hands.

This particular good forest tree had already yielded Joe-Blair two proper axe handles, a short shovel handle he made for Chauncey and a handle for a pitchfork. Right from the start, this piece he was working today was a hammer handle—almost, it seemed, destined from the seed, as if the limb had lived to produce just this one perfect piece. It was straight-grained, clear of knots, sinewy, strong.

He had been quietly working at it for several hours now, and had just passed the point where the wood had taken on a kind of life, a warmth and glow, of its own. To Joe-Blair, that was a good sign, the signal he'd been working toward and waiting for all along.

He now set about trimming the handle with a jag of broken window pane he'd saved. Like most folks around these parts, he never threw anything away that he thought would one day be of possible use. He kept a King Edward cigar box full of the glass shards in his corner ready for use.

Each stroke of the glass ran the unhurried length of the wood, shaving with the grain, taking only the very thinnest shaving from the wood, paper thin. Every curl was light and delicate and fell floating as slowly as dust into the lap and creases of his wash-faded overalls.

The sound of each pass was a silken whisper of wood, picking up the echoes of the distant voice of the vanished forest that had yielded the walls now sheltering him and his friends.

Every few minutes, Joe-Blair paused and hefted the handle in his strong right hand that had not lost its grip, looking vacantly about, allowing the feel of the handle to reach him fully through the hand.

When the pitch and balance of the contour sufficiently pleased him, he began to polish it with steel wool, stopping at times in between to rub beeswax and grease into the wood with his calloused hands. When the handle was smooth and friendly to grip—warm and eager of use, responsive, and so magically wedded to palm that it became part of his hand—only then did Graham stop, only then did he know it was time.

He picked out a drop-forged steel claw-hammer head from beneath the high corner shelves in the back where the coffins were kept and opposite the glass display counter where baby shoes of white leather waited in ancient dusty boxes. He then carefully set the handle into the head with eight-penny case-hard nails. He was satisfied. It was a good job and would last. It bore the marks of his hand, his talent, and sweat.

There at the store, about 4:30 of this fine late summer Day of our Lord 2003, Joe-Blair Graham presented the tool of his hands and his making, with no outward ceremony, no flourish of comment, to his young newly married grandson, who was just commencing to build the newlyweds' first home.

Young Bob Graham had driven in to the store to take his grandpa on back home, and to see him safe inside his old farmhouse one more time.

A short seven Saturdays into the future, the stool in the

dark corner of Kildee's store would be empty. Kildee and the men would leave it sitting there that way. They saw Joe-Blair Graham to his grave dug in the neighbourhood's red clay—patiently, reverently dug by one of their own, with a shovel he'd himself put one of his best oak handles in.

Kildee left Mr. Graham's King Edward cigar box of steel wool and window pane shards where Joe-Blair had placed it casually that last day. Its fragments of glass imaged a sharp shattering and splintering for them all.

But the grandson used Joe-Blair Graham's hammer to put up the walls of a home that was destined to shelter, no doubt, many Graham great-grandsons and daughters inside. From all accounts, it looked to be a happy marriage and complete.

In all of this, it occurred to Chauncey that human nature doesn't change, that nothing really passes away, that the spirit he felt in Kildee's old store was somehow basic and unforgettable, living in all of them there down deep, but detectable like a pulse. Perhaps, he thought, it was this same inner thing that was telling him to slow down, to look more carefully at the leaves as they changed, or to listen better to the tone of a voice, to pay better attention to people's words, to read better the silent spaces in between, to listen more than speak.

As Chauncey left the store this bright autumn day, on the first Saturday after they laid Joe-Blair Graham to rest, he stopped suddenly in the middle of the quiet road across from the deserted gin with the ghosts of men, mules, and wagons abounding there, to admire the silver ribbon of river that flowed deeply beneath him down at the base of the hill. In the distance on its rise behind the store he could see Kildee's farmhouse. There he could just make out Kildee's wife, Lula Bess, sitting in a rocker on the porch. All around him trees stood stoic, patient, and still, rooted in place. Today, not even a breeze stirred them. A young sparrow hawk on a high bare branch was surveying the land in a dying season of new gold. The stubble fields, honey-brown in the play of light, were precisely the color of the inside walls of Kildee's old store. To Chauncey, the fields and store walls matched precisely in some uncanny but thoroughly fitting and satisfactory way.

Chauncey paused long, feeling the diminishing warmth of the evening sun on his upturned forehead and cheek. As he stood there at the centre of a rich world, the spreading city seemed at the true one-dimensional and impoverished edge of things, the jumping off place of a jagged-edged, empirically diminished flat world that was poisonous decades away.

VI

Our Green Island Home

These old tales are like prayers. — Donald Davidson

In Kildee's big, comfortable old farmhouse, his assembled grandchildren had now settled down a little after supper. The women folks were washing and drying the dishes and putting them away, so Kildee had the chaps in tow. He knew that a story would do the trick to move them toward bedtime, and with much less racket from them and the least energy from him.

The community had just had a week of what the old folks called a September gale. It had blown from a hurricane far off in the Gulf. Much talk in the neighbourhood was of rising rivers and a washed-out bridge. So bending to his subject, he told a rip-roaring tale of rafting on the river in flood. This pleased all the boys.

He'd just finished off what he'd probably meant to be the first installment of several, when his wife Lula Bess, drying her hands on her apron and taking it off of her neck, entered the scene.

Fact was, in her own way, she was as good a tale teller

68

as her husband, with her own smooth style, but, bless her heart, she was usually so busy she didn't have much time to tell. So this rare evening they all gathered around her to hear another story of flood. And this is the way that it went:

"'Minds me of the time y'all's great grandma Liza Francis was a bitty child. Liza was too young to go to oldfield school, so she was playing with her little brother, y'all's great-great-uncle Jim-Madison, at the old homeplace on the Island, Henderson's Island, it was called, after us—playing games on the pretty white sand in the warm sunshine, such games as they knew. On this fair day, their child's play was mainly playing leap-frog, and rolling over and over on the clean sand and to see who could get to a set mark first, such a race made up by innocent minds. It was late in the fall of 1863, and a wild war raged, but Ma Liza didn't know. Their island home was cut off from the great world out yonder with no bridges or roads, and she was too little to hear and to fear. Only difference she could tell was that all the menfolks around her were gone, gone off to war.

"Now Henderson's was a big, big green island in the river Broad. It was a complete plantation with six hundred acres of fields, and forests, and orchards, and pastures for horse and cow. The big house was on the west side of the island—a large, two-storied affair, painted white, with green shutters, tall, airy rooms, and a great walnut-staircased centre hall, spacious and grand. The great island was a mile long and narrow and lush with deposited soil. At its closest distance to shore, the river was still far and wide. An emerald green Eden it was, cut off from the busy work-a-day world.

"It was a strange, strange year to behold. Lord love you, it was cold. Ma Liza was too young to compare, but her mama, your great-great-grandmama Sallie Glenn Henderson, could tell. The cold came on so early this year, with great blankets of snow in the mountains upriver above, the snow them up there later said was blown hip deep in valleys and coves, and ice-storms too, nothing like it in annals of old. When you get November snows, they are fast and furious, and then melt just as fast.

"Down country from all that, Ma Sallie had butchered this November day, had overseen all the chores with the black folks who kept at their tasks. She had had three hogs killed, a big busy scene. Ma Liza and Jim-Madison were at play on the sand as they saw the churning brown river rise. They ran in to tell their mama in excited treble: 'The river is rising! The river is rising!' For even at that age, they'd already learned to read signs of the river. The grownups all knew how serious a matter the river's way was on their island home, and was in constant communion the same, and the children intuited too.

"But on this busy butchering day, as there had been no rain thereabouts for a considerable time, Ma Sallie just kept at her work. Not knowing about the snow-melt, she only passed the report off as child's imaginative play. The second and third times the children ran to the house and sounded alarm, she still paid no heed.

"The fourth time, Liza said: 'Mama, the river is now most up to the gate!'

"With this, Ma Sallie stopped short, looked up, and said, 'I'll go down directly as soon as I finish the meat.'

"So when the greasy work was completed, hams put on their hooks in the smokehouse to cure, and the sausages hung in herb-fragrant festoons above neat, shining, green earthen jars full of lard, she picked up her skirts and stepped out in the dark (for it had taken all day). Yes, she went by the moonlight to see the deep river beyond. But she didn't have far to go, for sure enough there was the great roaring river in swirl past the gate right up to the yard. It carried in the silvery moonlight stray bits of the farms up above. 'Good gracious!' she cried.

"Rushing back, she called all the negroes at once, and they moved to the tall second story of the house. They were crowded within, whole families there, over thirty to a room. And it was only their weight that kept the house from lifting straight off of its piers. It anchored the clapboarded great ark on its sturdy foundation, and the giant tall chimneys kept it wedged in between.

"All else was afloat. When the new morning dawned, the world was all water, in dizzying motion. The swirl of water-driven trash and washed-away remnants of farms made the scene chaos; the froth of the water looked like new milk in a pail.

"They witnessed the slave cabins break from their

stones and circle away in the fast churning tide, lost in the eddies around the far bend, and leaving only stone chimneys to show where they'd been. The chicken coops and tack shed, the mule barns and corncribs were all floating away. One by one, the outbuildings broke loose from their moorings, circled, and then disappeared in the flow.

"The great log barn was the last, with chickens lined up on the cedar shake roof, like soldiers in row.

"Yes, what had happened was the snow and the ice of the big early storms in the mountains above had all melted at once on the subsequent Indian summer days. This freaky flood had come as the result—indeed, not known of before in annals of land.

"While all the family waited on the upper floor of the house, the churning water completely covered the island. The last soil to go under was the high hillock of family graves, with its final white marble tablet slowly submerged. An empty boat ran through the great double doors of the first floor hall.

"All the cows, hogs, goats, sheep, mules, and horses were drowned. They all washed away. Only some of the chickens and peacocks, who flew to the tops of the trees, remained safe and were saved. All the large brood of Dominecker biddies Ma Sallie had raised that year with Ma Liza and Jim-Madison were all swept away.

"For five days the flood raged and kept the island covered entire. A barrel of flour washed up and caught on the stair. The houseful of people had only this and green peanuts and apples and pears that luckily were up in the attic to dry, to keep them alive.

"One of our cousins up in Kentucky had experienced a similar flood. Her big brood of younguns had lived off of rabbits washed up in the flood. Ever after, their wide place in the road was called Rabbit Hash after that time. Ma Sallie then reckoned they'd have to call their place Flour Barrel, Peanut, or maybe Dried Apple and Pear.

"Little Ma Liza remembered mainly one thing, and that was sitting on the porch roof shingles and hollering to her uncle across the wide flood on the far bank to the west that she was hungry and please to bring her some food.

"Only think of Ma Sallie's worry and how strong she endured. When her pet cow Samantha's head went under the wave, she broke down and cried; but a brave lady she was to stand up and survive such an awful, strange thing. Yes, only that brought her to tears, for she said in her resolute way: 'No need adding my tears to the water, for already we've more than a-plenty of that.'

"Under her command, not a human was lost; and they all lived through the disaster to tell all the tale.

"When the water went down, there was tables and chairs and carcasses of animals from farms far up the country above caught on uprooted trees, that scattered all around.

"Lord, in all my borned days, nothing like that has been witnessed again.

"Grandma Liza was eight in the new months of '65. Of this time, she could tell me some more. Still on the island with Ma Sallie and Jim-Madison, she then knew of the war and the killing of Henderson men.

"The island protected them while the Yanks were a-prowl. From their windows, they saw smoke from burning houses in the countryside and a blood red sky in the night. The southern horizon was ablaze on one particular February eve. It was Columbia that night that they burned, as Ma Sallie figured the same. It had to be a whole city that size to make such a light. The minions in blue had ransacked and blistered our helpless land, depleted of men. Then Winnsboro went up in flames as the 50,000 came ever closer to their island home. These men's element was fire, not the water of floods.

"Ma Sallie killed all the roosters on the place to keep them from crowing and drawing attention to them. No lights were allowed. No fires in the kitchen or hearth to be made. The few livestock were hid out of sight. The Yankees threatened with pontoons to get over there; but easier pickings of hams, gold, silver, and such kept them away in their haste and their greed. Our people, your people, hidden away, could see sunlight shining off of the enemies' rifles and swords. They were just that close, just that near to catastrophe sure.

"Ma Liza remembered all that, and her oldest dead brother's corpse as it came home wrapped in a quilt in a box to be buried on the hillock at home. She vaguely had memory of her Father Henderson's death at the outbreak of war.

"The days they were troubled, and food was scarce. Most of the black folk as could be fed tried gaunt-faced to stay on. Each year, with the dwindling of acres and crops, a few more drifted away, like their homes, and the corncribs, and barns in the great snow-melt flood.

"Your great-grandmama Sallie moved off of the island and lived a good while. She was laid in her grave on the hillock by her kin, with her kin, and mourned by her kin. She had witnessed the flood and the fires and the sorrows of so many dead, but still struggled on.

"Grandmama Liza survived to have babes of her own in a world sorely lacking in men—a half of them killed or crippled and the farms and homeplaces all deserted and gone. Her struggle to live is the reason you draw breath today.

"Trials, and troubles, and sorrows your people have seen, and yet we're still here. We stick it out as best as we can and endure. Lord willin', we'll be here to see another century through. But to this day, none have lived on the island since then. The graves on the hillock is all that's left there to show the work of men's hands. But I reckon we wear the old days in ourselves. They says your grandpa is the spittin' image of all the Henderson men, tall and straight as a plumb line. The Henderson blood is strong to tell. And all y'all little ones in one way or another carry resemblance of the same. Something to be proud of, something to tell."

After a long pause as she stirred up the fire, Lula Bess asked, "I reckon y'all still remember how your grandpa got his nickname, don't you?"

"No, grandma, how? You told us, but we forgot."

"Ah. I'll bet y'all do remember too—just want to hear me tell it again. Well, his first name is Lyles, after his grandpa and pa, but as a teenager in the gangly stage, he just shot up. His legs grew and grew and wouldn't stop. He seemed to be all arms and legs then, and didn't know what to do with them. He looked so much like the Kildee bird, all pencil-skinny legs—bird legs, you know—that folks called him Kildee, after one of the leggiest birds that they knew. Nobody can remember who was the first to name him that, but it's stuck to this day. After we married, I called him Dee. Tall and straight, he's a Henderson for sure. So when y'all's Henderson legs start to grow, don't be surprised or alarmed. Be proud. It's just the Henderson's natural way. Y'all will find out in time."

For in truth, several of the boys would be approaching that age not too long from now, and Lula Bess was preparing them as best she knew how. It was a difficult passage, and awkward enough without legs sprouting that way. She wisely knew that their granddaddy's nickname would be a comfort and reminder that others of their kind had been there before.

There was another lengthy pause as the fire crackled and she let the story settle and nestle in minds which down the years she'd want to recall. Then gathering the little ones to her, she said, "Now, y'all come up close to your Lula Bess. Scrooch up here. Let's sit 'neath our quilts by the fire on the old heart-pine floor. And little Jim-Madison, I'll not tell you again: put them rambunctious hounds out the door."

VII

Shot-Face's Veil

On this fine sunny day, the ploughs and tractors of the community were busy. People were getting their ground broke and the smell of new-turned earth was in the air. It made all the world feel good. With all this activity, the floorboards of Kildee's store creaked seldom; and customers were less than few. So Kildee was in a remembering mood and had time to spin out a tale. His audience was a few of those regulars not able to take the field. To these, he invited his usual, "Light. Sit a spell." And they did. Some of the younguns joined in the circle, because Kildee this time had the look of going to tell a spooky tale. They were good to judge that way, and they knew that Kildee could tell one spooky good tale.

The story was about a local fellow named Shot-Face, and this is the way that it went. Settling back in his rocker, Kildee began:

"Now during the time I'm talking about, most of us had buggies and wagons; there were very few of us who had auto cars. So this fellow named Shot-Face walked everywhere that he went. That's what you'd expect of an elderly black man such as he. Some of y'all remember him, I feel sure.

"Down the dusty roads of our country, you'd know he was coming by the bird-shrieks of children, black and white. The word 'Shot-Face' was enough to make them seek the dress-tails of their mamas behind which to hide. From there they'd peer and hold on for dear life. Their fascination froze them and prevented them from not looking—not witnessing the scene. The grownups would greet Shot-Face, and with a little nod, on he would go.

"Shot-Face always wore a black muslin veil from his nose to his collar bone. It was this that gave the children pause, and the fact that he never spoke. No matter how often or familiar, the sight of Shot-Face always caught your attention, if not gave you a shiver or chill.

"For us children, the silent veil hid the unspeakable. We could never imagine what would be so awful that he'd have always to cover it up. So the blank behind Shot-Face's muslin was like the thick woods at night, the unlighted void of space between stars, the region of nightmare, the limbo land of where dead pets go. Unnameable things lurked there, unfathomable secrets. There lived the horror that could not be spoken, could not be faced or seen.

"The story goes that when he was a young man, Shot-Face was in a hunting accident and had his jaw blown clean away ear to ear. In some way, he survived. The flesh of the area healed and somehow he managed to eat. Out of modesty and a consideration for others, he straight off took to wearing his veil, so that now, years later, it had become natural as his identity, even inspiring his name. No one ever remembered what he was called before.

"He had seemed to be here forever and was part of the place. He was like the shadow a body cast in the sun, or the dark at the bottom of springs or wells. As a little child when I knew him, he walked quite bent with a cane. But my mother told tales of when she herself was a child, some half century before, and having felt the mystery too. To her even then, Shot-Face seemed old.

"Her parents were neighbours of Shot-Face's family, and this threw him much in their way. His family helped ours in the tasks of the farm. At harvest and butcherings and plantings, shoulder-to-shoulder, we all took the field. Then we all rested at laying-by time. So it is natural that mama and dad were involved and in a way accepted as their own what had happened, and its results. Life was that way. You took it in stride. Live and Let Live, and Help When You Can, were the rules of the day.

"Mama remembered a time when Shot-Face would sometimes be at their house for supper. It would usually be in the winter when Shot-Face's vegetables were few and round about butchering time. They had fixed him a little pine table in the corner of the kitchen, and by hearth-fire and lamp-glow he would eat to himself. In half shadow, and with back to us and facing the wall, he'd slowly unfasten and take off the veil. She never saw.

"And the corner. The children never played there or touched there a thing. Like the dark veil itself, that corner was a mysterious realm.

"Shot-Face kept a good garden; and he made what coin he could by doing odd jobs, or got paid for his jobs by accepting a meal, a cast-off garment or two. In this way his meager wants and desires could be met. He would never have begged, or would never have had to.

"The people around who took him as theirs, would help him in this way or that—in little ways as their circumstance would allow. Not many had much, and his distance from them in this way, truth to tell, was not far. When they had more than enough, like at butchering time, they opened their doors—not that they ever were really closed. Without naming it thus, their charity was real, more genuine than nowadays a check in the mail. When need has a face and a name, a gift is for real. Although on the rag-tag edge and margin, he was one of our own. Unlike the children, the grownups always looked him straight eye to eye.

"Shot-Face never had children or wife, and walked down his red country pathway alone. Despite his injury's loss, he was yet still intact and stepped with a sort of dignity even when bent—as much dignity as his situation would claim.

"Yes, he walked, then stutter-stepped on his way, till he lived a long life. On a bird-hatching morning in spring very much like today, when the farmers were all busy new breaking their fields, he took ill in the little log shack which his daddy and mama had built and where he'd been born. That same night he died in his sleep. He was found the next morn by Grandpa, with the low-burning lantern still lit, so Shot-Face didn't die in the dark. My daddy made his pine coffin in his wood-working shop, simple and honest as Shot-Face himself. I remember playing with the resiny, good-smelling curls of the pine from Daddy's sharp plane, there on the shop floor. Then Shot-Face lay in his new wood-fragrant coffin in state in our parlor for neighbours to view. And he went to his grave in his veil. The coffin showed Shot-Face complete as our memory knew him, still silent a mystery, modest, and veiled.

"I've been thinking of Shot-Face a lot now that I've gotten up in years, and I've taken to wondering what any of us ever know of each other, even those closest, or of the nature of things. Two and two does make four, but sometimes five and more besides. Who is given the light to know dark? It's like what's way down in the black of the great, deep moving river out back of the store. It never touches the light.

"This I do know: Shot-Face kept his secret, for we allowed him to take it to grave behind his black muslin veil, and I know that we did the right thing, to close out his chapter, and this tale."

The afternoon was getting on now and Kildee bestirred himself to get on home early to help his youngest son in the field. The gents stayed on as long as they liked, for Kildee never had a lock on his door. Last to leave made sure to shut off the light that hung bare on its cord.

VIII

Nails

~⌍~

Uproar is the world's only music. — John Keats

Chauncey and Kildee had an old friend from childhood who was a pure caution. The county was never quiet and relaxed with him on the scene. If he'd had a middle initial, it might as well been M for "Mayhem." Some of Chauncey's earliest memories were of his scary scrapes. Even as a child he was a mess. Now on this particular day, the old friend was amongst mostly rank strangers, so his talk was of a more formal cast, and restrained—quite the unusual condition for Triggerfoot. He was importuned by the lot to give an account of himself. In truth, his looks and intelligent blue eye had peaked up their interest to know. And this was his chance to spin out uninterrupted a tale of such things that had just occurred. The details and events were hot on his mind. So settled down comfortably, he began:

"For those of y'all don't know me, my name's Triggerfoot. Don't exactly know how I got it. Just is. Plain Triggerfoot. That's all. When the world makes its record of me, if'n it does at all, it should just write me down as *Triggerfoot Don't Know-How-Come.*

"I usually can cause a heap of trouble and even without aiming to try. After I make the mess and my name gets attached, folks just shrugs their shoulders and say, passing it off with 'It's Triggerfoot's doing and that explains why.' If somebody asks them why I've done this or that, they say 'That's just Triggerfoot. There ain't no rhyme nor reason why.' And they's mostly just right. Like an itchy trigger finger, I just does what seems at the moment to be the thing to do, just that and no more. No use to debate it or puzzle, no need to turn it over in the brain. No need to reason out why.

"Clay Bank's my home. Always has been; and if the good Lord lets me, always will. Don't have no car. When I ain't farming, I walks all about town getting into scrapes. Folks says they can tell where I been by the commotion behind me that I leaves. That wherever I've been, everything gets all connogled up. I just reckon that's true.

"Sometimes some fancy fine folk with a car will take me somewhere else. Some says they does so for their 'musement. As for myself, I don't 'muse much. Don't know exactly what they means. Maybe it causes them to 'muse on me, trying to figger old Triggerfoot out, to see what makes me me. If they ever does learn, maybe they'll tell me, then both of us will know, and maybe I'd care. And maybe I'd not. Old Triggerfoot keeps them guessing that way.

"They says I'm an independent cuss. Maybe is; maybe ain't. Won't say.

"I heard old Mrs. Jerrold call me an enigma. Well,

that's the most highfalutin' thing I've ever been called and it might surprise her to know that I knows what she means. She means she doesn't know what I means. And she is right, and I aim to keep it that way. Triggerfoot ain't the fool some thinks. He knows what he knows. And he ain't telling.

"One day an old she-pillar of the Clay Bank United Methodist Church said to an old he-pillar that considering my rundown, shackelty old farmhouse, I was one of the homeless and should have a Habitat for Humanity project created over my head. The she-pillar said that it doesn't look good to strangers coming into town to see me scouting around with my run-down shoes and weather-beaten clothes. That I needed a better place of my own mainly so maybe I'd stay there and be kept out of sight and not be an embarrassment to all. Old he-pillar agreed and knew the Reverend would too, seeing he was lately hot into humanity, especially when it didn't involve the gospel or losing contributions to that shiny brass plate they passes around. Some Wesleyan quadrilateral that!

"Them Clay Bank Methodists are a strange breed of cattle. The worst thing you could do to them is mistake them for a Clay Bank Baptist—a heathen maybe they wouldn't mind, but not a Baptist. In that way, they's just like the Episcopalians, only with 'piscopalians, you could throw in the Methodists with the Baptists. With the Baptists the worst thing you could do is to find fault with the basketball court of their new family life centre. Ain't many Luth'rans and Catholics around here, thank the Lord, but from what I knows of them, worst thing for both is for folks not to confuse them for each other.

"But old Triggerfoot is onto them all. He knows what he knows. But he ain't saying. He plays his cards close.

"Church she-pillars and he-pillars everywhere, they's mostly all the same. They just wants a nice feel-good place, a snappy church tchune, a country club with a cross, so long as the cross don't get in the way. So long as you can put it on and take it off depending on where you is, like one of those gold and diamond cross pins, so it'll just blend in, or be a decoration, and give no offence.

"But I didn't set out to talk about Methodists or any other of them sort of cattle. And that's the last you'll hear on the subject, at least for today. I'll leave the Clay Bank she-pillars and he-pillars alone till they starts trying to habitat me again or to pin me down. An enigma I am, and an enigma I'll just do my level best to stay. It's safest that-a-way—for them and for me.

"As I was saying, sometimes the highfalutin' set that tools around in them oversize cars, takes me with them for 'musement. It happened just this way some months ago. I got the royal tour and it ended for two of them in not-so-royal a way. Don't know what got into old Triggerfoot, but be-jesus if I didn't leave commotion behind me that day.

"You all knows H. Bethea McCall—in these parts, the highfalutinest of all. He's part bank owner, part chamber of commerce man. He's into everything: Kiwanis, stocks,

Rotary Club, bonds, Lions Club, real estate, American Legion, Masons, Republican Party, Limited Partnerships, Unlimited Partnerships, Shriners, Country Club, T-bonds, Civitan, municipal bonds, Rape-Pillage-Plunder Club, mutual funds, the Greed Society—everything that floats and some things that don't. Born Clay Bank Baptist, he graduated by stages on the ladder to Clay Bank Episcopal, in proportion as his bank account grew. He's sure got above his raising, the kind of man who now has to have his whiskey from a glass instead of the jug his daddy's been raised upon. As for his worth as a man, all vines and no taters, all bank account and no character, I say.

"Well, McCall had to drive to Columbia to meet with a big state agency or two on some sort of highfalutin' deal. They wanted me out of sight in town especially bad that day—the red-letter day that some automobile makers were touring to find a new manufacturing site—you know the kind that brings in its own to have the big paying jobs, with the locals like us to clean out the commodes. Some of them high-flying, jet-setting sort—so I couldn't be seen. The town had pulled out all the stops. The carpet was redder than red. And I was just disgusted and ashamed of them to see them fall all over themselves to sell themselves cheap. Such fawning. If you're going to sell yourself, I thought to myself, leastways don't sell yourself cheap. But seems they couldn't see.

"So McCall was drafted by the Clay Bank Chamber of Commerce to get me out of the way. Civic-minded as he was, and, oh yes, due to make a pretty sum for himself on the sale of the land, which he owned, so he didn't mind. It was just business as usual. I was the price he had to pay.

"He put me in the rear of his big black Lincoln car, behind the little window, on his way to Columbia. He and his driver, they set up front. There was a phone and a TV back there where I was, a doll's house of a refrigerator, and even a tiny little gold sink. Better than some people's home. But over all, to me it looked more like a hearse than a house.

"Of course, I wasn't invited inside to the big meetings, but just stayed in the car, locked in with his driver too. I couldn't get out if I wanted, cause the driver had the controls. The wall was between us and we didn't speak. With that little window shut, it was completely soundproof like a padded cell. The walls was all lined in smooth, shiny cloth like in the coffins I'd seen.

"But I had plenty to pass my time. I washed my hands and my face in the little gold sink, and dried them on them little towels monogrammed 'Bethea.' I played with the TV, fiddled with the phone, but made no real calls.

"With the little window open between us going to town, I had heard from the talk that on the way home we were supposed to pick up some nails for McCall's workmen, who were rushing like mad to finish putting a fancy slate roof on his ugly acre of house, and they were calling for rain. As I understood it, these special peg nails were only to be had at the big city hardware just on the edge of downtown. So we were to stop on our way. The forecast of rain made it crucial, or McCall, I don't reckon, would ever have dreamed to bother to stop. Too busy a man. For such as him, time is money, you know.

"Can't figure what got into me, but I just knew that I must. As is my way, didn't for second think any of it through. Just acted on spur like old Triggerfoot always does.

"On the fine little phone, I called 911 local and got through to the sheriff of that part of town. I told him I was reporting two men on their way. I used my finest and smoothest and crookedest politician's talk. Described our McCall and his driver and told them they'd just made a fast break from the State Insane Hospital on Bull. I got that idea as we drove by the brick gates of the asylum on Bull Street on our way out of town. I had known of this place besides and before, 'cause when some of them old ladies in town after some of my oneriest scrapes had said that's where I belonged. Should send him to Bull Street—Bull Street's the place for him and his kind, they would say. But as Chauncey once told one of them, the state university's on the other, south end of Bull Street. 'He's smart, Ma'am, but do you think he's that smart?' he would say. They just huffed off, but as for my own way of thinking, Bull Street is Bull Street, not much difference between.

"Yes, I described McCall and the driver smooth and complete, as I looked through my window, right down to the color and figures on Bethea McCall's tie. I knew McCall would be looking for nails. And I knew just where. The name of the store was Olympic Hardware.

"The sheriff had turned me over to an officer in command who was out on the beat, so I told him to rush out and look for them there, and that the men's looks would deceive, that they honestly thought they were banker McCall and his driver, and were dressed for the part, and would play out the scene, right down to persuasive fake I.D.s. Not dangerous the two, but serious delusions of grandeur and muddled in brain. They'd pulled this before and were experts right down to their high-polished shoes. Slick though they were, they were harmless to others, but needed safety of home, a roof over their heads, lest in their freedom they might do themselves harm. Yes, they needed attending. They needed their handlers, their medications, their doctors, their own safe and snug asylum home. They couldn't be trusted to stray or be on their own. I was so convincing, I near about convinced myself it was true.

"And pay particular attention, I said to the law: clearest I.D. of all, they had this titanic fixation—LOOKING FOR NAILS. Always, relentlessly, looking for nails. That would be key. Nails. Nails. Always looking for nails. For some crazy reason, known only to them, it would be Nails! Nails! Nails!

"The street it was busy at the rushing of traffic to home, parking spaces all jam-up and full. So while driver was squeezing the double-size hearse car through traffic in search for a park, and circling like black buzzard around, McCall he got out and went for the nails.

"Instead of nails, he got four uniformed officers whom he tried to convince who he was.

"'Call the Governor,' he said. 'He knows who I am.'

"'Sure. That's just what we'll do. Come with us. Step this way.'

"'Call the Lieutenant Governor. I've just come from a meeting with him and the chiefs of S.C.D.O.T.'

"'Sure thing. Walk this way.'

"'My limousine driver just put me out, to pick up some nails. All I'm doing is looking for nails. Just looking for nails.'

"Well, it was the nails that did it, that nailed the case down, so to say. 'Here, put on these nice silver bracelets,' they said as they whisked him away. He disappeared like smoke into air.

"'Sure you are. Sure you are,' they agreed. 'You're just looking for some nice old nails. We have them for you, safe and sound, in this little house with the bars. Now just quietly come along. We'll take you to your nails.'

"In truth, they treated him humanely and gently, but efficiently whisked him away in an eyeblink to pretended comfort of nails.

"McCall still hotly protesting, his I.D.s out of his eelskin wallet in a long plastic accordion string, his Gold and his Platinum Cards, Diners Card, Triple A, and his Rotary, Civitan, Lions, Optimists, and Shriners membership cards. Neither the secret sign of the Masons nor his protests to call Governor, Lieutenant Governor, and all D.O.T., not a whit did prevail.

"All was just wasted breath addressed to those who

would save him from hurting himself, knowing better what he needed than he. That he needed safe home above all, a kind of habitat for humanity. And certainly, most assuredly not nails.

"Well, our black buzzard hearse car circled and circled, but no Bethea McCall could be seen. He had vanished, indeed, like a puff of blue smoke in the air. The driver pondered and wondered, swore and mused on the scene. I could see his mouth move and his head shake through my closed soundproof porthole screen.

"This search lasted about an hour; and 'bout a block from the hardware, the driver finally found him long enough space then to park. He got out of the car and rushed down the street on foot to find Mr. McCall.

"When he told the nice officer outside Olympic Hardware he was looking for a man who was looking for nails, he too was whisked in a blink from the scene. Bingo! The police had secured number two!

"Abracadaver! Merlin! Ouija Board! Shezzam! No magician had better command. In a blink, he too disappeared—'Poof!'—without leaving a trace on the scene, not a greasy smear, nor a blip on the radar screen.

"So there I sat locked in the black buzzard car on the streets of Columbia for four solid hours way into dark, playing with the TV and entertaining myself with controls, and the potent contents of the little refrigerator, peeing in that little gold sink, till a red-faced furious pair was delivered right up to the door by the fanciest car I'd ever seen.

It had S.C.1 on its plate, and I recognized the Governor's bland, round, putty-white face through the screen.

"Narya word was said while we drove back to Clay Bank town. The two just fumed in red-faced fume. When a car would pass with its lights, I could see that little danger vein in McCall's swollen temple: *throb, swell, throb, swell, throb,* as the miles melted away.

"And no mention of nails, or the rain beating down.

"Well, just what was their beef? They were ushered like precious lambs by a shepherd to a safe charitable habitat for humanity. That was all. Why complain? It was a case of mistaken identity too, that wouldn't last long, and no less than the Governor had tried his best to make things all right. It could happen to anybody any day of the week, and without these same happy outcomes besides. Few would ever hear the Governor's apology or see Governor's tail lights grace any of their hard luck scenes.

"In their furious silence, I was not there in the car. They'd forgotten me complete in their anger and puzzlement and amaze. Lucky for me!

"In the pouring rain next few days, they'd all had to camp out, roofless, in the local Clay Bank Holiday Inn, which, to be sure, McCall partly owned. Roofs-a-plenty for all till he got back behind his big iron and brick gate.

"But for these few days, at least, he joined me, the homeless, while his workmen crew put up blue tarpaulin plastic to cover his acre of great soggy wet mansion house. And like me, he'd also been judged incompetent looney—at least for an hour or two, destination Bull Street, in earnest, not jest! I wonder if he learned a thing, anything at all.

"I'm sure he got a taste of this fact of life: that no matter how wilful and powerful, you can't have it always your way, no matter how tight and careful and tidy a schedule you've planned. For there'd just be some Triggerfoot glitch to make it all go to smash and fly to flinders like touch-me-not seed.

"But the best thing to come out of this all was that the meetings with the auto car factory locators were soured to the core by having to deal with a testy McCall. They had to postpone their interview with him because he got back so late, and when he met them next day, he was in mood that would make a sore-tailed grizzly bear seem friendly and warm.

"As the highfalutin' visitors left the Clay Bank courthouse the next day, I appeared and pulled out the stops in my raggedest clothes before all—me who they'd wanted to hide clean away. I put on my best, my very best play. So they and their machines never did come to our home to make more of their own buzzard hearse cars to set on the helpless carrion world.

"If I thought I had a part in blocking any of that, I could rest now at peace in the night, knowing I've just pure played a patriot's role.

"To this day, McCall and his driver haven't quite figured all of this out. And just because old simpleton Triggerfoot fool, a 'musement to all, is counted for nothing or less, I'm never suspected to have given a hand. I don't count and am as invisible as air—but, as you sees, quite as close as the air, and everywhere too, all at once.

"Fine and dandy with me, that I don't matter at all. They write me off, 'cause they think I'm not the brightest bulb in their fancy city marquis. Who would guess it was simpleton me who'd put in those three-minute calls, from the buzzard's own innards, the belly of beast, sitting right at their backs only inches away from their manicured heads, each hair lacquered in place—and with me pulling strings for the scene, a better Merlin magician, it seems. And who then was fool? And who was the fooled? Whose bulb burned the brightest that day?

"If they ever found out, they'd sure have me erased, I know, like some bad mistake, or have me shipped off by those men in the little white coats to old Bull Street, Columbia, S.C.—no forwarding address, no return. And with no toadying governor to boot-lick and shepherd me home.

"Locking me away would solve several problems all at the very same time—like the Clay Bank Methodist plan, just one other way to give me a permanent home, and keep from embarrassing them, looking bad before more visiting factory locators to our happy, dear, fair native town.

"In this tussle and struggle, my dearies, now hear. Put your money on Triggerfoot that he'll last them all out—old Triggerfoot who knows what he knows and is just who he is, and will thataway stay. If they'll live and let live, so will he. If they won't, they'll get worse besides. And that you can take to a bank that's better and sounder than H. Bethea McCall's own.

"Well, McCall and his sort of cattle won't win this one, that's sure. They's badly outplayed, and they'll have to admit it. But mark this thing clear: it's a sour tit, but they'll just have to suck it, if they have tit a-tall."

And Chauncey figured Triggerfoot was right. He nodded his head as he said, "Friend Triggerfoot, I reckon they just will."

IX

Triggerfoot and Flop-Eye

~⟋∾⟍~

"Well, old Triggerfoot promised y'all to let religion go for a spell, and he did. But after a while he just couldn't hold back no more, so here he goes taking out after the Methodists again. It seems that all of the pious in these parts have ganged up on my friend Flop-Eye Suber. They is after his hide and won't be done till his hide's nailed to somebody's barn. You see, he's like me and won't be tamed or used. We just won't be the easy pieces to finish their neat jigsaw puzzle of life.

"And they can't stand that a jot. You know how frustrated the ladies gets when they spend a whole week on a giant picture puzzle on the dining room table just to find the last piece is missing complete! Well, we're them last two pieces.

"We are just too much a living indictment of their kind, and point out their flaws. We're on to them—too much vines and no taters, as your friend Miss Goldie says— a big show, that's all. You know, Chauncey, going to church doesn't make you a Christian, like sleeping in a garage doesn't make you a Chevrolet. You know they's a powerful lot of empty people nowadays that has to fill up their emptiness with the show of doing good, when all along it's really mostly all about them. And Flop-Eye and me, we knows that about them so well, that that's why way down deep in their dried-up souls, they decide we've got to be gone.

"Seem like the latest Methodist obsession is this: they don't have their self-ordained Wesleyan quadrilateral, feel-good quota of colored folks in Methodist pews of a church Sunday morn. In fact, they don't even have one.

"Old Mrs. High-Horse Jerrold, church she-pillar number one, star of the amen corner, the kind of proper person who says 'John Donkey' to keep from saying 'jackass,' and looks at me like I was worse than dirt on a stick, goes about quoting Reverend Bugg that the Methodist Church is the most segregated place in town of a Sunday morn. Their bishop commanded them to get out the word and rope, like so many steers, some of them colored folks in. The whole congregation has gone on a great moral high-horse crusade, to the point of frenzy these days.

"Well, they've tried most all the wealthiest black folk of the town. Of course, they started at the top and worked down. Even got several to attend. Bettis and Viney-Mae Jeter were the first. They came to church several months back out of a genuine attempt to be friendly to all. In truth, Flop-Eye told me, they didn't want to go, dreaded it in fact.

Bettis had even gone so far as to think up some excuses; but since they were lies, and about church besides, he couldn't bring himself to tell them, and knew that he'd just have to go. He was backed into a corner, tied, bagged, and captured, he said.

"And Bettis and Viney Mae they found what they expected to find too, and even some more. The service and hymns, most all that they saw, seemed foreign and strange. And the sea of white faces around them, though most of them known, all of them smiling, and a few of them friends, were not like their own. And the preacher was over warm in singling them out in the welcome. Enough to make Bettis and Viney-Mae squirm.

"Then Bettis still vows that he and his wife was taken as text for Buggs' sermon on race. Seems the preacher had found it progressive humourous profound to say good black folks like the Jeters were just white folks with tans. He made no mention of what the bad ones might be. Jeter reckoned all black folks were, well, just themselves. Maybe as simple as that. Why does the world make everything simple so complicated, and reduce down the complicated to something too easy, tidy, and neat? Seems like we've nowadays got everything backwards that way.

"Yes, with their visit to church, the Jeters felt that they'd now done more than their share. They had politely come to show friendship, yes, had given their due. But they weren't going back. It was like they were saying, 'We've given at the office, and now don't ask me for more.'

"Well, this happened to three other families that I personally know. One was Pink Sanders. He owns a used car dealership in town. His wife, Thavolia, works at Bethea McCall's bank. They were ushered to the very front pew, with their four neatly scrubbed children, half-a-dozen bright shiny badges for the Clay Bank Methodists to wear. There they sat like eggs in a carton on shelf. Reverend Bugg beamed.

"Another was Mangle Gladney, the barber in town, and his florist wife, Rendy. We call her 'Ren.' The last, quite the fancy feather in the Clay Bank Methodist cap, was the councilman from Ward Number Three, Bonnet Sims. He came alone. All three families before found their going would be good for their own personal business cause. So did he, most especially so, but to her credit, the councilman's wife drew the line. She just wouldn't go. No amount of politicking from hubby could convince her a jot. Yes, Bonnet Sims came alone.

"Now, like the Jeters, all that had come felt they'd done their strict duty and were not going back.

"So, who was left? The bottom had nearly 'bout been scraped.

"The Methodist he- and she-pillars strategized with the preacher that maybe they'd started too high on the pole. If color was wanted, low-class color would do. It all served the same.

"So now it was Flop-Eye's own turn to do time on the cross. Well, they must shorely been desperate to try my friend Flop. For a feather in anyone's cap, he is not. And like me, he is onto their game. Both of us has seen cons and scams enough to smell them a mile. And we both like our pranks.

"As most of y'all know, Flop-Eye gets his name from a droopy right eyelid, and what makes him so uncanny spooky is the way he can move it at will, to flop up and down and gyrate around, while the other stands still at attention and rivets you straight. With all of your begging to put on this show, *that* he never will do. It can give you the willies, and is in the worst taste. Women will faint, children will scream, and grown men grow weak.

"I've seen it in action because we are friends. But even expecting and knowing, it can make my stomach turn queasy and give me a chill, even when it's done half-heartedly and like a youngster plays tricks just for fun. Flop's skilled trick of the eye, the rest of the world did not know. And Flop's own brand of charity was to keep it on leash, his own personal little gift to an unsuspecting world.

"So the appointed morning, it rolled 'round; and Flop-Eye was there. He was dressed in his Sunday's finest black-coated best, complete with shiny black shoes, starched, eye-hurting white shirt, and black tie. Old Flop-Eye, despite his eye, can look as dignified and self-important as an undertaker or old Bugg himself. Flop was quiet and pleasant, and the ushers missed not a cue.

"They took him as planned with great fanfare up to the front pew. All craned their necks just to see. He sat front row centre squarely beneath Reverend Bugg. Like a jewel he sat in the gold Methodist crown. The Reverend just beamed.

"Well Flop-Eye got the treatment all those of color before him received. Royal it was, and maybe all the more, 'cause our Flop-Eye was one of the 'poor.' He could thus possibly be two jewels in the crown. Condescension oozed like the grease from a possum baked at high heat in the stove. Bugg usually was oiley enough, but never quite like today. He plum out-did himself, it is said. From the start of ordeal, Flop-Eye, known for this dubious talent among his friends, had let out silent-but-deadlies to grace the fair scene. He had eaten his butterbeans, pintos, and black-eyes the whole day before, just to be sure.

"As one, the pew cringed and stifled their gasps. The fumes, they were nearly enough to set off the smoke detectors on the wall. It was just that bad. Even Flop-Eye himself was impressed. Then the pew behind got some whiffs and shuffled in seats, fanned with their bulletins, and coughed. The she-pillar, stationed right next to old Flop, with lace hanky, covered her nose. One time, she stifled a gag. Flop said he wanted to say, 'What's a little gas passed between friends? . . . Black and white, we's all human here.'

"Bugg at all this commotion was surely not pleased; he didn't know the cause. But when he launched upon race, he got even more. Yes, he got it both barrels, and has not been the same to this day.

"For at the moment of 'Reaching out hands and seeing

eye to eye with our black brothers,' old Flop let his eye go. The Reverend, of course, was just looking at Flop-Eye square beneath him, eyes to eye when he was greasily saying 'our black brothers,' and got it full in the face.

"While the left one riveted Bugg straight, the right eye jerked now its wildest, insanest, like it was to jump out of face. It took on life of its own, as it danced, cavorted, rioted, careened. The Reverend was stopped greasily cold in his tracks, frozen stiff and pale as a corpse in the middle of 'Race.'

"But Bugg had the stalwart zeal of crusader and vowed to go on, and that was just the latest mistake then of many he'd made.

"For in his usual line, when he got to the part that the best black people were just white people with tans, old Flop turned head in his pew to look back 'cross his shoulder to the whole congregation in behind, and let his eye go. This time, he really rose to the occasion for certain and sure. He outdid all of his performances soon or late.

"Like the eye of a snake that is charming the bird, they must watch, when it would have been better to bury their heads in their Methodist hymnals or the sweet innocent black child's beaming face on their bulletin cover today.

"No, Flop-Eye's eye had its charm and it held. But children murmured and cried. 'Make that man stop,' they told their mamas and dads. 'He's frightening me,' was the mildest they said.

"Then mamas and dads had to take their screaming

children out. First the pew behind Flop was emptied, then on to the next and the next, as Flop-Eye by the little ones could be more easily viewed.

"Well, we'd always joked with Flop-Eye that he was ugly enough to scare children; and this day we proved ourselves true.

"Reverend Bugg jettisoned sermon, skipped the prayer, and went straight into song. Flop-Eye turned his head 'round and sang with the best, sang loudest but slightly off-key. The sound set folks' teeth on edge.

"The one thing, however, would not be left off from the day, was that shiny brass plate that they pass truly religiously 'round to glean their rich harvest of greenbacks from those on the scene. It started at rear and worked its way up to front row, where Flop-Eye just took his time and picked out all the loose twenties and tens, and even some choice change. He left envelopes (with checks) all alone.

"During doxology, he straightened the bills, and at benediction, he tucked them away. He swears to this day he heard Bugg say, 'Go in wealth. Pay the Lord,' but I believe that a regular Flop-Eye invention or leastways a stretch.

"The congregation, decimated of children, was less lively, but in no way less hurried to get from the scene. And Flop-Eye left the building in both peace and wealth unexpected, like manna from on high in a wide desert scene—and far greater blessing, with no more greasy greetings and welcomes and fawnings to be suffered that very live-long day.

"To all this, old Flop had but one thing to say: 'You

know, Triggerfoot, you and me, we're alike and not much like all of them. We can see under scams. We know when feelings is false or is true. Some of my folks say they uses their color as black Visa cards, but all of us black folks, whatever the mood or the mode, has what I calls built-in shit-detecting machines. Triggerfoot, you knows, you're 'just black folks without tan.' And at that echo of Bugg, we both had us a good hearty laugh. Old Flop-Eye, he needed that too, after what he'd been through.

"Flop-Eye, he ain't often vulgar, and is usually discrete, so his 'shit-detecting' was a bit out of character, you must know, and forgive old Flop-Eye so. This thing at the church sorely tried him, you see, beyond his fair usual limits, it seems, and brought him to four-letter words. But them Clay Bank Methodists can count themselves blessed. They got off easy enough and were lucky this time. It would serve the congregation just right if he'd join. Then what would they do? Reckon we'd see if these vines had any taters this time.

"Hey, that's an idea! I'll see if old Flop won't write Bugg a letter and ask how to apply. That will most surely occasion a serious meeting of he-pillars and she-pillars around. Hey, Chauncey, what do you think? Don't you reckon it would be worth doing just to see if he'd get a reply?"

Throughout Triggerfoot's narration, Chauncey and he were seated in giant old rockers at Triggerfoot's hearth. In the coals, Triggerfoot had placed half a dozen fat sweet potatoes in their rich earthy-brown skins, so that the "vines and taters" image he'd just used had all the impact it could.

"While on the more important subject of sweet taters," Triggerfoot continued, after a pause, "roll one of them fat, oozing brown-jacketed beauties this way. They're sending up smoke signals to tell us they're ready to eat. Just look at that cinnamon color inside, darker and richer than the bottomland soil they grew in—and taste? Sweet as honey still in the comb, sweet as my own new-cut sugar cane at molassy biling time. No pitiful pale laboratory hybrids these. They ain't been educated inside at agriculture schools, never been inside them flourescent halls. Lived their lives out in the fresh air and sun. Triggerfoot wouldn't grow any of them sickly, worthless, pasteboard kind. They's imitations, that's all. Pure total scam. Improved in the labs? Yes, to take all the sweet taste clean away. Improved, my foot! Like gas-logs is a new kind of fire. Well, the joke is on them. And some of them calls *me* a fool!"

Chauncey agreed, "The genuine article, real taters, these."

Triggerfoot continued, "Yes, the very same vines that my great-grandaddy grew. I banks them in winter and saves eyes each year to year—like my daddy and granddaddy before. And I like knowing that too. It adds its own kind of sweetness to tongue. Won't get these at the Clay Bank Sprawl-Mart Super Store, nor none of them Winn-Dixie grocery chains. And why? They ain't efficient, ain't cost-effective for storage and shipping, the CEOs say. Won't pay. And Chauncey, you know 'bout how much I care for their efficient, cost-effective scene! But I don't need to say it all now, 'specially with real sweet taters sending up steam. Pure perfect sham and scam, that's all's needed to say, and arrogant besides, while the folks that buys them just props up the scam.

"Well, Chauncey, I reckon we're now about ready to have us a regular sweet tater feast! Stand back. Give me room. Where's the cow butter and cream!"

And the scuppernong wine jug was passed at the hearth, while the firelight flashed off of Triggerfoot's heavy, well-worn coinsilver spoons.

X

Our'n

Triggerfoot, as all who know him will testify, has his very own language. There is nothing remotely standard or standardizable about it, or for that matter, about him.

The Triggerfoot language fits Triggerfoot perfectly; both are downright unique.

We've all had occasion to witness how Triggerfoot's one-of-a-kind character gets in the way of the designs of those who demand and command a neat, tidy universe; but less common and more sophisticatedly complex are the frustrating and discombobulating results of Triggerfoot-speak. Well, this just happened a few months back and is a prime example thereof.

Officialdom has its ways, and Triggerfoot has his; and this latest Triggerfoot happening makes you wonder if ever the twain shall meet, except briefly perhaps under military law.

It seems that the latest economic design of the Clay Bank Development Board—Chamber of Commerce set is

Tourism with a capital T, Tourism to bring in the dollars, what they call the new cash crop. Official reports of how many greenbacks can be realized from every overnight visitor to town have been proclaimed in the local newspaper and celebrated near and far from Civitan Club and Kiwanis to town and county council. Statistics abound like weeds in the furrows after a summer rain. The local officials do their expert studies and get aided and abetted by the state, whose experts do theirs. Bureaucratic gobbledygook weighs in with its grandiose, mind-numbing haze. And eureka, what a surprise; they all agree. TOURISTS EQUAL CASH, an equation sure and certain and by which to organize a world.

What with the failure of these same citizens to land a much-desired auto-making plant for the town, they turned their angling from the big-game sporting marlin and swordfish to the common old cat. After such an ignominious defeat with the car manufacturer, they might even now settle for humble perches or gar. The Clay Bank Development Board now felt it had something to prove, and adjusted its lures, bait, and reels.

Triggerfoot, rustic poet that he is, had a better image for the game these officials played. "They aims to pick them tourists as clean as a row of cotton," he declared. He imagined it as just another kind of con game, a legal pocket-picking shell-game scam. For "scam" was the best single word old Triggerfoot could come up with to sum up the time. "My dearies," he'd declare, "Scam about says it all.

Everywhere that you looks is the scam, from politics to pulpit, from the school and the store to the shrine."

And speaking of shrine—it was shrine that set all of this latest Triggerfoot round off like firecrackers at Christmas or a big, costly, vulgar citified Fourth of July.

For the town was desperate for a historical shrine. It didn't have one; and tourists needed a shrine. Or more accurately phrased, for there to be tourists in town, there would first have to be shrine. Not until then would the new crop of tourist greenbacks grow, be fertilized, and picked.

So the Clay Bank Development Board and the money elite of the town, who had a true cash-register evaluation of all life, commanded, demanded a shrine right away. They were use to ordering and getting their way. They held up their money bags and cried, "My power is here. Make me a shrine."

A major inconvenience, however, was that the town hadn't produced any great, famous person whose birthplace could serve as a shrine. It hadn't been a battlefield site, or anything like that sort of a draw, so they had to dig deep. All this set the officials in motion, and to scratching their heads.

And dig then they did, or leastways Triggerfoot did.

Every spring, faithful as the sun rises in the east every day, old Triggerfoot still tried to put down rows in what remained of his family's fields now encroached upon by Clay Bank sprawl. Here he had his family's rundown old farmhouse, a falling-down barn, and about fifty acres left from a once large estate. In the old days, it would have been called a two-horse farm, that is, a spread that needed two horses or mules for ploughing and to keep a farm family of eight or more busy—"a livelihood farm," as it was called. On some of this land, he grew him some corn, and sweet potatoes, peanuts, sugar cane, tomatoes, field peas, and beans, but mainly corn. As Triggerfoot said of himself and family before, "We always liked to follow a mule."

It was all in and about the spring of this shrine-demanding time that he went several rows further into the bottom with his plough than was his usual wont. In so doing, his plough point struck metal and would budge not a single inch more. His old faithful mule Beulah refused to try.

Triggerfoot and his mule were a curious pair. One was about as stubborn as the other. Though he scolded and cussed, Triggerfoot only whipped Beulah with oats, as the old expression goes, because the two were a team. Stubborn, indeed, like him, she'd plough diligently enough all morn just for the privilege of giving a swift kick at noon. In fact, if the ploughing went smooth, you could bet that a kick or some other mischief would be soon on its way. But ornery as Beulah was, Triggerfoot did not go in for mechanization. He could get along with her because he'd learned her ways. He could talk to her, and her very unpredictableness made life interesting, to say the least. A machine was a different thing. Those who used them, he called "windshield farmers," and he didn't think much of them, and less of their ways. They were too much dependent

on the whims of loans and the unpredictable price of equip-
ment and gasoline. Besides, Beulah made free fertilizer too
instead of gasoline fumes.

Well, the object that Beulah had struck this day was a
curious old iron barrel which those who saw it knew must
be old. Triggerfoot got it uncovered by digging the clay
from around with the trowel and spade. There it sat, a perfect two hundred and fifty-year-old cannon with royal
signet of British crest and crown—for its age, in most
beautiful shape.

State agencies arrived, tipped off by the local elite, and
trampled down poor old Triggerfoot's new shoots of corn,
which he and Beulah stalwartly planted again. The town's
development and tourism boards made steady streams all
the day. Then came the reporters, "Like jorees," Triggerfoot
said, "small birds always scratching around in dirt." Beulah
seemed to hee-haw her assent.

When Triggerfoot was asked what he saw, he rightly
knew it was iron, but his honest, local Triggerfoot-speak
got misunderstood by the city as our'n. In his hillcountry
way, he spoke all his long i vowels as ah, and not eye. His
"It's iron" thus got translated a far different way than he
actually meant. They'd have liked to say back if they could:
"Ain't your'n; it's our'n," but they did not so dare.

For the getters and spenders, it was all about ownership,
of course. They had to plot out a scam, so they believed, to
make Triggerfoot's our'n into their'n, as a perfect centrepiece
of developing shrine. A delicate matter, this, for the land
was Triggerfoot's own, and he'd be able to make a case for

having all that was in it, too. Their battery of highly paid lawyer consultants advised solemnly against forcing the issue up front, but instead to take the circuitous route, with the end result of multiplying their fees.

Double checks by Clay Bank officials down at the courthouse showed that Triggerfoot had legal title to these acres, and the taxes on it were paid—paid late, but still paid. A small army of clerks and low-level officials poured over the books for more than three days. Not since they'd tried to get Triggerfoot out of town when the auto plant people came through was such attention given to him and his.

A most delicate matter indeed. And no one would go straight and ask Triggerfoot what he intended to do. They only reported that he'd said it was his.

So this self-created one-sided stalemate dragged on for several months more, till the officials brought in an expert from far, far away, to stand among Triggerfoot's now head-high corn. He authenticated the relic. "Existence-wise, a unique and unusual find, maximizing the probabilities the cannon is perhaps one of a kind" was among the most coherent of the bureaucratic pronouncements at the site while several cameras recorded the day.

Official meetings lasting deep into night multiplied like crows in a newly planted field. About these, Triggerfoot knew not a thing. He was busy making a crop and minding his business too.

He was pulling his corn when representatives from the state and local tourism boards approached him out in the field. One had a fine new leather briefcase whose sides bulged with bureaucratic gobbledygook, another a fistful of papers and pen. They had got desperate and now, as last resort, would just ask him face to face.

"'Course," Triggerfoot said as he signed. "Would be better to put it in town at the square so all who wanted could see. Glad you asked—I'd be honored—was thinking and hoping you might. What took you so long?" He didn't want to be so selfish as to keep all this community history to self. "Just ask!" The simplicity astounded them all.

Well, for their part in the deal, the officials got great commendations from all who mattered in state, and one even a promotion, and one in lieu of promotion, a juicy pay raise. They felt good about earning their pay. It had only taken about four dozen meetings, local and state, several reams of gobbledygook forms in triplicate, about 3,000 man hours, 10,000 miles of state-funded travel, at 65 cents a mile, and no more than the usual lawyers' fees. Quite a taxpayer's bargain, they'd say.

And as for our Triggerfoot, his iron became copper, because, despite his replanting and several months of inconvenience, he harvested a good crop of corn and the fermented variety thereof. "Farming in the woods," as he called it, he made some of the best mash that the country had known, and was just about to finish his still run. Now if there ain't any bad whiskey—some's good, some's better—Triggerfoot's was better. He aged it in great oaken kegs, with a few peaches and apricots from his trees placed inside. He bottled it up in mason jars with a peach in each jar. This flavored it and gave it a bright hint of the color of rose. It was so potent it would draw blisters on a rawhide boot. But for all of his artistry and hard work, it all went to smash this year after all, and most literally too.

For on his usually quiet acres, with all the ruckus that finding the cannon had made, half the world had come to his cornfield. "With more noise than the cannon had made when 'twas new," was old Triggerfoot's take. And right in its way, his assessment was true.

So about fodder-pulling time, the law found out his old still. Twenty acres weren't enough to quite hide the smoke and the rich, fragrant smell.

In the amber days of Indian Summer when the leaves were beginning to turn, they brought in their axes, and broke up his still, one that belonged to his grandpappy Tinsley, and Grandpappy's father 'fore him, an item some rarer than the cannon of crown, and almost as rare as the irony too. For the cannon was used to enforce King George's taxes on tea, in a big war fought for freedom from that sort of thing.

The cannon had indeed been certified as being from just that same war, and probably used by red-coated artillery men attached to Banastre Tarleton—known as the Butcher, the great Green Dragoon, who fired it against Triggerfoot's own, who'd bled with no quarter for the freedom of these few remaining acres of land. Oh, rich irony indeed.

Well, as you'd expect, they took our old Triggerfoot straight to the Clay Bank jail. As in days of the Butcher, still no quarter for him. They fingerprinted and booked him and put him in cell.

Through the bars of his window, he had fine sight of the square, and especially the cannon, now expertly mounted on expensive, authentic new green-painted caisson, and with freshly new-gilded crest of empire and crown—for all the world, the spitting image of the tax stamp for the colonists' tea. The cannon had been there but two days on view.

Triggerfoot, his hands on the sill of the window touching iron of bars, watched as a cluster of tourists, led by a guide, stood by the cannon in the square. He could hear the guide speak of the brave patriots of '76, and of the wonderful freedoms they'd won for us all.

And on this bright and cloudless winter's day, the sun gleamed merrily, reflected from the bright polished metal and especially off its gold imperial seal; and all those who saw, declared the weapon to be in great shape, and to look just like new. Upon that, most surely, Triggerfoot would have agreed.

XI

Triggerfoot Strikes Back

It took a few days for the word to get to Chauncey that Triggerfoot was in the hands of the enemy. Chauncey arrived on the scene in Clay Bank about midday to go his bail.

Triggerfoot looked some crestfallen, like a wet rooster in the rain, but the amber sunlight and fresh autumn air soon revived him. By three o'clock he had sworn revenge, and this would be all-out war, but waged in his own good time and on his own terms, with armaments, pistols, sabers, bowie knives—whatever—chosen by him. Like one of your serious lethal time bombs, Triggerfoot had been set to tick.

"Nobody steps on me without gettin' his foot bit," Triggerfoot had already declared, his eyes set in the slant of a hard squint; and Chauncey said he sure wouldn't want to be attached to the foot that had done the tromping. From Triggerfoot's comment about biting, Chauncey had in his mind the image of an old banner he had once seen, the Gadsden Flag it was called, a Revolutionary banner from the Carolina campaign that had on its bright yellow field a giant coiled rattlesnake with its lethal fanged head in a position to strike. Under the snake were emblazoned the words DONT TREAD ON ME. In keeping with visions of No Quarter Tarleton, recently discovered Revolutionary War cannons, and such, this flag fit the historical scene that was forming in Chauncey's mind, fit it right to a T. Yes, Chauncey kept thinking to himself that he wouldn't want to be in somebody's shoes, because Triggerfoot would come down on him worse than Judgment Day.

Triggerfoot was in a state of what you might call controlled rage. In his jail cell these last few days, his main problem was figuring out on whom to afix blame. That's what this new tyranny was like: a monster without a face, an enemy without a leg or foot to bite. The creature was so big and distant, complex and vague, that it was hard to know how to strike back, or at what. Frustrating indeed, and the frustration only built up his rage. In his cell overlooking the square, he had plenty of time to think and seethe. He had his guesses; but it would take him a while longer to get to the real root of it all, to see foot and face of the target at which to aim. When he did, as Chauncey well knew, the punishment would be swift and keen. The fangs would sink deep.

Triggerfoot had his ways, and within the following week he'd gotten to the bottom of it all, or at least sufficiently enough to know the heart of the cause. For, as Triggerfoot guessed from the start, it was more than making illegal whiskey that had gotten him jailed.

What he found out is that certain elected officials in

Clay Bank had leaned on the similarly elected county sheriff to find a way to rope old Triggerfoot in. He had shown
himself about town to be entirely too rambunctious and
free, and this had set them all off like Tarleton's artillery.
For they deemed him a threat just by being so free, though
they'd never use that word or admit, even to themselves,
that that was the cause. You see, Triggerfoot wasn't behold-
en to anybody, had been bought off by none, so couldn't be
trusted to be held in line; and that made him a threat to
their kind—subservient, dependent, dishonest, each one to
each, and with no honor among thieves.

Yes, whatever their rationalizations or views, they all
knew his sort was dangerous in the extreme. And then he
also had that nasty little habit of deflating their pretensions, of letting the air out of all their puffed-up bureaucratic self-importance, like releasing the air from a balloon
with the fingers in such a way as to make that loud, obscene
squeal. Not a few of the strutting ones all about town had
had cause to hear that humbling same sound. And some
knew the fingers at the mouth of the deflating balloon were
Triggerfoot's own.

Most of the *ins* and the *outs* of their tangled-up spider
web's plan he unraveled with help of Chauncey and a few
low-level courthouse friends in the know. A clerk and a janitor turned out to be his biggest aids. They asked about in
all the right places—of those who had been on the scene for
awhile—because they knew that the new broom sweeps
clean, but that it is the old broom that knows where the
dirt is. So Chauncey and Triggerfoot figured it out; and the

plump big daddy spider that sat at the centre of the web was the local state legislator, who had visions of grandeur eventually to sit at the top of the malodorous pile as the progressive governor of the state. As Triggerfoot knew, you touched this taut web and every strand vibrated from bottom to top and then down again, till the spider came out from his lair. This time Triggerfoot was the fly that shook up the threads of the scene.

It was too easy to pay the sheriff for his part in the scheme. He did the hard work that was dirty, and, handling the dirt, did not come away clean. That he wasn't clean to begin with is why he so readily complied with the plan.

But the one who set things in motion without sweat and with hardly six dozen words was none other than Senator Snipes, with his spider legs dancing in tangles across all sorts of webs, some of them his, some of them not. These often involved real estate ventures—land deals mostly—both great and small, that ranged from location of new industries and malls and new roads and schools, to the mushrooming offices for government agencies, state and local, under his palm, a palm that thus often got greased.

"Pizen as a spider and crooked as a snake," Triggerfoot described the Senator in his usual accurate way.

So Triggerfoot bided his time, for he knew the November election was not too far away.

And as justice would have it, the cannon he'd found would be part of this reckoning day.

The town had gone all out to make this as special a do as

Clay Bank could be capable of. It had been put together as a great campaigning tool for Snipes with a festival dedicating the cannon on the square. The Senator would be there to speak and campaign and do the honours of dedicating same, as usual taking as much of the credit as he could. This, as he knew, translated into votes at the polls.

This would be Triggerfoot's chance; and it took little to scheme, for his plan had the virtue of utter simplicity and down-to-earth, earthy, natural elements too. No elaborate web, no outlay of dollars and cents, no intricate networking or payoffs or threats, no lawyers, no forms in triplicate, no rumours created or strongarming or bribes. No favours called in. No favours paid out. The local newspapers would not be involved. No preaching from pulpits. No campaign posters or slogans or signs, no TV ads, no smoke-filled rooms, no noise of firecrackers, no skyrockets, no red-white-and-blue bunting, no imperial flags. Above all, no greasy greasing of palms. Simplicity's honest, elegant self was always Triggerfoot's way.

The day was a good one. The weather was fine. On the high scaffolded stage, the high school band was assembled, two congressmen national, the governor, his lieutenant and staff, all city and county officials of note, Bethea McCall, historical society, selected school children, and more. They were all scrooched up on the stage. It was one of the biggest turnouts Clay Bank had ever seen, a kind of festival, historical pageant, dedication, commercial, stump-speaking all rolled into one. The square was packed to bursting at the seams with folks having thus to seep into side streets just to get a view, radiating as it looked to Triggerfoot's eye like another great trembling web.

At centre sat the contented, fly-full big daddy spider, our Senator Snipes, wide smiling and just basking in glory before every voter in the town, assured as he was next week of a win. The polls had him double-digit percentage points ahead. People had on SNIPES OUR MAN badges. SNIPES OUR MAN placards were everywhere, on lawns, at intersections, in store windows, stapled flimsily on poles.

Over the stage was a big shiny plastic banner displaying the town's new slogan: HISTORY IS OUR MONEY CROP. The city council and Chamber took great pride in having come up with it all on their own. Its red letters floated on the breeze, altering the words in creases and folds. IS OUR became SOUR. HISTORY read TORY, like the Green Dragoon's own. CROP became OP, as in Good Photo Op. As Triggerfoot commented, "The town was aiming to milk this thing as clean as old Bossy the cow."

The mayor welcomed. Triggerfoot's shining newly placed cannon got duly dedicated in style; some fanfare was performed by the brass of the band. The imperial colours of two empires were paraded, and passed in review, again and again, then back once again. Revolutionary War reenactors fired noisy muzzleloading salutes. "The Battle Hymn of the Republic" was sung. Little Union Jacks fluttered and waved in peace next to thousands of Old Glories stamped out by the gross, like new-minted silver-coated coins. Then

Snipes stepped to the fore. His talk was a trendy one made to order for the easily led. Cliches abounded. They flew thickly like bullets or cannonballs in air. His speech hinged on his championing of all human rights. In truth, as we know, on this subject, no expert surely was he, or on any of the freedoms that had been extolled in this sham of a pageant today, and which he continued to mouth. And mouth them he did, round and round, like chewing a choice marbeled cut of prime rib, or a plug of tobacco, or the cow its ruminant cud.

All human rights, indeed! In his hillcountry accent Triggerfoot got it more nearly correct. "All human *rats*," he muttered to himself as the Senator spoke and he looked out at the scene. His image of spider now gave way to an oversized wharf rat wearing a gold crown. "I reckon it's a regular human rats festival jubilee we're having today and led by the king daddy human rat his own sorry self. And sorrier too, he'll soon be."

The dais was raised just high enough and in such a way for Triggerfoot to go in behind. One or two in the front row of the audience throng noticed that Triggerfoot took a wet-looking cloth and with it deftly brushed the Senator's right pants leg and shoe. Snipes was just beginning his talk in earnest now and with his own eloquence was carried quite far away. He was elated with big abstractions and thus too high in the clouds to notice what went on below, at his pants leg and shoe.

His rag-wiping done, Triggerfoot disappeared from the

scene. He was not idle though. In fact, he had just kicked into high gear motion, as he swiftly worked to untie a good many of the dogs he'd collected for this purpose all day around town.

There was a shepherd, a terrier, several redbones, a walker, a boykin, a bloodhound, a chihuahua, a feist, a lab, a poodle, even a dachshund or two. Of these, it must be admitted, our Chauncey and a friend had helped gather and keep hidden more than a few. And Chauncey loaned him his setters, and Kildee a few inquisitive beagles, pointers, and rambunctious hounds.

You must know that Triggerfoot's rag had been soaked by a few of the dogs, and it was this that got rubbed on the Senator's leg.

So each dog had its time in the spotlight on the stage, heisting its leg in review on the Senator's pants leg and shoe. Better and more effective than bullets or cannonballs, they let fly. And old Snipes made it easy. He stood still as a parked car-tire, fire-hydrant, or telephone pole.

Still carried away with his battery of words, he was quite too full of himself to notice the artillery below. And oh, how the fierce battle it raged!

The bloodhound looked so comically solemn as he did his dog duty in the sharpshooter's line. And his aim, it was good. The poodle and chihuahua, despite their diminutive size, performed heroically brave. Even the dachshunds rose to the occasion, quite literally too. The show was as good as some bizarre version of the Westminster dog show, in truth, bizarre enough on its own.

And thus the whole crowd witnessed a much more interesting parade than they'd seen earlier that morn. And they saw it all, too, and saw it to end, till the massive black lab and a greyhound in tandem ended the show.

Triggerfoot had a good view of the crowd, and he took it all in. Some of the faces were frozen with fascination, mouths agape, eyes wide, some nervous, some smirking, some stifling their laughing, some laughing out loud, some looking away; but they all had this one thing in common: of the Senator's bluster, they heard not a word, and of the dog show, they'd seen it full all.

Well, you can likely predict the results of this day. Who would vote for a man for whom even half the county's dog population had shown its disdain? The canines had each voted their tickets when they heisted their legs. Their cannons in effect had taken their soldierly toll, winning the day, as ex-Senator Snipes was laid out full slain on the field.

No, from what had transpired on this fair, busy day, as any reasonable man would easily see, one lesson clearly was learned and one absolute truth had emerged: you'd not tread on old Triggerfoot without getting bit and bit solidly good, or, as friend Chauncey said, without at least getting it wet.

If history meant a new crop of greenbacks, old Snipes was history too. Triggerfoot had harvested his crop of just judgment, with the help of his four-legged friends—dogs rather than plough horses and mules.

No doubt even better and more metaphorically appropriate new sayings than these would come from this historical morn. It would be left to the local wise wits, the sitters about square, the tale tellers and bards of the town, to frame up the way these sayings would go. Judging from their wit in the past, all of us knew they'd eventually get the images just right. For in truth they'd be telling this story for some time to come, enriched and embellished long after both Triggerfoot and citizen Snipes had played out their parts on the stage and passed from the scene.

Meanwhile, next day Chauncey, in his old pickup, met Triggerfoot walking in to town. Chauncey gave him a ride and they talked over yesterday's big scene as they drove.

"Triggerfoot, what do you make of all this?" Chauncey asked his friend.

"Just nothing," was Triggerfoot's reply. "Nothing from nothing leaves nothing, as the arithmetic book tells. But Chauncey, old egg, I've come up with a better slogan that'll fit the Chamber of Commerce and Board of Tourism both."

Triggerfoot paused to make his friend ask.

"Tell me, Trig. What slogan is that?" Chauncey finally inquired.

"SELL GRANNY! That's just it. That about sums it up to a T. And they just would, too, if they could get a buck for her old hide. They've already sold you and me."

Chauncey chuckled as he put Triggerfoot out at the hardware store, and drove on his way. As Trig grew smaller in his rear view, then disappeared, Chauncey began to whistle the same jaunty old tune Trig had been humming when he'd first picked him up on the road.

XII

Mad as a Hornet

Weeks now after the big HISTORY IS OUR MONEY CROP festival, the workaday world of Clay Bank had come back to its normal pace. Over the square still hung the giant new slogan, but its plastic was torn in several places and the banner now hung askew. It flapped and rattled in the wind.

Triggerfoot, after the Snipes triumph, settled down a little for a bit, but he wasn't through. Chauncey and Kildee and others who knew him figured that the time bomb still ticked. They wondered metaphorically in whose outhouse it would be placed and just whose dung would fly. It was not a question of if, but when, how, and whose.

Without Snipes as patron and protector, Triggerfoot knew there'd be easy pickings from a number of establishment men. The sheriff, the mayor, the head of Clay Bank Chamber of Commerce, the president of the Clay Bank Development Board, all these had had some hand in Triggerfoot's jailing, as he'd eventually found out; and it would most likely be one or another of these, one of them. We just wondered which.

But we'd underestimated our Triggerfoot—even we.

The Clay Bank Chamber of Commerce usually met each month with the Clay Bank Development Board. They met in the board room atop city hall. But this monthly meeting was to be a truly big summit. It included the Clay Bank mayor and his staff, the sheriff and his biggest cheese deputies, county council, tourism commission, some state officials, and more. Because of its size, they had to change the meeting room to the judge's big courtroom at the county courthouse. This space could comfortably seat two hundred or more.

Triggerfoot kept up with details through his low-level friends at both city hall and the courthouse itself. At the latter, he was friend with the janitor, an important old fellow, who had all the keys.

This one wasn't much of a challenge, so the story is brief.

Triggerfoot, nature boy that he was, knew where half a dozen large hornet nests hung on persimmon and cedar and oak boughs. He often rambled in the woods with our Chauncey, 'cause Chauncey learned much of his woods lore from him there. And Chauncey, who'd learned his share from his friend, contributed knowledge of half a dozen nests more. The tally made twelve, a nice apostle's number, but with this one difference sure. There wasn't a Judas in the bunch.

The day of the big summit, Triggerfoot, with a long

tree-pruner and black garbage bags on a poled contraption he'd made, snipped each giant nest into a bag, and collected all twelve. One measured a good two feet across. Its paper walls throbbed like the engine of a great logging truck. Triggerfoot didn't get stung a single time, for it may just have been him who originated the local saying, "Never hit a hornet's nest with a short stick," which meant to Triggerfoot that you shouldn't get too close to the chaos and mayhem you're about to create.

His janitor friend, after all the workers had gone home for the day, let Triggerfoot in at the alley door in the rear. Black garbage bags were naturally the janitor's stock and trade, so nothing was thought, nothing was said. But peculiarly today, these twelve bags were going in, not the opposite way.

There was a small closet in the courtroom where the judge's robes hung. In there he dressed and undressed for his duties of court. To this room, Triggerfoot had the key. And this is where the nests were deposited too.

The in-door would be Triggerfoot's fast escape route. The out-door opened into the courtroom. This would be the escape route for his mad, buzzing hot-tempered friends, who in truth were genuinely now riled.

Eight o'clock sharp and the meeting commenced. These business and bureaucrat types had nothing more to do than to get to places on time, so there they all were, near two hundred strong.

The sheriff sat on the front row, he in his bright shining badge and dressed fit to kill. The mayor was shaking hands and smiling a big toothy smile, since there were no babies to kiss.

The county council were doing statistics on taxation mills and figuring how they could get away one more time with raising the property tax. The development board was alternately weeping and shouting "Industry! Industry now!" They for all the world sounded like the frenzied fans at a football game.

Boosterism reigned. The chamber officials glowed, like the charcoals on their suburban gas-powered grills. It was truly a booster club bureaucrat's utopian heaven on earth. Cash registers played a "Hallelujah Chorus" at which all assembled dutifully rose. An "Ode to Joy" chimed out from the clinking coin. Flashbulbs spewed and cameras whirred.

This dog-pony show and circus had it all; overhead cam projector, e-mails projected on screens, statistical charts looming like strange ghosts hovering before them like ectoplasms on the front wall. "Just look at the full pews. The worship place of Mammon," Triggerfoot thought as he prepared, like old Samson before him, to bring the great temple down. "They's as mad as my hornets or the mad folks they've got locked up on Bull Street at the big crazy house. In their own way, they's madder, seems to me."

The town clock on the Clay Bank opera house chimed out nine and prepared Belshazzar's own doom. The hand came out of nowhere and once again wrote its MENE in the shadowy statistical charts projected on wall.

Triggerfoot had once again proved that everything that goes sneaking around in the night ain't Santa Claus. Instead of a pack, he had his twelve garbage bags ready. They hung from the judge's long peg rack, where he kept his wardrobe of black garments for court. Triggerfoot had untied the bags' tops and had placed through each top a cord. Pulling this from the back door, all the hornet nests would be yanked from the pegs and drop to the floor.

Before the assembly arrived, he'd taken the pins out of the hinges of the closet door that opened onto the courtroom and had corded the door handle from the inside.

Just as the development board's president boomed out "Industry now!" to the room's wild, mad applause, Triggerfoot pulled both the cords.

The crowd scarcely heard the inward fall of the door, for they were madly applauding and looking wildly out of excited wide eyes.

But the scene quickly turned even wilder and madder as over 12,000 mad hornets, seeking the lights and human smell of the room, made their presence known to each one and all.

Triggerfoot's only regret was that he hadn't been able to witness the scene. "A man just can't have everything he wants in this world," Triggerfoot told Kildee and Chauncey the next day. "But, I swannie, you can bet it would have done my old heart good—better than winning the biggest prize in the governor's silly dam-fool lottery once every week for a whole calendar year." In this last,

Triggerfoot was referring to the state lottery created just the year before, as another tax on its gullible citizens who couldn't think beyond. But as in most things, as was usual, Triggerfoot immediately saw the scam, while the many around him got fooled.

As Chauncey rocked at his ease at Kildee's potbellied stove, he looked over at his friend and asked, "Well, Triggerfoot, how did all this come out? Did your hornets pronounce judgement in the courtroom yesterday?"

"Well, Chauncey, I swear, you don't listen right good. As I told you, how'd I know? I was gone from the scene. But my friend at the courthouse, who stationed himself cross the square, said he'd heard applause, shouts of 'Industry,' a pause, then lots of blood-curdling screams.

"These lasted a good while, because—icing on the cake—I'd on leaving locked up the courtroom's giant front double doors with the keys my janitor friend loaned for the purpose of same. The door to the hornets fell off its hinges and thus couldn't be closed. The big doors leading outside to relief would not open, so the hornets calmed down a little, knowing they'd not have to hurry and could pick then and choose their targets in relative ease."

Triggerfoot continued: "I hope they enjoyed Sheriff Ketcham's fat face and rear. Thinking of that just gives me a warm feeling inside.

"Well, after I left the scene of my crime, I just walked straight on down to Clay Bank Memorial Hospital and sat in the nice new waiting room at the door to the emergency room. Some of the swole-headed assembly that soon showed up noticed me sitting there at the door, but most of them didn't, 'cause they were fidgeting, burning, scratching, rubbing, frantic to get some relief, as if doctor could help them to some, now that the damage was done. Ain't it just like these dam-fools to think that their money could buy some magic technology pill to make them all happy, warm-fuzzy comfortable again!

"So you see, I did at least get to witness some of the results of the scene from the crowd pouring in. The swole-headed mayor had a bigger than usual swole head. McCall's face was redder than red. He give me a glare as he whizzed through the door, so fast I didn't have time to ask him if he was searching for nails.

"I was looking most close and could see on some of the patients-to-be, swollen lips and eyes, ears red and swole-up twice their natural size. Some of the faces were puffy white, with only little black slits of eyes. Sheriff Ketcham qualified as one of these, and one of the swollen up best. He saw me there, and I was glad, for that gave me the very best alibi too.

"And I just couldn't let this chance pass me by, so I said to old Ketcham right there: 'Ketcham, looks like you've got more to do tonight than bust up a person's great-grandaddy's still.'

"He just cussed me and rushed on inside. Mad as a hornet, by golly, I reckoned, as I laughed to myself. But the hornets weren't finished. As I watched him disappear, last thing I saw was an unsatisfied, fat, golden hornet peep out from the back of his coat collar, and eyeing Ketcham's bare tender neck, still spoiling, he hoped, for a sting. And I had a tender feeling for the little buzzing trooper, hoping he'd succeed, for all the hornets had in fact played better part of a friend, than arya one of the humans who sat in those fancy lacquered and polished, money-sanctified pews.

"Then I heard Ketcham's shrill 'Yow. Yow. Yow'" and I knew the darlin' little critter had connected for sure. I heard Ketcham slap and thrash.

"As you know, Chauncey and Kildee, my dears, a mad hornet's got a hay of a sting. And maybe when the swellin's gone down on these fancy folks' usual fat swollen heads, it'll stay down awhile, and they'll get back their sanity too. Now Chauncey, what's the lottery chances of that, does you think? Slim, I reckon, and I'd be willing to wager on that one!"

And Triggerfoot's mason jar sparkled in the light and gave a satisfied gluck.gluck.gluck.gluck.

XIII

Accent Reduction

~⦿~

It took several months for all the dust to settle down from the mayhem occasioned by Triggerfoot's incarceration and his subsequent retaliations. Now on one fine spring day, Chauncey and he were walking from Chauncey's to Cousin Kildee's store. Triggerfoot had been helping Chauncey line his rows, as Chauncey had just helped Triggerfoot line his. Straight as an arrow they were, and they took a country man's proper pride in this.

On their way to the store, they took their time, noticing everything as they went—from what neighbours were doing or had done in their fields to the fresh new color of the woods, a green that was golden, for the tender new leaf shoots, as yet unfurled, were as yet more yellow than green. This color reminded Chauncey of a snatch of a poem whose name he couldn't recall. As he walked, its rhythm got mixed up with his feet and stride, and the words kept on going through his head: *Nature's first green is gold. Its hardest hue to hold. Its hardest hue to hold.*

"Most surely so," Chauncey thought, but didn't say aloud, for there was plenty of quiet on their walk. He and Triggerfoot were comfortable that way. They didn't have to be talking every minute of the time.

One particular red buckeye tree by the side of the road caught Triggerfoot's eye. It was in full brilliant bloom, its splendid scarlet candles peeking out from the edge of the wood. It burned brighter than maples in fall.

Triggerfoot broke the silence: "Looks for the world like a burning bush. Bet it was this kind of tree that old Moses saw."

"It most probably was," Chauncey agreed, knowing full well that to argue with Triggerfoot on the matter would be to get nowhere fast. And in a way, the tree must be speaking to him in a manner Moses would have understood. But a red buckeye growing in a Middle Eastern desert was something Chauncey's mind took a while to adjust to and grasp. Finally, though, accept it he did. It was somehow more Triggerfoot's world than his, and Chauncey played by its rules.

"Them red buckeye candles could light up the world," Triggerfoot declared.

As they passed old farmer Caleb's, they saw him distant in the fields with his sons.

"Look over yonder," Triggerfoot said. "Bossy as always, I declare."

In truth, Caleb was busy directing the work, too busy to see the two walk by, and it was too far to holler or shout.

So they walked on unseen. On such a day as this, to shout that loud would be worse than disturbing the peace, more criminal than the new noise ordinance just enacted in Clay Bank town.

To be fair, that law was aimed at juking loud car radios, CD players, and such, which neither Chauncey nor Triggerfoot thought much of.

"Dam-fool worse than me," Triggerfoot would mutter when such a vehicle passed him by, the whole car vibrating and rocking, the driver making dance motions with his shoulders and head.

"Dancing in the car. And without a partner. What next?" Triggerfoot would say.

But, for all his dislike of annoying loud music forced on the public, the new law raised Triggerfoot's hackles just the same. "Guess we better mind how loud we fart," he said, "or we'll be farting in jail. I sure don't have the ready cash to pay them big ordinance fines, and I eats lots of butter-beans and peas. I've already warned old Flop-Eye, and he's toning it down."

"You know, Chauncey," he continued, "I don't have no pickup, like you, to pawn if I gets in a tight. Don't have no jewelry, nor stereos, nor TVs. Wonder what Beulah would bring."

"I don't rightly know, Triggerfoot," Chauncey replied. He smiled at Triggerfoot's as usual outrageous, but logical, take on things. At the core of his wildest tomfoolery lurked an even more outrageous truth. The world's absurdity could only be expressed by Triggerfoot's own theatre of the absurd. *Waiting for Godot* had nothing on him. But then he reckoned Triggerfoot's drama was more like an old Mummer's play, acted on village square when country and local villages were still centres of life.

The white, fleshy petals of a big-leaf magnolia caught Chauncey's eye. Its flowers were showy as they bloomed on their bare black limbs. "Blooming its heart out," Chauncey said out loud.

The flowers looked like giant white lotus blossoms or water lilies floating among inky branches of trees. Big as plates they were, a levitation of flower spirits in the woods. When they got fully ripe, the seeds' red, fleshy coats dangled on yellow cords, as if they beckoned him to pick and plant.

For the last fifteen years, in off times, Chauncey had been collecting the seed from the tree's great purple cones. He'd learned how to plant them in buckets, then when they'd come up, transplant them to pots, grow them up for a summer or two, then set them out in the woods. He'd now set out more than three hundred on his land. On his walks, he would mark the progress of their growth. Some had now gotten much taller than him.

For some reason, this particular tree seemed like a cousin to Chauncey, some kind of close kin. There was no real explaining the attraction. Maybe its three-foot-long leaves, he supposed. Or maybe because one day Hoyalene had broken a branch in full flower and brought it inside, and when she fell ill, he did the same for her, placing them fresh in a vase at her bedside. Or maybe it was just its joy in sending up giant fresh blossoms, each a work of perfection, that would last only a day and be gone, yet that fact not holding it back from doing, no, not a jot. It bloomed impractically, lavishly, in a spendthrift celebration of life, not measuring or calculating the cost, not weighing being against reasons not to be. He spoke none of this aloud, though Triggerfoot, perhaps even better than he, would have understood.

Now Chauncey had begun to give the potted trees to friends, who liked having them too, and planted them around. In days long ago, this tree had been common enough, present in groves scattered here and there, but with all the ravages of planting crops and tree-farming the land, loggers clear-cutting everything every twenty-five or thirty years, only a bedraggled few had escaped before Chauncey went on his tree-planting rampage. After Hoyalene had died, he poured all his grief into this scheme. It helped him get through, making a thing that she loved, to live, when she could not. In some small way, she lived on in these trees, which he now spread far and wide. They fanned out from his farm like the rays of the sun.

"A regular Johnny Magnolia-seed, is our Chauncey," Triggerfoot said. He was amused at his friend's trying to learn the Latin names for all the plants around. So at other times when Chauncey was in a *Magnolia tripetala* or *macrophylla* planting mood, he'd call him "The Macrophylla Kid," like some desperado of the tree-planting kind.

Although Trig might joke about his friend's interest in

trees, he approved. They both were aware of the earth's manifold productions, the richness of variety and individuality in nature, as they admired it in women and men. No two the same.

Then Triggerfoot had one of his moments. "If I was to die," he declared, "suddenly, right now, like that there magnolia flower, out of the bare sticks of my body, I'd break into bloom." To that, Chauncey could make no reply. Birth, death, and rebirth. Yes, a solemn Mummer's play.

As they walked on, dogwoods were everywhere in bloom. So were the redbuds and yellow jessamine vines, spilling in long ropes down oaks and pines. The jessamine's yellow bells smelled better than anything bottled by men. The world, after a cold winter with several big ice storms and snows, was ready for color and fragrance and life. So were the two who walked at their leisure down the road. Winters in drafty old houses made you rejoice fully and properly in spring. It taught you the meaning of joy.

Chauncey had seen the joy in nature too. The first warm night breaking the winter's more than usual cold, he had spotted with his headlights a field of deer. The new-born young were frisking, almost like they were jumping up in dance, clicking their heels. Chauncey sat in his truck by the roadside and watched them for a long time. "Joy," he had said aloud. It was this same feeling that he felt with the coming of warm days. The two friends walked on, and the smell of new-turned soil came on the wind. From further off, a whiff of burning broom sage.

Now there on the roadside grew a large patch of iris—

"white flags," they were called in this place. Every old house in the neighbourhood had a few, and some even had rows. They'd mark where old houses had been, many years after the structures were gone, and along with jonquils, lenten lilies, and buttercups and snowdrops, still showed where the garden paths had been. Often they'd crop up on roadsides for just no reason at all. They endured toughly and faithfully over time, thriving on neglect, it seemed. Triggerfoot said that to them they looked like the face of hope.

Indeed, their cool, watery white petals reminded Chauncey of Easter and of Hoyalene too. She'd break large bunches to decorate the altar of their church. She'd go there with armfuls of dogwoods and blue-bottles and iris. He remembered one clear Saturday before Easter when she was decorating the church. She wore a white flag in her raven black hair. He was helping her at the altar, and a gleam of sunlight coming through the bright blue of the stained glass robe of Christ in Gethsemane Garden fell on her face and white blouse, and turned the iris in her hair strangely to blue. It was just like yesterday and he felt himself suddenly catching a breath.

As was his wont, when he thought of Hoyalene, his hand went automatically to the locket at his chest. "Hoyalene," he almost spoke aloud, as if to get her attention across the table at suppertime.

Instead he called back the image of the stained glass altar scene. WATCH AND PRAY, the base of the window read, and Christ was kneeling in long blue robes with his hands clasped in prayer outstretched on a flat grey rock under olive branches, begging the Father to take this cruel cup away.

"But Thy will be done," Chauncey, breaking from his reverie, said aloud, before remembering he had a companion there.

"And thine too," Triggerfoot replied—sincerely and not in what would have been his usual flip way, for he'd caught Chauncey's mood.

Then there was the store. It materialized like some familiar ghost out of the woods. The resident hound sat at its entrance. Every such store had at least one such stray that had come out of nowhere and which the store more or less owned. In the absence of anyone else, the store reckoned it did. Actually, it was kind of the common property of the neighbourhood, friendly, but independent, and sometimes aloof. Sometimes you wondered if the store and neighbourhood owned it, or it owned neighbourhood and store.

But then it was not necessary to reason or say. Like the great magnolia blossoms, it would be there for its eyeblink of life and be gone, but just for its brief time, at least, levitating on the banks of the great river, it would joyously stay. "Everything to its season and purpose," Kildee would declare.

The hound came up friendly and slowly to greet the two familiar men. It sniffed at their shoes, then went back to its seat at the door.

Inside, there was the bustle of a spring morn. Kildee was staying busy at the counter, totting up purchases, joking, and visiting, receiving and passing on news, passing on greetings to other family members and neighbours and friends via visitors there, receiving greetings via them. Life was much more a matter of this than business with Kildee, as all around knew.

So Chauncey and Triggerfoot were the sole masters this day of the realm of the potbellied stove, at which few visitors this planting season had luxury to sit. Spring ploughing was the busiest time of the year. In fact, the two old friends had it mostly to themselves the whole day, with only an occasional cameo appearance from Kildee or a brief malingerer or two.

Into this eddying of the quiet stream of their day Chauncey cast a baited line. The water was as calm and blue as Christ's stained glass robe, as placid as water could be. He knew Triggerfoot would bite at his hook with the relish of a great, hungry, ten-pound bass in Chauncey's pond. So cast it, he did. The line played out this way.

"Triggerfoot," Chauncey not so innocently began. "I've got a suggestion that would save you lots of trouble and grief, lots of times. If you'd known about this before your cannon explosion, you'd have not been subjected to such an ordeal."

"No big ordeal for me," Triggerfoot replied, "at least when measured against them others that got visited by dozens of doggies, and millions of mad stinging hornets, and such."

But Triggerfoot was playing with the bait, nibbling along. He was curious to know what Chauncey was up to with him.

"Unravel," he said. "I know they's most likely fixin' to be some nonsense from you. What is it today?"

Chauncey chuckled at this, for as usual his friend had once again caught his mood.

"Over yonder in Georgia, at a big university night school," he began, "they're having a fancy class called Accent Reduction 101. I wonder if you'd better not enroll. If you'd just have said i-ron instead of our'n, properly, you know, like the fine folks in the Clay Bank Chamber of Commerce and Development Board, you'd not ever lost your great-grandpappy's still, or landed in jail."

At this, Triggerfoot's eyes widened, but he made not a sound. He just waited for Chauncey to dig his hole deeper, before he'd explode.

"Yes, indeed, old pal, they have what they call a Speech Pathologist to teach the class, and that will treat the nastiest language disease. While I was over there last year with Hoyalene's brother, I saw the class description my own self, brought to my attention by my brother-in-law's friend, who taught at the school. A Speech Pathologist, he said, can just cure any such raging disease, even what might seem to be terminal ones like your own."

Finally, this last was too much for old Trig to hold in. His eyes narrowed into a glare—a signal that Chauncey well knew was prefatory to dishing out damnation and hell. "Chauncey, you're a liar. There's no such of a thing as—a what? Speech Pathologist, did you say?"

"No, honest. I'm in dead earnest, Trig. The real article, a Speech Pathologist that can cure your disease. Don't you think you should enroll, or get a doctor's appointment, or whatever they'd call the thing? Then you could talk like Snipes, Reverend Bugg, Mrs. Jerrold, and the Clay Bank Chamber of Commerce and Development Board."

For once, Triggerfoot was almost speechless. But after a considered long pause, his eyes narrowed further into a furious steely squint as he began: "Change the way that I talks and my daddy, and his daddy 'fore him? Why, I'd first sooner cut off my head."

After another long pause, in which he was building up steam—"I knows the way that them Commerce and Development folks speaks, or tries to, at least, to sound like them goons on the news on TV. But they ain't foolin' me none. All their fancy no-accent's an accent, sure as God's in his heaven and his world's gone to hell."

There obviously wouldn't be any accent reduction classes in Triggerfoot's future. From his vehement tone, no crystal ball was needed to see that. Of course, before Chauncey brought all this up, he knew there'd be no rush to enroll, but he wanted to hear how his friend would stand up for himself. And he wasn't disappointed a whit.

He looked over at Kildee with a wink, and said: "I believe old Triggerfoot *would* sooner cut off his head than to bow to that upwardly mobile crew."

Yes, Chauncey was pleased with the way his friend had answered, with his comment that in effect he'd rather die first, for in a real sense, he would be dead if he changed. He'd no longer be Triggerfoot anymore.

"What you reckon these folks over yonder have in

mind?" Kildee asked. "I hope they don't come nosing 'round here looking for speech disease. We got fools enough already in Clay Bank and down Columbia way, than to add more to their numbers with the PhD'd kind. You know that big university down thar with all them fat paying salaries for being dam-fools. Well, all them degrees, my daddy used to say, only puts you in kinship with a ther-mometer of the rectal kind."

Chauncey had already thought about this question for sometime, of why they'd want to change, and he and broth-er-in-law Clint had concluded this way: "They do it to make themselves able to get more of the things of the world."

Chauncey continued, "One of their Speech Pathologists said to Clint: 'Well, Mr. Blair, you get you a new and more fashionable hairstyle, don't you? You learn better table manners too, get you a new suit of clothes—to be more socially acceptable, you see. Why not a new way of speak-ing too?' As if accents are bad manners, or you can put on speech like a new suit of clothes. Change as easy as a hair-style in an hour or two. The nerve of such cattle, I say. They act like those little green lizards outside the store that change color to the wood or the leaf they happen to pause on. They play-act their way through the world, so every-thing they do is just fakery and quackery and pretense at the core—everywhere that they go. Who'd want to know them? There'd be nothing to know, like a wisp of fog in the wind. They'd have nothing to offer but vowels pronounced in a one-size-fits-all sort of way. Uni-race, uni-sex, uni-world, like the Ebony-and-Ivory Uni-race Uni-sex Hair Salon. Why, they're nobody at all. I sure wouldn't trust anyone whose life was put on like a play, or put on or took off like a fashionable or unfashionable coat. 'I expect,' my brother-in-law says, 'they finally are changed out of existence and always take their color from the world, having none of their own.' They sure don't have no place to call home, and that's what's the matter with them. They're not from anywhere. And I expect the young fellow's just about right, but maybe a little too kind. If the world had only their sort, there'd be no color left in it at all."

Yes, Triggerfoot's "rather cut my head off first" was the dead centre answer, like the bullseye of the dart board on Kildee's store wall. If Trig played the chameleon, then Trig wouldn't be Trig anymore.

The Speech Pathologist would have called the way all those around Kildee's store talked, "nasty drawl." "Y'all" would probably cause him to try to crawl up a wall. "Nasty drawl," that's what he called what Hoyalene's brother had, indeed, as if diagnosing a bad virus or cold. His sales pitch was that the course wasn't going to cost him but 750 dollars to get rid of it too. Quite the medical deal. That is, if it could be done in only one semester, not two. And even then, compare that to a top surgeon's fee. Then all the increased salary the student would make with better jobs and promotions would soon pay it all back. "One of the best investments, Mr. Blair, you could ever make," the

Pathologist declared. A neat sort of pitch. He had it down pat, as just an investment, and a sound one too. "Have you seen what's happened to stocks of late?" the learned Pathologist threw in as final argument in a most knowing way.

"Another fool scam," Triggerfoot weighed in, "like a Yankee peddler's of old, to separate innocent dam-fools from their coin." He continued, "I mind what my grand-pappy was told, that in the long, long ago, peddlers came down to these parts in wagons selling their wares. Tin pans and frying pans were tied all over their wagons and vans, a kind of portable moving Kildee's store with horses and wheels. You could hear their clanking and jiggling long before they were seen. Grandpappy said how they'd pass off mahogany sawdust as cayenne pepper, and have nutmegs carved outen wood. He was savvy enough for the most part and only bought tin pails, that is, after he'd tested them to see if they'd hold water without too big of a leak. But one time he got bit, and got bit bad, just the same. He bought a dozen two-inch-long pumpkin seeds that were guaran-teed to grow fruit of a humonstrous size, a titanic great pumpkin that would be the wonder of these parts around.

"And Job the old peddler made him a mint in these parts, it was said, from the sale of these seeds, Grandpappy heard tell—that is, for the first season only. 'Cause them seeds never come up. They rotted in the ground. Like them wooden nutmegs, they was carved outen wood. Grandpappy cussed for a year and remembered it to his dying day.

"So, my dearies, be careful with these peddling men types. They's born just to cheat, and cheat you they will. They'll sell you a flummery of goods, and call it better manners, smooth speaking, a new hairdo, or a new suit of clothes. Iced up with the cake icing of promises, you won't know what you've got under that icing till you've got your cake home. It might be devil's food cake, or the devil himself. Might be chocolate or it might just as likely be dung."

"Kildee," Triggerfoot changed his tone and declared, "Don't you reckon it's about time for a new hairdo for your twenty-four hairs?"

To that, Kildee answered, "There's only one hairdo around this old store. Hare do this! Hare do that! Or it's what Lula Bess will do to my hair when she thinks it gets too long at my neck. When old Jayber the barber died some time ago, she bought his second-hand clippers from his estate sale, and learned on her own. It was that or drive all the way to Clay Bank to the Ebony-and-Ivory Uni-race Uni-sex Hair Salon, and I've got better things to do with my time."

Triggerfoot replied, "From appearances, looks like Chauncey cuts *his* own hair, too, and in the dark of the night, withouten his glasses, and when there's no moon."

To that, Chauncey stayed silent, because, truth to tell, he did cut his own, ever since Hoyalene's death; and did a good enough job. As he said, he wasn't trying to make

Gentleman's Quarterly or the fashion magazines.

Jim-Jesse Sims, who'd just come in the store, and hearing the conversation, said that the other day he "seen a new hair-styling place," with the curious name of CUTTIN' UP on its sign. But he didn't cotton much to the name, "'cause that's what folks 'round here calls their female dogs when they's in heat."

Triggerfoot laughed. He'd seen that same hair-styling salon, and knew that same phrase. What caused him to laugh most expressly was that, honest to God, as luck would have it, it was located right next to the Clay Bank Dog Hospital and Vet.

"There at the Vet," he said, "you get your dog fixed. Then, no more cuttin' up, lessen you go next door and wants a trim."

Triggerfoot went on: "What if you was to get the two places mixed up on a high lonesome tear, and your head all muddled from the corn, and you went in for a trim but got the wrong office and came out singing soprano when you went in singing base."

This talk about cuttin' made Chauncey uneasy. "Enough about cuttin', whether up or down," he laughed and chimed in. "Hairdoes and cutting off heads and accents, and neuterings and bobbittings, and speys. Friend Triggerfoot, we best get on our way. I got to drive you back home to your farm before milking time."

"Well, Chauncey, what if one of them Speech Pathologists was to get hold of me and cured my disease, give me a new hairdo, cured my table manners, and put me in a grey flannel pin-striped new suit of clothes. A Marx Brothers suit. Would I be me? Reckon you'd recognize me then?"

"Mr. Triggerfoot, don't you mean Brooks Brothers suit, not Marx Brothers?" Jim-Jesse broke in.

"Marx Brothers, Brooks Brothers, I knows the difference. You think that I don't, but they's all Larry, Curly, and Mo just the same, with Karl and Groucho and Chico and Harpo thrown in to boot—pin-stripes, grey flannel or no.

"Chauncey, I just wants me a hairdo like Curly, or maybe Harpo, from the Ebony-and-Ivory Uni-race Uni-sex Hair Salon, a kind of Marx Brothers Afro, and maybe even a new name for myself with it all—maybe something like, oh— 'Hairpo, the Accentless Wonder,' with kinky locks greased and lacquered down with a fresh coat of polyurethane paint, in a new pin-striped suit, and cured of my nasty draggledy drawling disease. Or maybe a combination of mullet in back and dreadlocks in front would do? I'd just have to see what would suit my classic profile. So much to choose from, so little time!

"Like one of them freaks in a side show, or one of them Speech Pathologist rectal thermometered Ph.D.s, maybe I could get me a fat, easy salary or two, give up farmin', get a wide, fat arse from sitting at a desk, sell the old farmhouse, and go live at a travelling college, or better, go live fair to fair in a circus tent and give the bearded lady some competition for cash. Maybe some budding romances with lizard women or bearded ladies would then be in my crystal ball, provided I don't get too near that Cuttin'-Up-Dog-Vet-and-Uni-race-Uni-sex-Hair Salon. *"Rat this way, ladies and gents! Eighth wonder of the world. See 'Hairpo, the Accentless Wonder.' He can set a table with all them salad forks at just the right place, not drink from the finger bowl, use napkin rings without dropping a one or lobbing them at ole Blue, not dribble redeye gravy or sorghum molasses or grits, or better yet quiche, on his new grey flannel pin-striped lapels, say grace like the parson thanking but always a-asking for more, and nevermore break wind at the table—leastways till everyone's eating is through."*

But to the delight of most of those gathered, Trig wasn't done. His eyes still in that steely squint, he continued resolutely on: "The crowd at the fair would look skittish, but the barker would proclaim, *"We lets him outen his cage now and then to roam out on his own, don't even need a leash or a chain. We taken the bone outen his nose, and the spear outen his hand. He ain't cooked and eat no one in days."*

At this, Jim-Jesse bowed out. The talk had gotten a mite beyond him. A literal, most sober fellow, he couldn't take any more. Like his famous high-powered corn liquor, Triggerfoot had to be administered in small doses, and carefully too.

But Chauncey and Kildee got a big kick out of it all, and an especially good laugh at "Hairpo, the Accentless Wonder," now unleashed and off of his chain; and then Chauncey and Triggerfoot, after themselves bowing out, set off on foot on their own way home. They had a smart way to walk till they got to the truck, and were glad that these spring days were now getting long.

XIV

When Shall the Swan

When will that day-star, mildly springing,
 Warm our Isle with peace and love?
When shall heav'n, its sweet bell ringing,
 Call my spirit to the fields above?
— Thomas Moore, *Silent, Oh Moyle*

Triggerfoot, for all his roughness and occasional crudeness, could be as gentle as a shepherd with lambs. Like most of us, he had his boisterous moods, but could be elegant serious too. He was special with children—the children he had wanted but never had—and they flocked to his feet. This fine autumn Saturday found him seated at the tree-filled Clay Bank courthouse square at his usual stand, or, I should say, his usual park-bench perch.

Released from the bonds of school, children's voices trebled in glee. On bicycles, on foot, taut-energy-driven, they were all over the square. That is, until they fell under Triggerfoot's powerful sway.

Several dropped their bicycles and gathered around. They sat on the warm rose-colored bricks at the foot of his cast-iron bench. Then there were six. Then there were ten. They accumulated as naturally as the leaves falling from the largest oak tree there.

Magic transformation was all about in the air. The cooling

of summer, the coloring of leaves, like the rising flush of color
to cheeks. The growing up of children, their magical quiet-
ing down after noise of the day. And Triggerfoot's own
magic was well on its way. He was becoming their age,
transforming himself in reverse of the aging of seasons, himself growing back into child. An artist, magician, just so.

At length he became one with his audience. "Negative
Capability," the celebrated poet would say, to banish self
and become for a time what you described—in Triggerfoot's
case, to become the imaginative age of the ones described to.

And as such, as one of them, he began:

"Old Triggerfoot, my dearies, has a story to tell. Don't be
minding his broken old hat and his tattered up clothes. Sit
around him and listen of the long, long ago. You'll remember all this in later years, I vow. When you've babes of your
own, you'll need this golden-coined treasure for them.

"Now dearies, you hear the church bells of our old town?
They can ring you awake or to sleep, if you listens closely
for them.

"If you listens right, they each have a voice. You can
learn to tell them in time, like voices of friends. The
Wesleyan bell has a tinny brass sound. Trinity's rings silvery hollow, like silver forks put down heavily on lace; old
Ebenezer's bells sounds like birds chanting each to each on
a bright August day. St. Eustace echoes the peal of pipe
organ within. The Baptist bell has the sound of coins hitting big collection plates.

"But in the olden days, my dearies, the greatest voice of

them all was from our old First Scots. You see its twin towers there right behind me, just over my head. Yes, her bells,
they rang true and rang long. They had range of ten tones, at
least so say the people of old who to us passed the knowledge
on down. In one mood, the bells could be sombre like the
chimes from a far, misty wet valley in spring. In another,
they could sing out a blessing on land like the voices of children at recess or released at last for the day—happy free voices like yours in glee. Their sounds carried the faithful like
wings on their great voyage beyond. They comforted mourn-
ers, and widows, and orphans, and the daughters of men, and
promised meeting again. They strengthened the sons to take
up the plough or to measure and mend. They sang of
redemption and the joys of rightful God-given blessings to
men. But most of all they sang the song of the free.

"Old Scots' voices were like the sound of waves on the
shore, like the lap of waters on land. Like the fluted, rhyth-
mical breathing of the loved-one at sleep by the side.

"But that was in the long, long ago, back before the dark
evil day when your great-grandfathers and uncles and
brothers lay dying on fields, or stretched out cold and
white on their biers.

"It was then that the bells of First Scots left their twin
towers to ring out no more, to be melted for shot and ball
in defense of the land. Blue-clad men came with their
swords to burn, pillage, and steal. And the towers were
silent. They fell under the sway of ruin and stark grey
decay. And the silence was so fierce and loud that it hurt

hearts of the daughters and sisters and mothers of men.

"Yes, old First Scots vowed no bells. No new bell would then ring from its towers again till the freedom of land, till the curse of invader would lift with his leaving and the people be free. Other churches restored then their bells; but First Scots had made its decree. No voice from its towers would ever be heard till the land would be free.

"For thousands of months now the gaunt silver moon has waxed and then waned twixt the dark brooding towers, now empty of bells and their sounds. Not even the birds will utter a note from the towers' stones. They too honor the silence of sadness and grieving of loss. Like the stopping of time and enchantment of hours frozen in limbo of a night that never can turn into day, it's like the day star, in sympathy, refuses to shine.

"It was in the time when the bells left the towers in defense of a woe-beset land that a daughter of the town grew into her most beautiful own. Midst all the strife, she bloomed suddenly forth like apple blossoms on tree, surprising the unsuspecting, taking their breath clean away.

"For of grace and perfection, there was none like her in the town. Her name too was as rare as the beauty of face and her form. It was Finnuala, a name from the lore of the people of long days before.

"Finnuala's story, like her life and her beauty, like all life and beauty, was tragically brief. As she blossomed in majesty, she seemed to know it herself that 'twas doomed. The sadness at moments would shine from those perfect larkspur blue eyes, or be caught in the trace of a tear occasioned by the heart of the maid, who could never bear suffering of any of even God's smallest things.

"Tender-hearted she was for the bird with the broken, spoiled wing, or the timid mouse in her mother's cruel trap. Her mother might grumble, but Finnuala could only see how its tiny features showed its final sharp pain.

"Finnuala was desired by all men who witnessed her beauty. She had no protector, for her father and brothers died in the cruel hard war. She had laid them on biers among flowers and had wept them and mourned, as their fatal wounds oozed scarlet through cerements and bandage and clothes.

"Her own chosen young man, grown up with from childhood, had asked her to marry, and she had agreed. They would have soon wed had he not also been killed, sacrificed on the invader's cold steel.

"Now in victory the blue-clad hoards were swarming among them, burning and stealing, and forcing by sword. She was hotly pursued by an unwanted new suitor among them, as her own chosen young soldier lay dead on his bier.

"Truly, the usurping new suitor was the best of the invaders, but in his desire, attended her cruelly there. He had used the hard confusing time of her lover's own death to pursue his desire. Yes, he courted her even as she wept by his side, her head in her hands, and her untied billowing black hair streamed down dishevelled like dark raven falls in the mountains above. So distressed then was she.

"Her silence he wrongly took for assent, you must see, so just at the moment the soldier thought he'd won her fair hand right there at the bier, her dead lover's wounds opened anew, and bled through the linen profuse scarlet fresh blood. Finnuala saw. The victor may have thought he had owned her, but, in truth, no master was he.

"And the moment usurper reached his hand to the face of his prize, she was gone.

"In her place was the form of wild swan, like no other creature the folks of these parts had ever seen. Her suitor was stunned, grasped and grappled the air, and then fled like a thief from the scene.

"For fair Finnuala had been turned into the most beautiful and graceful and saddest of birds. Swan's beauty was like beauty of all, inspiring sharp sadness at rareness and briefness, and the fact that it truly is not of this world. The kind guardian spirit of a woe-beset land had had mercy on her and had taken her thus to her own tragic and bleeding sad breast.

"And the old story goes that Finnuala was made to wander certain dim lakes and secret recesses of hidden grey rivers, and at certain mystic, mysterious times could be seen, and still can to this day.

"It is said she's to wander until old First Scots' bells ring out again and on her mystic far lake, she can hear their fair sound. And that can only be when the curse of the land then is lifted, and it is free. Then she will be transformed back to her own, released, and her same faithful soldier in grey will be released from his bonds to bend face to her own in a kiss.

"Now don't you weep, my dearies. A century or two is so short a time, an eye blink to a rare magic wild swan. But until that time, bells will be silent. We must wait for their sound, and their magic release."

As Triggerfoot finished his tale of the long, long ago, the children sat entranced as the last copper beams from the sun glinted through oaks, still disrobing of leaves. The whispers of their fall on the now quiet twilight of deserted square broke the potent magic of Triggerfoot's telling, while the violet shadows of the twin empty church towers had edged toward and included them now. In little groups or alone, the children left in silence walking toward the comforts of supper and home, biding their time with the grace of sad swan, and later in sleep in their beds, dreaming the joyous music of transforming bells.

XV

Chauncey Cuts Loose

Chauncey kept chickens about his farm. He had yellows and russets, grey speckleds and browns, and a lot in between. They went by no particular breed name, not Domineckers, Leghorns, Orpingtons, or Rhode Island Reds, just a hearty mixture of all. Their feathers shone rich green tints—a sign that they were well fed on the richest of nature's own foods. He let them roost where they would. Some flew up in the tall cedar trees, protection against cold and sleet in winter, and hiding from minks, weasels, possums, and such.

He built them a dry hen house, but the weasels would always find a way to get in. So the chickens thought better to risk it outside. And if you know weasel nature and what they do to a hen, you'd understand it was instinctive to the breed.

Plain old-fashioned yard chickens they were; and he mixed them in with bantams, silkies, araucanas, and guineas, and an old peafowl hen. Their eggs were as rich as the sweet new-skimmed cow cream. The hens were thus in modern lingo "range-fed," and the egg yolks' color was never that pale sickly lemon yellow of the eggs that you bought in the stores.

Because chickens couldn't, they'd not know how good they had it. Sure there were possums and minks, but that brought only death, not the living death of cramped chicken houses and hermetically safe cages and pens. All there was in the latter was done by machine—mechanical feeders and waterers, mechanical collectors of eggs, the feed all spiked with chemicals and additions to make them grow fast and produce. The desired finished product was not good chicken but fast dollars and cents.

No, he would have none of those lines of white robots squatting over slots for the collection of chemical-fed eggs.

Lives lived in the grass put Chauncey's yard chickens at ease. There, as was their nature, they could scratch and find a fond worm or grub. Life was variety, and not the sameness of cage. As Chauncey soon learned, you could even tell in a chicken when a creature found joy in life. With them, this was just so.

And Chauncey saw first-hand the results of the cage. Some pullets were so cramped that the bones of their legs grew crooked and bowed. This came from the poor creatures not being able to rise, to fully extend, to stretch out their legs, so cramped as they were.

And Chauncey thought about this more often than he would like.

On one summer day, he drove down to the crossroads to

visit a neighbour who'd been ill. As he met the usual array of pickups, from beat-up to new, he raised the customary first finger from the steering wheel in friendly hello. Some of the drivers, he knew. Some he'd known only in this way on the road. He seldom failed to get his greeting returned, no matter the speed of those he met. As for Chauncey, on this day, he drove particularly slow. He looked at the faces no matter the speed. It was more than casual with him, this saying hello.

He had brought the family a good mess of beans and some fresh okra he'd overmuch of. And this okra was prime. The seed had been passed down in his family for many generations, and from his father to him. Chauncey never harvested without thinking of his kindly old dad.

His rows needed cutting each day to keep on producing, and he hated to see any of it go to waste. So off he went. The farmer had got sick before he could get his okra seed planted in. Chauncey knew that, and was "taking up the slack," as the folks round these parts would say.

A large chicken truck with its living cargo of thousands of white young fryer Leghorn hens was either broken down or just stopped at the crossroads when Chauncey went by. He'd stayed on his visit a full hour or more; and when he drove back, that same truck was still sitting, unattended there in the sun.

It was hot August, and the birds in their crowded condition were panting worse than old Bo on a run. They fought with each other just to get head out to breathe. He didn't know what got into him, but he guessed it was the example of his old friend Trig. He found himself muttering to himself, "Let go. Just let go."

So he promptly got out of his car and opened the levers to every cage. It took near an hour and he risked more than embarrassment there, if he'd have been caught.

The birds wandered off, for, in truth, they had no proper strength to fly. They'd never been out of a two-by-two space, and had no real reason to know. And they'd never touched soil, or seen grass or a tree.

They were the funniest things, blinking amazed like going from pitch dark to bright light, exploring a strange world like a babe first time let out of crib, to crawl and get into everything as it learned on its way.

Well, these chickens eventually made it to the pastures, fields, and the woods. They'd not eaten today, so they pecked, scratched, and found bugs, ate chickweed and grass, for the very first time.

Chauncey saw how fast they'd taken to chickens' natural ways. No matter how iron-deep man's unnatural, artificial conditions had been, they still had that instinctive fathoming centrally inside, at a place reduced down so tiny, but large enough still to be there, and be free basis of life.

All this did Chauncey's heart and soul a wonder of good.

He placed all the money he had in his wallet on the truck driver's seat and was gone from the scene.

A year later his farmer friend shut-in was out hale and hearty to the tasks of his farm. His okra was high, and he now had him a real bevy of white happy yard chickens that had chosen his place for a home. There were white yard chickens and white yard chicken biddies scattered around on farms for more than a mile.

They kept down all the beetle and bug population in the farmer's vegetable garden that year. No poisons were needed by him. Chauncey had learned that fact already about the benefits of fowl, but the liberated chickens were now spreading the word.

"What if I'd been caught liberating chickens?" Chauncey mused. "I'd have been put, like poor old Triggerfoot, in a cage of my own." He never regretted the choice though, for as rough on the outside as he sometimes might seem, he'd a tenderness to all creatures that suffered that redeemed so many shortcomings besides.

XVI

One Lost Sheep
~·~·~

*A single death is a tragedy. A million deaths is
a statistic.*— Joseph Stalin

At the store today, Kildee and Chauncey were talking
about the big, puzzling world outside their own. Their
own, in truth, was baffling enough, but this other was
beyond the pale. With the help of farmer Lyman and a
shifting gallery of a few farmer or hunter customers who
came and went, the faithful trio were trying to make at
least some modicum of sense of the how, where, and why
that world just didn't agree—didn't line up at all—with
their own. They concluded that that other realm was not
concerned, as they were, to know the difference—that it
probably didn't even know theirs existed, or if it did, it
would view them at best with condescending amusement,
or with bafflement and utter disdain.

"Yes, we people in the flyover country probably don't
make much of a ripple in their stream," Lyman said. "They
don't care much for things that don't pay."

"Nor do I," he continued, "Only the pay is a different
sort of a pay."

Chauncey and Kildee didn't need any explaining to know just what Lyman meant, and the conversation got no undue encumbrance for taking the time to elaborate or explain.

That's what Chauncey said he liked the most about the fellowship around the potbellied stove. Lyman put it best: "You know, talking to these other folks just tires me out so. Wears me to a frazzle. They may be good in their hearts, but having to explain every little thing wears a body out. I don't have that kind of patience no more."

And again they made no further comment. They knew just what he meant, for they'd been there before.

There was silence as Kildee put another piece of wood in the stove. The only sound other than the metallic clank of the stove door was the crackle, spew, and settle of wood and a winter wind that whispered its own deep tale about the store eaves.

A few minutes later, Chauncey picked up the trail of Lyman's thought. "Then after the explaining," he declared, "they'd most all the time look at you in wide-eyed puzzlement, or pure amaze. My days is too short to waste time on them that don't really want to know."

After another long pause, Lyman concluded, "No, we just ain't made alike, I reckon. Our bodies are forked the same, and we stand upright on the same hind legs, but that's about where the likeness begins and it ends."

"The very alpha and omega of it all," Chauncey agreed.

The talk then ranged from the Time-Is-Money,

Hurry-and-Worry values of city folk and their squirrel cage jobs, the way they lived, their pastimes, their extravagance and waste, to the kinds of superstitions this way of life was built upon.

"For them," Chauncey reflected, "it seems that truth and money are one and the same. If it makes a heap of cash, well, then it's true. If it doesn't, then it's false. What kind of equation is that to live out a life by?"

"Well, in my book, that equation would be a master superstition," Kildee declared. "And these folks don't give much caring heed to the world them two legs walk upon. Everything's bigger and better, and bigger *is* better with them. They just don't seem to do anything human scale."

Lyman shifted his weight in his rocker, and after a pause, added his concurrence: "Human scale? Take their buildings. They just dwarf me. When I'm among them, I look for the sun and it's gone. One time, I accidentally brushed up against a pre-poured concrete first-floor wall of one of those great towers, and its pebbly surface took off the skin of my knuckle and wrist. Just grated it in jags and shreds clean away. Like cheese on a grater, I'd say. I won't make that mistake ever again. As for me, I like wood, not concrete and steel. Wood's more forgiving, and I like that in things, as well as in men."

"Well, Lyman, cold cathedrals of commerce, them towers, where the watchman watches in vain. You're lucky not to have to traffic there much," Kildee said. "It's a perilous place."

"Yes," Lyman replied, "A doctor's appointment or two when old Doc says he can't or won't do, and sends me to town. That's the only time I goes. I never have the slightest wish to go to these new-fangled climate-controlled malls. Like space bubbles on the moon. But we ain't on the moon."

No answer was needed to this.

"Those high and mighty practical-minded brokers of men think they've got the entire situation figured out and in their control," Chauncey declared. "They think they're just so flaming rational and efficient in every act that they do. Their rational take on the world determines everything from business decisions to high and mighty government plans—and all built on assuming unlimited resources and unlimited profits therefrom. They have no normal human feelings of gratitude and humility, or guilt over things they might have done wrong. For ruining lives, 'Nothing personal, just business,' they say. Their great Bottom-Line is the world's religion today. Bigger and better, indeed! As for loyalty to community, neighbourhood, land, or the things thereon, you'd might as well fart in the breeze. They don't take satisfaction in the things that they do. They settle for making things half-assed, and then praise them as good and sell them to you. They don't care a damn if they damage the world. WASTE is their big middle name. Hot-toe-mighty damn, if I don't hate them for the mess of the world that they've made. And to call what they do practical and rational too! To my mind, they're the craziest of all!"

After this bit of spleen venting, there was a much longer than usual pause. There was some uneasiness, anxiousness, at the agitated tone of Chauncey's words; but things eventually settled down to its accustomed jog-trot rhythm and sway. Not that anyone there disagreed with Chauncey. No, not at all. They knew well what he meant and that he'd had reason to feel some of this sharp edge because he'd for a time had the misfortune to see this other world up closer than they.

Kildee put another piece of cherry wood on the fire. Cherry made the best fragrance of all and the brightest and hottest red coals. The fire spirit came from the heat circles of wood and stood there among them as Kildee pokered the flames and sent dancing sparks up the flue.

Kildee had their attention and opened the pack of great tales he had always there stored close at his call. The moment was quietly magic, as if frozen in time, and he gentled the scene with the gift of a tale.

"Well, gents, 'minds me of a story," Kildee began. "My Great-great-granddaddy Henderson kept a passel of sheep."

The men always marvelled at how abruptly and from out-of-nowhere these tales often began. They had their curiosities piqued to see how a passel of sheep could ever mean anything relevant to what had been the subject at hand—how sheep could ever mean anything to them.

"Yes, Great-great-grandaddy Henderson had a rounded number flock of one hundred of these fluffy, walking wool balls. I've never been around sheep much myself, and don't know much about them excepting they're not right bright like a horse or a dog. As y'all know, we don't raise them around here no more. But in those old days, they were on most of the farms 'cause we all made our cloth for everything from blankets to clothes. Raised flax for our linen right in the row, cotton in bolls in the furrrow, and wool on the hoof. Lula Bess still has some of Great-great-grandmother's coverlets in chests by our beds, looking almost like new. Linsey-woolsey's the stuff they're made of—a soft, long-lasting collaboration of linen and wool, both made on the place, and dyed with indigo or black walnut hulls and in patterns to make your eyes dance in the design. Great-great-grandmother Henderson made them with her own hands on her big loom. Lula Bess takes them out and uses them on our bed or on one of the younguns at Christmas and other special family gathering times.

"Great-great-granddaddy Henderson was a loving, gentle old man, so it is still told. He took his faith seriously and humbled himself to the world. He had what those around him called the sympathetic mind. He handled folks gently, both those he knew, and those he did not. And this extended to the creatures and non-breathing things of the world, things seen and unseen.

"He was a good farmer and raised all that the family used. If he didn't grow it, they didn't need it, and thus did without.

"As I said, he raised sheep. It seems that one day, a solitary one of his flock of a hundred wandered astray. It was during a storm, and the animal was nowhere to be seen.

"Great-great-grandpappy would have it no other way but to look high and low till that one sheep was found. And find it, after much looking, he did. While he searched, he had to leave the rest of the flock unguarded and open to dogs and the dumbness of sheep who'll just take off and go. They'll run over a cliff to their deaths, each one and all. No, it was not out of ignorance that he left the ninety-nine alone. Like Amos of old, he knew how swiftly dogs and wolves attack, so swift you can't beat them off, so that all you might be able to pull away in the struggle would be a sheep's ear.

"But Grandpappy was just that way. He valued each sheep, one sheep at a time, not in the rounded-off number, and not for the wool just alone.

"Well, these generals and presidents and CEOs today, I reckon wouldn't suffer old Grandpap for long. They'd never make an all-out search for the one if it meant putting the rest of the flock at a risk. The great bottom-line: NOT COST EFFECTIVE, they'd conclude.

"Like you says, Chauncey, they think they're so practical-rational all. But not Grandpap with his sympathetic mind. They'd probably be angry and baffled with him. Their kindness and mercy just don't cover the bed with a linsey-woolsey coverlet of magic design. But to my way of thinking, it's this weave that'll outlast them all."

With this declaration of faith in the old tried-and-true, hand-woven ways, Kildee concluded his tale. The tone around the stove was now mellowed to quiet and gentle cheer, with some genuine occasional cherry-red sparks of real joy in the scene. In the words of a dramatist, some catharsis was had, some satisfaction achieved.

For a long time, silence reigned, as the assembled relished the glow. Casualness set in like a much-needed gentle spring rain on newly-sowed fields, or the soft feel of a family coverlet on a warm winter's bed.

Then Lyman rose on his cane to take leave for the day.

"Yes, a different sort of pay," were his parting words that fell like a benediction on the scene.

And his cane made its familiar tick-tock tick-tock on the old foot-polished floor in perfect rhythm with Great-great-granddaddy Henderson's big eight-day clock ticking its music on Kildee's store wall.

XVII

The Day D-HEC Made Kildee
Take the Flypaper Down

~~~ ❧ ~~~

    Chauncey was busy breaking some rows for his big win-
ter garden. He was putting in a large, happy plot of turnip
greens. He about loved cornbread and turnip greens in the
winter best of all foods. He saved his usual purple-top
turnip seeds year to year and mixed them in about a two-
to-one ratio with mustard greens. These gave him the
cooked greens he preferred; and he was a connoisseur of
greens. He was also breaking up four rows for collards. He
was known all around for growing good ones too. These
rows would feed a passel of folk, for he liked to give away
these crisp, white sweet heads near about New Year's.
People all over these parts, each and every one, had collards
to insure plenty of good luck the following year. Some
cooked them with hambones or ham hocks, which was the
best way. The squeamish, on diets, or too lazy, used canola
oil. This Chauncey would never stand. "If I live one year
less, let me enjoy my collards with ham while I do," he
would say.

For the purpose of ploughing, Chauncey had borrowed Triggerfoot's mule. Triggerfoot had walked her two days ago to Chauncey's old barn, and after supper, Chauncey had driven Triggerfoot back home, with a big mess of fish Chauncey and Kildee's oldest son had caught in Chauncey's pond. Now today, with his ploughing all done, Chauncey had walked and ridden Beulah on back. In split-oak "thankee baskets" slung over her rump, Chauncey had packed Triggerfoot four gallons of his best last year's scuppernong wine, and a mess of crowder peas still in the hull.

At Triggerfoot's, the old friends swapped a few pleasantries, some news, and several tales. They had them a sip or two of Triggerfoot's very best corn whiskey, put up with a whole bright-red Elberta peach in the jar. The whiskey was smoother than smooth. And the peach set it off.

Then Chauncey hitched a ride with Triggerfoot's neighbourly young neighbour as far as Kildee's store. Like all of them did, the neighbour gave steering wheel waves to everybody he met in the road. This lightened the drive, and made friendly and pleasant the scene both inside and outside the car. The conversation was cordial and easy, starting out with the weather but ending with the very personal problems the young man was having at home. He had a new baby girl and bills coming in, about to smother him like an avalanche of snow; but his wife was his strength. She never complained and could stretch a dollar as far as dollar could go. They were doing their best so she could stay at home with the babes, but they feared she would soon have to find her a job. And what for the children then? They didn't want strangers to raise them, no matter how kind. Chauncey confessed that he regretted that he and Hoyalene couldn't have had at least just one child, but maybe it was best. He wondered if he could have raised a child alone. He laughed and said he had hard enough time raising himself, especially at six in the morn.

"Much obliged," Chauncey thanked the young man as he took leave at Kildee's door. "No problem," the answer, "Any time." The way it was said, you could tell it was meant.

Inside the store, Kildee was behind the counter, fiddling with removing the gauze cloth from off a new hoop of cheese. The aroma filled up the store. Kildee greeted our Chauncey with the usual "Well, Chauncey," to which Chauncey returned his usual "Well, Dee."

But there was something in Kildee's look that didn't seem quite right. The tone of his voice seemed the same. But was it? Chauncey wondered on second thought.

The store had its usual accustomed ring of rockers 'round the potbellied stove. No fire, of course, in this month of August, but still it was the centre where all gathered the same. The rockers were unoccupied, and the several dogs were mostly asleep here and there. Quiet reigned.

This was not unusual at all, for quiet was the commodity of which this community had most. But still there was that lingering something in Kildee's look, his voice, even somehow in the look of the place.

Chauncey gave it some time, and the two friends exchanged news. Chauncey told Kildee of his escapades with Beulah—"Her Royal Highness, Queen Beulah the Stubborn," they had named her even when she was young. And now she was even more contrary and ornery with age. "Intractable" and "recalcitrant" were also words he could have used. Kildee was filled in on all the details of Triggerfoot's most recent scrapes and they shared then some cold fried chicken and potato salad Lula Bess had sent from home, and thin slices of newly cut cheese. They passed 'round two sweating mason jars of tea.

But Kildee didn't eat with his usual relish and still had a touch of the hang-dog look about his eyes, just barely noticeable for a split-second, and then it was gone. It was almost as if he looked a mite guilty, but the look would quickly pass like mists on a river shoal.

Gone! Chauncey realized then what was missing completely from the store—from over their heads. Usually, on a breezy day in August like this, with the doors all open wide, Kildee's signature brown molasses-coated strips of flypaper would be floating, flying, fluttering in the breeze. This always seemed to Chauncey to make the store cheery and gave it some down-home class. It made a strong statement, and that statement in bold letters read: HERE WE ARE OURSELVES AND LIVE IN OUR OWN WAY AS WE PLEASE. YOU DO THE SAME.

But today, all of the strips, each and every one, were gone. Because Kildee was looking so unusual, Chauncey decided not to bring it up. He honored his friend's feelings, and resisted the temptation to ask. But Kildee, a reader of people, truly skilled in the art, knew Chauncey had noticed and was minding "what manners he had." So at the right time, Kildee began to spin out his tale.

It seems that today, a shiny new car with an official gold seal of the state on its doors had showed up at the store. A fellow named Sheridan was inspecting, sniffing around the neighbourhood, and now it was Kildee's sad turn to come under his gaze. He was from D-HEC, pronounced D-HECK, as the state called its Department of Health and Environmental Control. Most all was in order, but the strips of flypaper had to come down, or if not, the doors of the store would be closed. Kildee rejoindered, "But I don't ever close them. I don't have no locks for the door."

There were some warm words, then a few hot ones, and Sheridan had gone so far as to write out the paper that would shut the store down this very day. And Kildee would have to provide the locks himself, so it could be secured. The official word was that a building like this could not be left unattended and unlocked and presenting a hazard to those who might just wander in.

"As if they didn't already," Chauncey said.

Kildee backed down. The flypaper would go. What else could he do? And with the help of his creaking old wooden stepladder, he removed every one. The ladder was by far a more serious hazard than any flypaper had been.

"Wouldn't do to have flypaper hanging over the cheese,"

narrated our Kildee, "would be better to have flies." But the man's regulation book said nothing of live flies; it covered only the dead. And they violated law.

Through Kildee's solemn narration, Chauncey said not a word, but his look also took on something of that air of hurt and grief in it too, to show his old friend he quite understood. It was more than flypaper and flies, living or dead; it was more than inconvenience and bother and work. Yes, they both understood; and both looked by turns angry, then guilty, but mostly frustrated, because, in truth, what could they do? What was it today to be free as a man? The word stuck in their craws, and was too painful to say.

Triggerfoot would no doubt have little trouble finding some choice blazing words for the agent's folderol rigamarole. They could at least look forward to that! And the words would be worth remembering too. Kildee and Chauncey made up several outrageous but very possible scenarios of what Trig might have done or said were he Kildee and in Kildee's place. They tried a few jokes, and a few of them took. But Kildee closed up early, and they called it a day. It had been a long one for both. Chauncey with Queen Beulah; Kildee with King Sheridan.

The next week, Kildee's youngest son brought him in an empty three-foot hornet's nest, cut complete with the limb to which it was attached from over the river in back of the store. This Kildee mounted on a wooden block and placed high on top of a tall glass counter in some sort of strange symbolic way that satisfied him some. For all the world, it looked like a monstrous, giant butterfly's cocoon. What sort of super butterfly would come out of this, it would take a real imagination like Chauncey's or Triggerfoot's to say. Next to the hornet's nest, Kildee placed a large, cleaned-out yellow jacket's hive, full near a foot square, that he'd dug from the ground himself a few months ago. The hive was gridded and layered like the meshed coils of some air cooling machine. Chauncey described it as looking like some devilish waffle you'd cook up in hell.

Cousin Kildee finally got a handle on D-HEC's visit after struggling awhile. He and Chauncey never mentioned it again. But privately ever after, this day was always remembered and went on the calendar with Kildee as THE DAY D-HEC MADE ME TAKE THE FLYPAPER DOWN.

XVIII

Houses on Wheels

We have stayed at home.
        —Ben Robertson, *Red Hills and Cotton*

It was deep Carolina summer. The Fourth of July had just passed, but there was no firecracker celebration at and around Kildee's store. Kildee and the folks in his parts paid little mind to this day. It was like just any other to them. Their folks before them hadn't either. As the oldtimers said, "We tried for our new July Fourth with all that we had, but got killed and invaded and burned out for our pains. Now we're still paying the price. From the looks of it, we farmers around here still ain't free. Free to get put out of business. Free to starve maybe, but not free." Kildee and Chauncey, Jeffersonian to the core, were coming to the conclusion that their country had been hijacked and the results of the theft were raining down around them like a lethal nuclear fallout or some worse kind of more caustic acid rain.

So the day went past in peace and quiet. No giant cookouts or beer. No bowing to consumerist hype on blaring TV. No hitting the road travelling hither, thither, and yon, or plans for the same. *Vacation* was not a concept around here. Going to Hawaii or Cozumel could not be conceived. They vaguely knew others in other places did, but it registered little, and bothered them less, that they'd not join in the train.

Out on the big highways, when Chauncey or Kildee would venture in their pickups, they'd see motor homes, regular caravans of them, particularly this time of year. They'd be heading to Charleston, the beach resorts, or down I-26 and I-95 to Florida, mainly from the North. Their tags said Illinois, Michigan, Indiana, Ohio, Minnesota, Wisconsin, the land-locked taking their fastest corridor to sea. Kildee wondered why they'd need to come so long a way, why they'd go to so much trouble and expense to leave home. How unhappy and dissatisfied they must be, to fly so fast on the road, looking so frantic to get away. It was like they were evacuating in the face of some gigantic disaster, fleeing ahead of some terrific storm.

These giant motor homes amused Kildee. Some of them were almost half the size of his store. They had kitchens and bedrooms and bathrooms, the latest in all gadgets, everything up to date. In fact, in having a bathroom, they were one step ahead of his store. He wondered just how much such vehicles would cost, and what amount of gasoline they'd guzzle up.

They and the people who drove them became the subject this lazy day at the store.

"Them things just tickles me," Caleb said. "I've lived

eighty-eight years and in all them years I've never seen nothing more foolish frivolous than them."

"Caleb, I'll have to agree," Lyman concurred, "sort of like house trailers, that nowadays they call mobile homes. Who'd take the risk of going into your doublewide one night to sleep, and wake up the next day in another state? Not me. I don't want a house set on wheels that somebody could hook up a truck to, and in a blink of the eye, move me away. And a motor home is a sight worse."

"Yes," Caleb agreed, "and the number of house trailers getting to be around is pure astonishing. I'm beginning to think we live in a crazier than usual time, when the old cars all sit up on blocks in the front yards, and the houses sit on wheels."

Kildee chimed in, "Clay Bank County, where the cars are on blocks, and the houses on wheels! Bet you'll not hear that slogan from the Chamber of Commerce or Clay Bank Tourism Board."

Chauncey, who'd just come in and seated himself in his favorite rocker there with the men, said that last week he'd been on the interstate with old Bessie, as he called his beat-up pickup, and nearly got blown off the road by the motor homes barrelling down southward on this Fourth of July vacation, headed for the beaches, like true lemmings to sea, hellbent to get there in the most frantic rush. "And what for?" Chauncey asked, and then answered himself, "To relax!"

To go to all that trouble and expense and frantic hurrying to relax just did not make any sense to him. "They rush and work extra hours to take off on vacation and then rush and rush busier than before. They have to pack all that relaxing and vacationing in, just to convince themselves that it's been worth it for making a hell of their lives the rest of the year."

"Smells like somebody's getting scammed," Lyman declared. "Chauncey, I'm like you. I can't see how rushing forty-nine weeks of the year to get two weeks of rushing vacation makes any sense."

Lyman continued in this vein with more words than he'd usually use: "Maybe if they didn't buy motor homes, big fancy houses and cars, and all of them things that they say we've just got to have, then they'd have time to slow down a little and come up for air."

Chauncey added, "And from what I've seen, they're not happy at all. Last week on the interstate, several blew horns at me, irritated, I reckon, at my slow travelling as they flew past." He remembered one particularly angry red face in a motor home, a face that had looked down at him about ready to explode.

Chauncey continued, "Or maybe they're just mad at themselves for being dupes. They've just bought all that consumerist hype. If not happy, the advertisements will say, just buy my wares. Unhappy? Then go shopping and buy me. Then after buying, and you're still not happy, the ads will say, 'But you didn't buy the deluxe model. Do that, and then you'll be happy for sure.' So they work overtime, and buy the super deluxe model, and find they're no happier than before. What then? They rush about on wheels searching for it, like some wild distracted beasts lost from off their natural range. No wonder their faces are red. Maybe from frustration and anger, or maybe from shame."

"'Stress' I think they're calling it nowadays," Lyman said.

"Hollow," Caleb gave his reply. "Hollow at the core."

"There's something missing for certain, but it's not things," Lyman agreed.

"And neither of the regular or deluxe model kind," Kildee weighed in.

The day that Chauncey and old Bessie nearly got blown off the road by the Florida-bound motor homes, he'd noticed the same bumper sticker emblazoned on at least three. I'M SPENDING MY CHILDREN'S INHERI-TANCE, they boldly declared.

Kildee had to agree that no truer sticker had ever been stuck to a bumper.

"It's even a lot truer than they understand, I expect," he said. "Yes, and in more ways than one. They're not only just spending off their bank accounts that one particular set of younguns would receive, but all the substance of the land for more than just a few, and for more than one isolat-ed time. This spending's for a long, long time, and for more generations than one."

"Deadly serious stuff," Chauncey added, "So they pass it all off as a bumper sticker joke. A perfect and fitting saying for the 'Me Generation,' still just as selfish as they've been all their lives, and they'll never change. Great squanderers they are—escaping, rushing about, getting things, then as quickly discarding them, getting more, bigger and better, and more up to date, the old thrown by the wayside, wasting the world. They're like spoiled children who don't take care of their toys. They don't have to, you see. New, more, and better will come.

"It's an awful sin to waste things," Chauncey continued after a pause, "but I wonder why they don't realize they're being wasted too, in the same ugly scheme. I wonder if they know they're being moved about, rather than choosing to move, not just moving around, but being moved. Maybe that's what makes them so mad. Maybe they *do* know. To find out at last when it's too late that you've merely been tools and have lived for the great industrial machine just to be used. Lives lived at the beck and call of jobs that you hate and over which you have no control, going where the jobs are like gypsies, forced job moves, promises of happiness, promotions, more money to spend, bigger and better motor homes, longer and further vacations, faster speeds, and then finally with a big empty nest sold off in an exclusive gated suburb, to live lives now completely on wheels, not even having an address to call home. Yes, my face would be red too, from both anger and shame. And not at that poor hayseed bumpkin driving the forty-mile-an-hour minimum on I-26 in his beat-up old truck.

Chauncey was warming to his topic: "They've bought everything that they've been told to, obedient to the last. Now through all this pretense of pleasure seeking, they find no pleasure is in it and the joke is on them. Then who is the fool? Me in my old pickup? Or them in a travelling, motorized, gas-guzzling floating home?"

"Running from responsibility, more the like, seems to me," Lyman concluded as he got up from his rocker, said his goodbyes for the day, and then walked from the store.

Chauncey commented that nowadays it was common to nap on a jet liner and wake up on another continent. Caleb remarked that when he went up in the sky, it would only be with Jesus, and not in a machine.

Chauncey had been reading a biography of Bach, his favorite musician from the olden time, and learned he never left his little homeland, not even to visit elsewhere. Neither did Shakespeare, nor Virgil, nor Dante, nor Chaucer. The list went on and on. Maybe they gained something from that, he mused.

This new phenomenon of restless mobility interested Kildee, who had not even a tiny bit of such desire in his bones. Today, those at the store were unanimous in deeming this wanderlust unwise in the extreme.

"It's a moving age, for certain sure, but people had better stop somewhere," Chauncey declared. "One day, sooner or later, they'll learn they can't run away from themselves."

After a pause, Caleb concluded, "And they'll be rooted at last, you can be just as sure. They won't move in the grave."

Although the men didn't articulate their understanding that it required long-term commitments to make life even more moderately worthwhile, they all knew full well that it did, and did their best to honor this truth with their lives. It came naturally to them.

Grief might come in the bargain, but so could real joy. They all knew from birth that a goodly part of life was to be tightly involved in a long sequence of lives, lived out in one place, as there was no real escape from responsibility without hazarding self, endangering who you are.

Kildee declared that he and Lula Bess had decided early in their marriage that what they'd inherit and build up, they'd pass on, or do their best to. If it meant sacrificing, then they would. They would trust their children to remember from whence that inheritance came. It all was finally a matter of faith.

Lula Bess was good that way. They named their first child Lyles, after Kildee and Kildee's granddaddy Henderson, too, who first opened the store he now ran. When Lyles was born near thirty years ago, Lula Bess had said, "Dee, I'm not one of these moving kind. I know we got to provide for Lyles, and I know we want a houseful of daughters and sons, but I reckon we can do it right here, if we're smart and careful how we live."

Kildee remembered even now how that declaration had overjoyed him, reflecting the same wish as his own on the subject, in part and in whole. They'd both had an idea they'd each wanted the same as the other in life, but in their youth had never yet really put their wishes into words.

They'd also agreed that if they chose to move away to

a town or city job, they'd probably both have to work. Then their children would be without parents all day. This placing their younguns at a distance in the hands of strangers was no way to do. They also needed their grandparents at hand.

And this the children had had. Both pairs, when they were finally not able to take care of themselves, lived at one time or another with Lula Bess and him, making three generations of Hendersons and Blairs under one roof. In retrospect, what a treasure and joy this had been, and for all concerned, the younguns not the least.

Lula Bess had rightly said, "You know, Dee, if we choose to move and start lives faraway, then we've taken away the choice for our younguns of whether to stay here or go. We'd be making that choice for them before they'd had a chance even to say." He'd not thought of it that way, but she was right. They'd let their children choose, and would have faith they'd choose right. All you could do was to raise them up properly well. They knew that to teach by example was always the best way.

Even when two more sons and three daughters followed little Lyles, and it became a scramble sometimes to make ends meet, and Kildee mechanicked on top of his farming and the store, they still stuck it out. They stayed. And they'd held on to their fields. They had added cows and a poultry yard too; and Lula Bess and the children had all pulled their weight. They'd finally even had enough left over to buy in some few more acres around them when these went up for sale from a defunct timber company.

And this they'd needed, for the sons had built houses nearby and farmed too. Like their father, when they had to, they worked at small jobs. A daughter had married and she and her husband farmed on the family land. Two young daughters were still with them at home. One was engaged to a boy a few miles down the road. His father farmed and the new couple was planning to build a house on his land.

So with Kildee and Lula Bess, spending your young-guns' inheritance on motor homes travelling about was not a thing to be joked at, no, not at all. Instead, to do so, to them, was serious and childish folly, not befitting grown women and men.

"A wholesale attempt to escape obligations, seems to me, this moving around," Chauncey reflected after a pause. "A man's going to be remembered in one way or another— either burden or help, either squanderer or passer-on-down, either true or false to his kin. That's the choice as I see it today. And it's that's been the choice all our days. I don't want to be remembered as a liability. None of us, I reckon, do."

Kildee rose to take care of a customer, and in his absence there was silence to reflect. In this pause, Chauncey thought of the anatomists—the inventors of convenience and rapidity, and figured that the rightful end of their busyness and laboring would be to make us all senseless and undesiring as animate stones. As he frequently did, he offered up a prayer that man be spared the logical consequences of his folly. Then Chauncey had a strange vision of Dante's ninth circle in hell, where traitors to their kin lay half buried in ice, up to the pubic shadow, where the doleful souls were sounding their chattering teeth like storks.

His mind then moved to a book he'd just stumbled upon, a slim volume by C.S. Lewis that he'd immediately taken to heart. He had jotted down this passage on a scrap of paper and pinned it to the wall of the little alcove where he kept his modest collection of well-used books. "It is the same with all their machines," the passage read. "Their labour-saving devices multiply drudgery; their aphrodisiacs make them impotent; their amusements bore them; their rapid production of food leaves half of them starving; and their devices for saving time have banished leisure from their country." Here in the store with his friends, that passage describing the industrial nightmare about summed all this motor home business up for him. He was impresed by the fact that a sophisticated famous author could sound so much like Lyman, Caleb, and Kildee.

The talk and tone had grown a mite heavy 'round the cold potbellied stove as the shadows lengthened outside and the long summer day was reaching its close.

Today, no one, not even Kildee, had offered up an anecdote or tale. And this was a most unusual thing, strange of itself, like motorized houses on wheels. Instead, they all puzzled at the great unsteady, hurrying world in the flux of uneasy motion outside their door. With this mystery, eventually no doubt a story or stories would come, for that was their way of making what sense they could of the sometimes senseless actions and motives of men, but today there had been none.

"Unsettled and unsettling," old Mr. Caleb finally declared.

After the last of his friends and visitors had gone, Kildee turned off the naked light bulb that hung from its cord, and sat for awhile in the dark, alone but for his thoughts and the pair of dogs lying on his feet, as if to keep him nailed there.

He was musing a bit somberly on all that was said. He'd seen those same bumper stickers too, and knew they were put there by "senior citizens," as they preferred to call themselves now—women and men, not too much older than he, who didn't like the "elderly" word, and, heaven forbid, being called "old." To Kildee, wheels, and the freedom of youth that wheels gave, were quite surely a mixed blessing, if blessing at all, and freedom from what?

This was the question he left the store with, as he walked the familiar red clay path to Lula Bess, the children, and the supper waiting at home.

That path had been made and worn clean now for six generations of his family name. As he climbed the rise to the house, with the great river shimmering below, he knew that very same sight had been seen by all those who came before. He had a notion that if he looked over his shoulder he could see them, all trooping behind him down the years, close enough to touch their shining faces with his hand.

Now his footsteps fit and echoed theirs, and this Kildee felt was as it should be. Their steps validated his, and his own proved that theirs, in this well-loved place, had been unquestionably solid and right. He thanked and blessed them as he walked cross his front porch and opened the screen door.

His footsteps on the wooden floor sounded like a gentle drum, announcing the presence of a walker there. No doorbell was ever dreamed of, for the front door was always open to let the breeze up from the river blow through. The summer supper table, its blue checked cloth moving in the wind, was set in the open breezy hall.

"Home," then he spoke, letting Lula Bess know who was coming in. The screen door made its greeting slam. Inside, the clank of dishes and the cheerful voices of his daughters, no doubt chattering about some detail of the upcoming wedding of his eldest, let him know he was coming on time, that they'd not have to wait supper for him.

XIX

The Road

Clint Blair was home from college this summer and on this Saturday had walked up to the store from his family's farm a right good piece down the road. He had his black and tan with him, following close at his heels. Her name was Towse, and it was clear that she was overjoyed to have him home.

Clint was Hoyalene's youngest brother. His ma and pa, and now Hoyalene, had gone. His sister Clarissa, whom they called Clarsie, had married and moved a county away. That left his oldest brother, Joe-Pratt, and his wife, Sally, and their three younguns to hold down the place and keep on farming the family lands. Clint helped out when he was home, but the two brothers knew that the place wouldn't be quite big enough these hard days for farmers to support two families on, and Clint, loving animals as he did, had always wanted to be a vet anyway. They talked it over with Kildee and Chauncey and the folks around there, and figured he'd have enough business to come back to, with his home base on the old family land.

Clint and Towse arrived at the store and were gathered in; warm greetings were passed around. It had rained an awful lot lately and the old road to the Blair place, three miles off the paved road to Kildee's store, had washed out again. It took a four-wheel drive to get in and out; and Joe-Pratt, Sally, and the younguns had been off on a stock-selling trip in the truck that had lasted for several days. This had left Clint without proper wheels.

The lad was taking care of the place in their absence, but this Saturday he'd needed society and had come in to the store, his morning chores done.

The mud that was splashed up on his pants legs told part of the tale.

"Wonder when they're going to get around to paving that dirt road of your'n," an old fellow said.

"Don't reckon we matter enough," answered Clint, who then added with a smile, "and hope we don't ever. It's just fine with us that-a-way. Good enough for Mama and Papa and Grandmama and Grandpapa before."

Lyman chimed in, "Clint, y'all Blairs have always had the best of good sense. Paved roads are the ruination of the world. I wouldn't give nothing for the four miles off the black top we are. It makes going mighty rough to church and back, some of these times, but that's about all."

"Tell you what," Lyman continued. "People who live at the end of a dirt road like we do learn mighty quick that life's a bumpy trip that can jar you plumb down to your teeth sometime. You learn early that life ain't tidy and neat."

There was a pause. Then Clint answered, "But I reckon

that bumpy road's worth it, if you got a good wife, happy chaps, a couple of cats, and a dog like Towse. Every acre of asphalt is one less natural place to love."

At the mention of her name, Towse raised up her head and her master placed his big hand on its crown.

Lyman continued, "Tell you what. The education world wouldn't have near the trouble in these modern schools if the children got their exercise walking dirt roads and having to learn how to get along on the way. When they got there, they'd be too settled down to sass."

Old Mr. Caleb was listening intently. "Sure would be less crime. A thief wouldn't walk two muddy miles to rob you or do any meanness at all, 'specially if they knew they'd be facing eight barking dogs and a double-barreled shotgun at the door."

Lyman chuckled, "There'd be no drive-by shootings, that's for sure."

The group joined him in his laugh.

This was all they needed now to get them to pour it all on.

"Divorce rates would go down," said Kildee. "Too much trouble to find love interests outside the home. Too tired and dirty to be in the mood if you tried."

Lyman added, "Makes you satisfied with what you got. Too much trouble to look for fancier or more. Weighed against the trouble, the old tried and true would look better and better each day."

"Teaches patience," old Caleb said. "Maybe even values too."

Clint got into the game. "This way, you value your chaps more than your car, our dad used to say. He never cared anything for new vehicles. Whatever he had was fine, as long as it'd go. He always said that a house with a three-car garage was never likely to become a home. Hoyalene once told me that she thought that the number of miles on an odometer is a good measure of how far we've gone from where we belong."

Kildee, who'd been listening from the counter in between serving his customers there, now had a lull, so he could add his own two-bits of wisdom to the coinage piling up there in a gold treasure trove. "Well, drivers were shorely more courteous on dirt roads back then," he declared. "You didn't tailgate by riding a bumper, or the fellow in front would choke you with dust or break out your windshield with flying up rocks. You're right, Mr. Caleb, taught patience, it did, and courtesy too. None of that road rage, we hear tell about."

"Guess the best thing dirt roads do," Kildee continued, "is they slow people down. The world's too much in a hurry, and usually with no place to go. Everything flies by in a blur. And people get to where they don't belong anywhere and ain't from no place at all."

There was another long pause.

"I reckon that's a part of the values and character dirt roads teaches," Lyman said.

Clint, who'd been reading about the Amish and Mennonite way, could tell the little gathering, to whom both Amish and Mennonite were strange, foreign words, that when folks from outside asked them why they used buggies and never drove cars, that they'd answer, "We've just always done it that way." That was proper enough of an answer, but if pressed to think of "reasons," they knew that the community was defined by the distance a horse-drawn buggy could go in a day. That circumference determined your neighbourhood, and each community changed with the individual centre from which its radius was drawn.

Old Mr. Caleb said that made a lot of sense. He'd finally learned that a day's buggy distance was about all the heart could fully take in. You could love just that space well and no more, and maybe learn not to abuse it in time. When things got too big and distant and abstract, that's when the problems set in. Trouble for sure.

Now away at college, Clint was learning just how smart his people had always been. Strange. The older he became, the wiser his ma and pa got as he grew. This environmental questioning of BIGGER IS BETTER was nothing new with them. And dirt roads may have been the key. On a dirt road, you sure didn't waste. Hopping in a car to go to the convenience store for a loaf of bread or a quart of milk just made no sense. On a dirt road, instead, you walked to the barn and milked old Bossy, and you baked up the bread. When it rained, and the dirt road washed out, you stayed home and had family time. You talked and learned values and manners and how to get along. You made up games and played them without spending a dime.

You played on the fiddle or banjo and sang songs learned across no telling how much time. You told stories and made sense of the world with the telling of them, and that included the young. You sat down at the table and said grace at the meal. What you didn't see before you, you used the imagination to gain.

Another long pause.

"Paved roads lead to trouble," Lyman declared. He remembered his own youth: "Dirt roads lead to fish in the river and a swimming hole."

Chauncey had just come in from his fields and today had driven the few miles to the store. He'd picked up on the drift of the talk and could add some of his own feelings thereon. "And paved roads take people away," he said. "And sometimes they stay." He looked over at Clint, who knew what Chauncey was saying to him.

Before Hoyalene had died, she and Clint had talked long and serious talk. Clint, now that his mother and father were gone, was toying with leaving for greener pastures and the great world outside. Their talking settled young Clint down, and his sister had passed on her love of the place she knew she was just about having to leave. Maybe Clint had never quite seen Hoyalene's favorite hill from her kitchen sink in quite this same way before, or the little touches of light on the crown of the oak, the familiar glint of the river in flow, the impress that their people had made on the land.

The talk between brother and sister opened up the

world that they knew, their own world, so rare and dear to them all. When she died, she merged with that world, and Clint now saw his sister in all that she'd loved.

In this, Clint and Chauncey found a bond, and Hoyalene had made Chauncey promise he'd look out for Clint, and this Chauncey had taken seriously and did. Clint had become the brother Chauncey never had.

It was clear now that Clint was coming back home after his schooling. He'd make a fine man. After another year at his college, he'd be getting his homecoming degree. Hoyalene would be proud. The black top would in his case lead finally home. And this, Clint now knew, was as it should be for him. Clint called up Towse and after good-byes, they walked on their way. Joe-Pratt, Sally, and the younguns were expected later on that day, and Clint had the evening chores to do, so they wouldn't have to. He knew they'd be tired out from the drive.

XX

Miss Sparta Mae

~⟨∾⟩~

It was another hot, dry day in August, a real "pea rip-per," as the old folks would say—hot enough to bust the pods of blackeyed peas in the field. "Hot as the hinges of hell," Chauncey contributed his own. The corn leaves were roped up in the rows, and old Caleb vowed that the river was so low they were having to haul water to *it*—or that a catfish swimming upstream would have to send a bullfrog to take soundings ahead. Even the neighbourhood children were at home taking voluntary naps. There were none this day at Kildee's store. It was too hot to play.

There had been a week of temperature readings at the three-digit mark; and Cousin Kildee was at his store count-er in his khaki cut-offs. This was not the usual sight that greeted us there, and Chauncey commented on the fact as he came into the store. Grown men in these parts didn't customarily show their knees. But today Chauncey was also in abbreviated attire, with his khaki Duck Heads and a blue checked shirt, its tail hanging out, as if to make up for half pants.

To show a kind of solidarity with his friend Kildee, and greeting him as a mirror thus, he lifted his shirt to reveal he was wearing short pants too.

Well, as you know our Chauncey, he's a bit spacey at times. Well-intentioned, he often just has his mind elsewhere and forgets practical things. Before coming in, he'd been out behind the store to take him a whizz, and had forgotten to zip up his pants.

Seeing the state of Chauncey's relative undress, Cousin Kildee greeted him with "Well Chauncey, you selling hot-dogs today?"

Old farmer Lyman, seated in a rocker nearby, added his own two-bits to the scene in his usual deadpan way: "And bet nobody's buying, I 'spect."

There was no laughter. It was too hot even for that. There was brief banter about nekkid knees that produced some genuine good laughs. Then the three passed off some minutes with pleasantries and some little news. Much of the talk turned on the weather—the heat, the drought, the effect on pasture and crops, the toll on farm animals and men. Then the minutes became hours, as the hot August day slowed, unraveled toward noon, halted, near stopped, slowed in the long afternoon like pouring winter molasses from a jug.

Cousin Kildee's hounds were at their ease too. His country store had never seen AC or even screens, so the dogs moseyed in and out at will, just as they pleased. Today, they even had some local neighbourhood dogs with them as guests.

Mostly the hounds were all in rather than out, lying on the cool of the old floor. They were watching, waiting, in their hound-trifling way, in between many a short snooze. The hounds, like all creatures this day, had sought out the shade.

These were the Dog Days when Sirius blazed bright in the heavens at night; and the sun had a peculiar shine during the heat of the day. It was now that wounds and scratches were slow to heal; fanatics grew more fanatical, the insane crazier, as at the full of the moon—and even dull and sober common folks did crazy-peculiar and original things. Not a good time to mend an old quarrel or pick a fight "lessen you wanted one," as old Lyman would say. It was time too for inspiration. As the ancients were wont to say, it was the time of poetic frenzy under the sway of the scorpion's sting.

The head-baking, dull glare outside in the heat of the afternoon gave everything under the sun the metallic sheen of the aluminum and galvanized tin of the pots, pails, and buckets that hung on nails in a jumble from the store rafters over our speakers' heads.

Cousin Kildee, in his rocker, had now settled into his fixed remembering pose. I reckon the Dog Star was having its effect upon him too, because he looked driven to tell. Chauncey and Lyman sat in their rockers to hear Kildee out. Others were gathering too. Kildee's "Come on in. Light a spell" inevitably settled them in. "Sittin's cheaper than standin'," he'd say. "Too hot to be traipsing around." It was always worth listening when Kildee looked serious-inspired in this way. The assembled sat motionless still in their chairs. It was too hot to rock.

Kildee's story was about a lady from Clay Bank. She was a woman of means whose family had helped found the town several centuries ago, and one of Kildee's own distant kin. She had no truck with the Development Board-Chamber of Commerce set, whom she knew to be just what they are. If town had its queen, it was she, Miss Sparta Mae. She'd been born deep in the last century and lived on strong and tough up to their time. She had outlived two sons.

For tough she was, and tough-minded too. Kildee recalled one of her comments most particularly today. She had criticized the mayor and, in fact, several high rankers in town. In a kind of blanket condemnation, Sparta Mae said that all those fellows in the town and county offices were just like the legislators in the state capitol, running about like three truckloads of beanpickers without a fore-man. And as for questioning her for saying so, came her memorable answer verbatim complete: "You know, things have come to a hell of a pass when a man can't kick his own jackass." For tough and fiercely independent, she was. If the world had gone to the bad, she didn't have to follow suit.

Kildee remembered her clearly from her last years, in her nineties, and her great, bulging car. It was a sparkling white Cadillac with finish like a diamond—one of those monsters with a pair of flairs at the rear like fish fins.

The whole town knew the car—man, woman, and

child. The very sound of its engine was known. The bright flash of white was noted, taken for granted, by all, and became part of the town scene, like the giant willow oaks of the square, or grey, carved-granite obelisk centering there. Like church bells or opera house clock chiming time, Miss Sparta Mae and her Cadillac car meant home to them too.

Now it would be an understatement to say that Miss Sparta Mae, bless her heart, was not the best of the drivers in town. Sometimes she would take her allotted half of the road squarely in the middle, straddling white line. She would swing in great arcs when she cornered or turned.

So the bulk of the town, as was its old-fashioned, easy-going, tolerant wont, handled things gently. At the moment the white fishy monster emerged from its green leafy sea cave, the lesser fishes pulled off of the road. They stopped and gave Miss Sparta Mae wide and clear berth. Some pulled onto sidewalks as she obliviously passed. Their usual comment, like as not, was "Bless her heart," and they'd go on their way. This went on for years.

But Miss Sparta Mae was old, they reasoned. They'd not have to do this forever, they knew. What little inconvenience this was in the short term did not weigh in the balance to hurting the feelings of one of their own such as she.

And then she *was* their town. More than the elected officials, and the boosters and promoters, she represented the place. She held its traditions, was their story's own keeper, and was at the same time generous, imperious, opinionated, tolerant, and kind. In her life and person, she was them all. There was never a question of police or patrol or the sheriff to come on the scene.

For she was their character too. And the town loved its characters. It's what made it their own. Coupled with Triggerfoot Tinsley, Miss Sparta Mae in mirror reverse, they were the eccentric two sides of a home-minted coin. There was nothing of the coppery Abraham Lincoln on their currency, and they were more valuable than cold faces of green. The powers that be might not like them, but the rank and file felt comfortable having them there.

The town indeed had its well-stocked treasure chest of characters from which amply to pay the new bribe against sameness which increasingly few places nowadays could pay. How lucky they were!

Now in the 1950s and '60s, as Kildee remembered, when Miss Sparta Mae was driving her Cadillac car, the one driver who'd not budge an inch in the road, also oblivious it seemed, was the old gent who still drove his A-model Ford, bought by him when still new, and looking just as it did the day it was made.

He had the cheerful habit of smiling and tooting the A-model's horn at everything he saw, at all breathing things and some that did not.

He would toot at the cats and the dogs, at the towering monument in the square, at trees, at mailboxes, telephone posts, and carriage-mount stones, at gentrified horsehead hitching posts with rings, at lawn jockeys, and the occasional painted concrete yard chicken and urn. His favourites were the little painted concrete negroes seated eating slices of watermelon or holding cane fishing poles. At these last, he would both "toot-toot" and wave.

His last name was Williams; and the town, if they'd ever known that his first name was Lewis, had forgot. For they all called him Toot-toot. That was the sound that he made. So Toot-toot Williams his name.

And you would know he was coming long before he was there, for his "toot-toot" would announce him, "toot-toot" coming or "toot-toot" leaving the scene. It was this that may have saved him from Miss Sparta Mae's great white shark-finned machine.

As often they passed, there was never a scratch or a dent, none of her white paint on his black, none of his black on her white, no mayhem, no problem at all. A few of the town's more serious sort may have worried about such a meeting, but they still kept their peace. They left it to Providence, and in Providence's care. For this was awhile back, as you know.

So Toot-toot greeted Miss Sparta Mae; and she jangled her gold bracelets at him in her customary spirited wave.

For, as Kildee recalled, bangles and bracelets were Sparta Mae too. She wore her long, age-thinned-out arms full of them, each on top of each, and both right arm and left. She had gold ones, and bakelite, and brass ones, and silver. She had enameled ones and turquoise, pewter ones with rhinestones, platinum ones with diamonds and rubies, and jade.

Yes, from middle age on, bangles were her trademark imprimatur, and adorned her wherever she went.

Like Toot-toot's trumpeting before him, her bracelets announced she'd arrived on the scene. You could make no mistake she was there.

Sparta Mae was a mainstay at the tall, elegant-spired old Episcopal church in the town. Its rose-pink stucco was mossy with the history of the place. Its floors had been polished by pilgrim's feet for a century and a half of slow time. Its great altar window glowed, and cast cobalt and ruby shadows on all. The glass had been run through a cruel war's blockade in Charleston and carted through 200 miles of sand, mud, and clay, up to the town. Its high burnished cross bloomed at the top of its steeple, a flower of grace to bless all of the town. The children who grew up under that cross all seemed special and blessed.

Inside, of a bright Sunday morn, when the sermon would grow longer than patience allowed, Miss Sparta Mae would rustle the leaves of her father's old leather-bound *Book of Common Prayer*, setting her bangles to clang in a riot of sound. Sermon then ended, hymn was sung, offering, prayer, and blessing swiftly followed treading toe upon heel.

It was also reported that the kindly young rector had once said from the pulpit when she bangled his sermon to end: "Well, I see Miss Sparta's ready to go, so we'll just quickly conclude."

And no doubt more or less this was true. Kildee had had the story from one who was there.

When Miss Sparta Mae finally joined her kin 'neath

the crooked crosses and angels and carved marble wreaths of roses in the town's burying ground, there was great empty silence and a gap in the town's heart, of something now missing, indefinably gone, like the bells no longer were ringing, or the old town clock no longer ticked out the time. It was like the brooding grey-granite obelisk on the square had been stolen away one night by thieves.

Her daughter, an excellent and most sensible driver, inherited her white Cadillac car, and it took several years for the town still not to pull off the road as it neared. And in that truth was summed up so much of our tale.

The daughter has moved on to a distant big city now; and gone also the car. Toot-toot has driven through the great pearly gates and, like Miss Sparta Mae, is motoring his golden A-model on that highway celestial too. St. Peter greeted him with a personalised GoldCard for all the gas eternity would need. Heaven for Toot-toot, indeed. No doubt he is "toot-tooting" at angels and harps, "toot-toot-ing" at great golden yard chickens pecking up pearls, and gilded-over little negroes with sweet ruby watermelon slices and sterling silver fishing poles.

The town, like everywhere this year 2003, is now covered in United-We-Stand One-Nation-Indivisible flags, flying from every house, every store, every pole, everywhere you look, flying on cars, at doorsteps, in windows, on car lots, at the feed-and-seed, the hardware, the florist, ice-cream parlour, all but the new Chinese and Mexican restaurants on the town square. The latter sported its Mexican flag. It was Dog-Star insanity, a frantic obsession, and could not be rightly explained, except perhaps as making a stage set, some media-manipulated scene. To Kildee, it all moved as in a dream.

Best Chauncey could figure, as he said, is that they're trying somehow to take the place of Miss Sparta Mae and Toot-toot, trying desperately hard to fill up the blank of their leaving by bringing flap, flash, and flutter to the scene. But he knew that for all of the busy jumble of stripes and the too-many stars, the scene was just cluttered and hidden with the same busy blur of the flags and their poles, with the place sadder and solemner, colder and emptier— more vacant, more neutral of persons and things. Chauncey concluded that for all the United-We-Stand flash, the world has become blander than aluminum and greyer than steel, and the new officious breed of politicians and bureaucrats have multiplied themselves into even more truckloads of beanpickers without foremen—or a clue.

As Chauncey said, "Today in this new jangling order of empire flag-flying world, no doubt Miss Sparta Mae and gentle old Toot-toot would have their driver's licenses taken away. 'A public hazard,' the official citation would read, and 'Protecting them from themselves,' would be the excuse." Both Kildee and Lyman sadly agreed.

"The times is evil," Lyman volunteered a word.

And nodding agreement, Cousin Kildee concluded with wistful tone: "These stamped-out slogans and star-spangled banners of sameness don't like Miss Sparta Mae's or Toot-toot's sort, nor I suspects me, Chauncey, nor you. Their jackass sort never do. They'd like to be shed of us all. We ain't part of the progress, so the squadrons of cars with their snap-on flags rushes to pass us on by, like they would want to run us off of the road we'd no right to be on. They're like arrows shot straight at the moon, and they'll get where they're going 'bout as soon as I'll get to tread Mars. What a sight! Zooming around in circles. Chasing their tails like Old Blue."

The conversation now having turned weighty and gloomy, our Chauncey thought to half lighten what seemed to be Kildee's considerable load.

"Well, Kildee, old friend," he said, placing his hand on his friend's shoulder, "nobody'll make you fly one of those homogenizing flag agents at this run-down old country store, here on the forgotten, jagged, rag-tag edge of the world. They'll not try to convert or get shed of you, 'cause they don't even know you are here." And making one of his usual attempts at a pun, he concluded, "We're the fly-*over* country you know. We won't have to fly it here."

The rocker creaked as Chauncey rose to go. Looking back, he declared that, yes, as long as our own Kildee drew breath, the world would never be empty or bland, for Kildee in his own way, if necessary, could out-toot-toot old Toot-toot, could out-jangle Miss Sparta Mae's bangles and bracelets, in order to enliven the scene. The flag that he flew was never printed from cloth by machine or either stitched by the hands of woman or man.

But then all of them there, including our Chauncey and good Kildee himself, yes, all of them knew what they knew. "The times, they is evil," old Lyman said once again, and all of them gauged precisely what he meant and silently agreed.

Under the blaze of the hot sun of August, and the ancient scorpion sting of the Dog Star at eve, those few there gathered at the forgotten, jagged, rag-tag edge of the world would just have to wait the madness all out, and just see.

XXI

September Gale

Rain and more rain. It came down in buckets, and had been raining buckets just this way for several days without a stop. Folks around these parts called this a power of rain— a trash mover and a split-rail fence lifter. The air had a soft feel about it and was balmy warm, the wind thrashing high in the trees. As Chauncey said, the air felt like that time when he went to Florida. He wasn't far wrong because this September gale, as the old folks in Upcountry Carolina called this kind of extended rain at this time of year, was the remnants of a big hurricane tearing northward to them out of the Gulf of Mexico. Though the storm was now over a thousand miles from its breeding grounds over tropical seas, it brought the soft, strange feel of the tropics with it.

Farming activity had slowed because of the weather, and more folks than usual were gathering at Cousin Kildee's store to pass the time of day. Kildee had a small fire in the potbellied stove, not so much for warmth, but to dry things out some and provide a little cheer.

"If you sit still too long, you'll mildew," he declared.

"You've heard of rolling stones gathering no moss. Well, don't move much today, and you'll start turning green. Better check your north side when you leave."

"And watch out for spores," Chauncey agreed, "or tomorrow you might have ferns in your clothes." A few of the men chuckled at the near truth of the stretch. By now they had come to expect Chauncey's spritely imagination, and knew how to take it, as familiar as the worn old rockers about the stove, or the weather-beaten store itself.

It had been a welcome rain after a dryer than usual summer. Everything around looked tired, just about worn out from the long summer's heat. The animals, even the trees and vegetation, looked a mite exhausted. So this long rain had come at a very good time. It was a blessing, and now they could draw a long breath.

The store had visitors during these rainy days that the regulars seldom saw. They were neighbours and kin, but for one reason or another, they didn't make it to the store very often. For those regulars who came most every week, and some every day, it was a rich treat to have them.

Among the visitors this day was Uncle Dick Gilliam, pronounced Gill-um in these parts, and "Dick Look-Up" by nickname, a venerable old black gentleman who lived on the river in a small weathered and unpainted house built by his grandpa many years ago. Uncle Dick had the reputation of being a fine teller of tales, but the white community didn't get to hear them that often. These were reserved for his many grandchildren and kin, and the folks at his Seekwell A.M.E. Church.

So this rare, strange day of unusual weather and new folks in the store was suited to the tale that he told. It began quite naturally as a response to the clatter of rain on the store's metal roof.

As the torrents came in a particularly hard gust and blow, there was a lull in the talk. All got silent, conscious of the sound of unseen things happening outside.

Uncle Dick had sat quiet up until then, a bit out of the circle to the side, with his chin on his sturdy homemade walking stick cane. But with this hush occasioned by the lull in the storm, he began.

"'Minds me of one September gale my grandpappy used to tell about in days gone by, long time before even when he was around. He remembered it as a chile, and the story he told us chil'ren was about his own pa, my great-grandpa, who I never saw.

"You know all us Gilliams have always been close to that big river out there—lived by it, fished on it, worked on it, listened to it, talked to it, night and day, summer and winter, old and young. It's hardly ever out of our eye. We learned to watch it close for all that it would tell. And tell it did, and in more ways than one. We depended on it mightily too. It was as natural to us as kin.

"Grandpappy's pa was a boatman in slavery times. That was his job for his Marse Jim, carrying big loads of Marse Jim's cotton down stream on his flat boat, piled up high with many four-hundred-pound bales. He was a good boatman too, from all the hear-tell, a big strapping tall man with great, powerful wide shoulders, ropes of muscle, and big hands, made all the stronger for poling the boats.

"He had plenty of excitement in them unusual days. After a rain like this, oft-times the water would be deeper than a tree is high. Where there usually was stones and rapids, you could glide straight on over. Not even a ripple of rock showed below.

"It would take five boatmen to a boat. The steersman steered, and four others poled. They made the poles to suit the job. Some were short, some were long. Some broad and flat at the end, others blunt, others sharp. When the river ris' up, the waves sometimes got as high as this old store. Then it was a real man's job to help handle the flat. With water roaring and foaming, it went round you like a mad tiger blowing his breath. Grandpappy said that his pa declared how sometimes his legs shook, he was so scared.

"Sometime that river would take your flat 'round and 'round like a carnival merry-go-round till you got so swimmy-headed that you'd have to bring up all the vittles you'd eat. Then the boat would lurch and swing from that swirl into a fast stream that would send you flashing like lightning a mile-a-minute straight downstream. You'd see a big tree right dead ahead and you aiming to hit that tree square, so with a well-aimed pole, you'd glance off and sail right on by. Power it took for all this, power of body and will, and bravery too.

"Marse Jim would say, 'Boys, we got enough splinters at the fireplaces at home. Let's don't make no more out of this here raft,' and sure they would all pole.

"Grandpa's pa told him of how on one of their trips they went up the river real narrow—plumb into North Carolina, a place they'd never been before or since—like millions of miles to them. I ain't even been there myself. When they went up, well, the river, she looked like a lamb, and the boatmen they breathed the cool mountain air. But the great rains came like this, in a September gale, while they was gathering their wares, and they had to get the flat back over a hundred miles home, loaded with barrels of apples and tobacco and fat kegs of chestnuts too.

"Them narrow banks they went up on vanished, he said; and the boat went tearing down that valley of water faster than a wild stallion kicking the boards of his stall and let loose from his pen. The boatman never had to hit a lick on the poles, but the flat went so fast that they was so scared they couldn't take a long breath.

"Finally Marse Jim called out, 'Boys, see the tops of them willow trees down yonder? We'll steer her over them so they'll slacken our speed.' They did just that, with a great thrashing sound, but it didn't at all deaden their speed. Great-grandpappy said that Marse Jim shook his head and allow, 'Just bound for hell, I reckon, boys. Bound for hell!'

"They got to Cherokee Falls, with the water so high they couldn't tell there was falls; and Marse Jim say, 'Lay her to the right; we can't wreck this flat without putting up an honest man's fight. I'm bound and determined to get us all back home. If we break up, we'll sho' go to hell.'

"The boatmen tried to swing her by grabbing to a willow, and they broke a lot of limbs in trying, but at last they did swing her and the flat ran a hundred yards without no steering. Then the bow landed on a little mountain of sand like the ark, praise the Lord. There were great tall-legged sand-hiller cranes walking all around, with silvery fishes in their mouths.

"Marse Jim allowed, 'Ain't never seen such an ocean of water outside the Atlantic, damn if I have.' He looked at Great-grandpappy with a devilish twinkle in his eyes, and said he: "Don't know whether Charlie Gilliam is scared or not.' Great-grandpappy said he was setting his foot on the sand at that point and so he was brave to reply, 'No suh, ain't scared; could have come down this lamb of a river in my little one-man batteau.' Truth is, he told Grandpa, he was so scared to death, that he wasn't scared.

"All the men's legs wobbled on land, so long it had been since their feet had pressed earth, and so scared they had been.

"Well, they laid over on that sand mountain two days, to let the water go down. They lived and moved among the sand-hiller cranes, and lots of all kinds of other animals, all at peace that in other times was at each other's throats. They said how strange it all was, like in a slow-motion dream. Great watersnakes there were, lying next to half-drowned field mice, and like neither aware.

"The men had taken their rations such as meat, bread, and cabbage, and caught all the fish they could stand.

Besides they had the barrels of apples and chestnuts, and could roll them some good fat cigars. They had nice coffee too. They made fires of the driftwood and had them a time.

"During their rest, the water had done receded a little, and so they got down to Lockhart Shoals, near thirty miles, in one day, with no mishaps or loss. The water was still so high that they ran over the shoals without so much as a tremor or shake. They come sailing on down to Fish Dam Ford and went over the old familiar zig-zag of rocks and never knowed it was there. They zipped past Henderson's Island, where they were close enough to see candlelight and lanterns in the parlor windows there, and old Mrs. Henderson herself, reading her Bible by the fire, and landed the flat in the dead of the night, at the road down here nearby, with everybody safe, but still a mite shaken and scared.

"All of the men that made that ride knew that each could be trusted. Great-grandpappy said that ever afterwards they formed a real bond. I reckon they gave meaning all around to the old saying y'all probably have heard the old-timers use for folks you could depend on. 'He'll do to ride the river with,' they'd say. And I reckon the Gilliam crew already had.

"There were two Charlie Gilliams in them days—my great-grandpappy, and a poor unfortunate other one too. Some years after they got home safe, the other Charlie was hit by a poleman on cutting the flat when he got in the way of the poleman's pole. It caught him spang in the temple

—some said in the ear—and he fell over in the water stone dead. Warn't narya drop of water in his lungs, so they knew he was killed then straight out and never suffered none. No one was to blame, but Grandpappy's pap said how sorry they all was, and how long that they grieved. The kilt boy was a strapping, young innocent fellow who was just learning his way in the world. They jokingly called him the baby because 'spite his age, he was probably the biggest, strongest, and bravest of all, just caught for an unlucky moment unawares. They declared what promise of life that he had, and now it all ruined, snuffed out like a lamp.

"When they laid him to rest in the ground, Marse Jim read the words from the Book and said words of sorrow and praise, and they shed many a tear, big men with strong shoulders shaking in grief. And Marse Jim said that there was no shame in none of that neither at all, and shed big tears of his own.

"Marse Jim and all of them felt just as sorry for the poleman that had killed poor Charlie too. He meant Charlie no harm, and they was allus good friends—the best of good friends, who'd been part of the trials by water and hairbreadth escapings from hell. He never quite got over that day, nor did my grandpappy's pa."

As Uncle Dick finished his story on this sad note, the wind was still blowing in torrents of rain. A big drop would sometimes trickle down from between the old warped weatherboards and fall. Every now and then, a wind gust got caught in the downspouts and made mournful sounds. At these, Uncle Dick looked up and said, "Voices of the dead." It was as if his grandpappy and his pa, young killed Charlie, and all of those men from years long ago were right there with them in the sound. And the old store sighed but weathered the gale like a stout ship at sea, waiting for dove.

The men too were conscious of Joe-Blair Graham's empty stool in the dark corner of the store. He had been dead now a year, but the memory of him presided from the stool as regal as any throne.

Now it was time to call it a day. Night was showing its first signs through the cobwebs and dust of the store's dingy window panes. This time of year the days were shortening down and night came on fast. Because of the weather, Chauncey had come to Kildee's this morning in his beat-up old truck. It was raining too fast and furious for Uncle Dick to walk himself home, so Chauncey drove him on down the road to his house on the river bank.

There the river had already begun its gradual rise; and, before leaving, Uncle Dick had some wisdom to share with Chauncey inside the truck door. Chauncey was in no hurry, and listened to the old man's slow, measured talk.

Chauncey waited till Uncle Dick's kerosene lamp reflected in the shanty's panes. Then the truck's taillights reflected from the silvery sheen of the rain-covered road as the great river brooded in flux just below. From his rain-dotted rearview, Chauncey gave it a long parting glance as he turned the last curve.

"Bound for hell, boys," he recalled from Uncle Dick's tale, as he envisioned Jim Gilliam on his flat-boat riding the waves, standing firmly wide straddle-legged and strong-voiced as the boat bucked and roller-coastered beneath, and his five burly polemen and steersman laboured on, frightened nearly to death, but having the ride of their lives.

XXII

United We Stand

~ ∞ ~

And when the danger comes, as come it will,
Go as your fathers went with woodsman's eyes
Uncursed, unflinching, studying only the path.
— Donald Davidson, *Sanctuary*

Be not conformed to this world. — Romans: 12

Some miles away, in another land, another world (it might have been deemed another galaxy), our Chauncey stood at a bus stop in the grey shadow of metal and glass office towers, now in the act of disgorging, emptying their inhabitants like so much cargo, into anonymous dusty streets. The buses of the city transit system labored to zoom and whiz city-folks on their busy getting-and-spending ways. The buses weren't having much success though, bogged down as they were in a blended quagmire of vehicles that only moved slowly as one, like the flow of hot lava or grey molten lead at the precise moment before it cooled and congealed.

Just as in Chauncey's county-seat town, the cars here were also madly flying their wind-stiffened flags. So were the buses and buildings. Every street scene had them; every pole. Traffic stilled to a halt, making a four-laned parking lot of cars as far as the eye could see. Massed as they were bumper-to-bumper, they all strained and throbbed as one.

Chauncey wondered what his friends Kildee and

Triggerfoot would make of this land beyond Damascus, were they ever to see. One thing he knew: they wouldn't be pleased; but it would almost be worth putting them through it to hear what they would say. They'd have some original choice words, he knew. At least about these serious, straight-ahead faced people, he knew Trig would volunteer one of his favorite expressions, "No ham and all hominy," meaning all work and no real let-down play.

A woman stood at the bus stop where Chauncey waited. He wore a camo jacket and shirt. Before he thought, he nodded his head and said "Afternoon, M'am," as he naturally would if he were at home. The woman looked quickly away.

She must have taught at the big university looming behind them, for she wore the look like a badge. She was past middle age, had on wrinkled, shapeless pants and a sloppy, ill-fitting denim shirt. She looked amorphous like rubber and sexless as an amoebe. She carried a paperback text with red post-it note markers on its pages, a red that matched her AIDS ribbon pinned over her heart. Thirty years ago, it no doubt would have been a MAKE LOVE NOT WAR slogan and a peace symbol. While he waited, Chauncey ruminated on the fact that, to his mind, most of the people around this centre of learning had about as much raising, as much a cultured way to act, in their whole bodies, as the folks out around Cousin Kildee's store had in the tips of their fingers. And this was no compliment to the towers behind him, or the things that went on therein. He had an image of a giant, long trough at which the unsuspecting students fed. They had their heads filled with the swill of every kind of *ology* known. When they were full, or mostly so, they were told to go where the job is, when what they were needing were homecoming degrees. He'd heard of casting pearls of wisdom before swine, but here the pearls were not pearls and the swine didn't necessarily have to leave the trough as swine.

Chauncey had now come to understand that the three greatest superstitions of the industrial culture of such cities as this was that it will come up with solutions to the problems it has created, that all knowledge is value-free and neutral, and that education in these universities makes people better, that you can make people better through science, pseudo-science, technology, and fat government grants.

Chauncey eyed the book for its title, and found there quite incredibly honest on its cover, emblazoned in the same red as the post-it notes: *Race, Gender, and Class,* the new sanctioned Bible of a secular religion, the text no doubt for a psychology, sociology, or anthropology course. No matter, they'd be all the same. They'd study and adjust the surface environment, as good social engineers, split hairs and tinker with the externals, never thinking of what may be inside, or what couldn't be described by statistics or proved in a lab—B. F. Skinner writ large. They cared nothing for empirical nothing, they'd say; and Chauncey would answer that that manner of thinking led straight on a path to nothing itself. More swill at the trough. He had an equation for them, and of which they might even approve: "Thinking nothing of nothing leads to nothing." What about that?

He was beginning to understand more clearly now that

the state and its grant-seeking university minions wanted to impose *Race, Gender, and Class* in order to control society to make it conform to the managerials' view of what it should be, never thinking that what was utopia for one might be hell for the other. Here was puny, wilful man at it once again. What were once private and free social spheres were no longer sacred and free, for the State would intervene, ever expanding into a widening range of human relations that had been strictly off limits before. In the Skinner formula, what was wrong with technology was that it had not been applied properly to the interior man.

Chauncey had also come to the startling realization that the managerial State wished to cripple any social group not under its strictest control. Those whom it would "empower," as they called it, would then owe its status to the State and hence its allegiance too. For what the State giveth, it can as easily take away. He and Hoyalene's brother Clint had talked about this and agreed that the managerial elite, as Clint called them, had in this way concocted obedience pills. "Hard to swallow," Chauncey had said, but the lad had demurred. "More like suppositories," he declared. Clint was learning the ropes.

They agreed that what this place needed was a good reality check, or maybe just a swift kick in the pants or pantssuit, or, better yet, to cut off the funds that paid for the swill—expensive stuff, but still swill, and far from nutritious, mainly hazardous to health and well-being of soul. Ists and ologists indeed! Pumped up with self-importance, their do-gooding was usually all about them. Chauncey had seen enough of their kind. So had Clint, who knew these ologist sorts very well. He caught on quick, very quick, having Chauncey and Kildee to talk to and discuss. The more that Clint learned, the more the young fellow feared. He'd gotten now where he wouldn't say much around others, and just shake his head.

Some of the deeper meanings of all this were mostly beyond Chauncey, but not so the message of the way the woman at the bus stop stood, the superior unfriendly look of her, ignoring him quite in a stiff-necked way to show that she was ignoring him and wanted him to know. In his part of the world, people looked each other in the eye and said hello, even waving when meeting metal-encased in cars. That included strangers too. Doing so was only a modicum of good manners. You learned that early and never forgot. It got so natural with you that when someone didn't, it jolted you, hit you like a slap in the face.

"Hell," he muttered under his breath. No doubt she was a bra-burning Viet Nam protestor thirty years ago, but now stuffed, satisfied, and complacent, with too much success in the egalitarian smug empire she had helped to create. She and Little Joanie Phoney Baez, or better yet, Hanoi Jane, he thought, but no tight-shirted, mini-skirted Barbarella she. She stood there overweight and shapelessy complacent, smugly perched on the brittle fortress of her power, from the very citadel of Paradigm, and looked down her nose at all around and outside. "You're just so outside the paradigm," her refusal to look at him was aiming to say.

Chauncey entertained the notion that she would have been at home in combat boots. He passed the time of his wait imagining her thus, and thinking up downright mean thoughts threaded from his experience of country talk at Cousin Kildee's store. He fought the meanness but sometimes just couldn't help it. "Yessiree," old Jim-Jesse might say, "she's so unpleasant, even the tide wouldn't take her out." Or old Bob might add, "She acts so ugly, bet when she was a chile, her poor mama had to borrow a baby to take to church." Hell, Chauncey thought, back home she wouldn't even make the first five finalists for Fat-Back Queen.

In this way, our Chauncey could help neutralize her look and counter the engulfing gloom. Still, he knew there must be a person way back in there somewhere, and if he had the time or chance he'd make an effort to find her out. But like all else around him here on the grey street, she was a part of the flux, and like a leaf, in an eyeblink, would be swept casually away. It was that kind of age; leastways here in the city it was. He found himself touching the gold circle of locket at his chest.

The troubled Year of our Lord 2003. These past few months, all the news had run riot on the Middle Eastern scene. Wars and rumours of war. Under mammoth polyester displays of red, white, and blue—too many stripes, too many stars—politicians were sabre-rattling, enlisting to conquer Afghanistan, Iraq, then on to Syria and the Saudis, to win the War on Terrorism and bring the conquered, as they declared, out of their barbaric, unenlightened ways. Veils and harems, indeed. Injustice, oppression, inequality, the dark ages of men. To topple the old, replace all with what they called "Liberal Democracy," to make all the weary old outmoded world in their own image of the bright, shiny new, or, at least all this the excuse.

As symbol of this future, Chauncey imaged a new-minted Lincoln penny that would soon smudge and turn, and almost as worthless too, the gruesome face upon it, a great bearded, base-metaled statue of mammon to be worshipped by all. "Regime replacement" and "Preemptive Strikes," the Big Wigs of empire had smugly called their program at a news conference today. He imagined Preemptive Striker Children at a school playground scene. All the youngsters were laid out before a single brawling big lad. I got them before they got me, he was saying to the teachers there. Not convinced, the split-lipped victims called him names, and "bully" was the one most often heard. Preemptive strikes. Ridiculous indeed!

And if these faraway places didn't play ball and just give in? Then who's to stop the preemptive bully? The Mideast would be turned into our private own self-service gasoline pump, one columnist had had nerve to say. "Yes, who's to stop us?" was the question that hovered on screen like the ghost of all imperial conquerors from empires long past, and up until now. Self-service would be the word. No need to have even a lackey long-robed Arab to pump the gas at our efficient new station. No thanks; we'll just help ourselves. Self-serving as always. "Under New Management" the bold new sign would say. Such happens during so-called "reconstructions" to colonies always.

Chauncey's own Southland gave him the clue, for he knew his history taken not from revisionists' books but from his own family's experience in time.

Through Chauncey's mind kept running the old promise, that when a people's ways please the Lord, He makes even their enemies to be at peace with them. Chauncey held up the plumb line against his own, and found them to be less than just and upright, and fearfully ripe for just chastisement. The land flying these thousands of secular flags had gone from the Church of Your Choice to the God of Your Choice—a polytheism at best, in keeping with a tolerant, multicultural plan. He'd just heard of the national service that placed the Koran on the altar of the nation's own church in D.C. Had they not been cautioned many times of old? As Chauncey saw it, who could not but prophesy? He knew full well all the time that few would listen, as with the prophets of old. What else was new!

The new prophets of progress were smug, complacent, and fat. "Never trust a fat prophet," he remembered his father's saying of old. Daniel and Jeremiah, Ezekiel and Isaiah, they were all gristle and backbone.

With these and like ruminations, Chauncey mulled it all over while he waited. Most emphatically he thought this "War Against Evil" a ludicrous thing. It presupposed that evil was always the other, residing only in other peoples of other lands, and that it could not be inside. This war to exterminate evil, when looked at aright, was a death wish for all. Only armageddon could bring such a result, and he had nothing of the suicidal in his nature. Just more of the culture of death, like those three thousand abortions each day, he thought to himself. "In love with easeful death"— a snatch of poem came to his mind, but this death would not be easeful in any way.

The buses had on them large computerized message boards that spelled out their words with bright yellow digital dots ever lit and running nervously down their fronts and across their sides, like nervous tics on a guilty face. The message that flicked off and on in this time of the "War Against Evil" was UNITED WE STAND. Instead of message, it was more like command. Chauncey thought it should read UNITED WE LIE—as in THE BIG LIE. Hypocrisy and humbug, sham and scam; and self-righteous above all, a "titanic pride," as Triggerfoot might say. He felt that small knotted circle of nausea start to grow in the pit of his stomach, as his ab muscles tightened 'neath his belt, and his belt became loose. He hadn't eaten all day in his haste to get home. Scam, and again scam, was the only word that would come to his mind, scam the best single word that would best sum up the scene. He kept the circle of nausea in check, by an exercise of the will.

The UNITED WE STAND slogan had replaced the name of the bus route and destination, so that he was not altogether sure what each bus was.

Chauncey wondered if the UNITED WE STAND bus

was going as far as Iraq and toyed with asking the driver the same. Instead, he turned to the woman and inquired cheerily, "Are you taking the UNITED WE STAND bus all the way to Iraq?"

Of course, no answer was made. He didn't expect one. Any other question, and the result would have been the same. She continued to act as if he still wasn't there.

A bus with no destination, it was clear. Yes, the slogan-command had supplanted its designated route. He refused to get on it thus blindly and out of pure faith, not knowing where it would go. This blind faith in the actions of men, right down to their blind faith in their government's paper specie, was idolatrous, sure. Chauncey put no faith in the distant governments of men, their enthusiasms, their utopian dreams disguising mere lust for power—raw, cruel, and extreme. He only rendered unto Caesar what Caesar took on demand—Caesar with his hooded falcon perched on arm, the falcon now unleashed and not hearing the falconer, the falcon a far different thing than a red-tailed hawk back home.

A faith in this war? The world had gone mad. Who wanted to wake up in an Iraqi desert, staring at your own over-sized self-service gas pump we'd just made out of some one else's home, with backdrop of nothing but bomb-pock-marked sand, people crouching in caves, mounds of smoking ashes from newly burned veils. And to be there in this desert with this stone-faced woman whose look a veil would have mightily improved. To be stuck on a bus with only *Race, Class, and Gender* to read. "No, I believe I'll just walk, thank you, m'am."

The street was clogged with the cars of travellers now desperate to get home. The scene had all the look of a massive evacuation from some great disaster. The drivers sat in their fume-heavy vehicles with windows all rolled. They looked straight ahead almost as far as to see the Afghanistan hills the invaders had been successful in doing as they promised they would—bombing the land back to the Stone Age. The drivers sat, each one like the other, with their stiffened necks and fixed, unseeing stares, as if turned to pillars of salt or stone. Occasionally, Chauncey could hear the muffled throb of a CD playing inside a car, the wailing voice like the sound of a smothering man. He could feel the vibrations through the car's metal and plastic skin louder than the sound. A lethal mixture of dust and fumes took the breath from out Chauncey's clean lungs, accustomed as they were to a different place.

As he walked, Chauncey thought to himself: "Chemical weapons and weapons of mass destruction? We've made up our own! Who needs to fear theirs? We're intent on exterminating ourselves without even knowing it, it seems. Our own worst enemy, us, and the evil within."

The scene all about already looked for all the world like a desert to him. What once had been Isaiah's fruitful vineyard now only yielded concrete and weeds. Chauncey envisioned the curse already upon it, its wall trampled down, its watchtowers gone, yielding a waste fit only for briars and thorns. In this land of dead asphalt, he mused, briars and thorns and nettles would even now sure be a great treasure trove. Faith in the scam. Yes, the world had gone mad. His hand was at the locket on his chest once again.

XXIII

The Eighth Circle

~∞~

In his progress on foot, Chauncey continued to make faster time than the city bus. As he passed under the shadow of its lumbering shape, he glanced up at the digital screen. UNITED WE STAND and GOD BLESS AMERI-CA interchangeably, alternately ran—the first a command, the last coming across as a shouted demand rather than prayer. The empire's nervous tic was just as discernibly nervous as ever on the bus's digital screen.

Once again he caught a good glimpse of the hard face of the woman he'd met at the bus stop looking straight ahead like the sharp piercing point of Liberal Democracy's leveling arrow on its militant flight.

She looked at him from her trance for a split second and then quickly away—straight into the hazy gas-fumed ether of utopian space. As he looked at her, a passage from Jeremiah came to Chauncey's mind, concerning God's judgments, and the failure of those chastened to be contrite: "They have made their faces harder than a rock."

All in the bus seemed to be sedated into a daze. It was

as if a yellow drip I.V. to drug them into stupor was attached to the vein of each passenger's arm. Their eyes were all fixed ahead, as if studiously avoiding engaging another's there. As Chauncey walked, he ruminated on a line he'd just read that people these days always preferred comfort to joy, but Chauncey found it ironic that in their obsession for the former they had neither. It was as if they'd cocooned themselves against all danger and pain, and even sweat and exertion, but the irony hit Chauncey again full force that peril and discomfort were all around. And it was as often as simple a matter as breathing the poisoned air or crossing a narrow painted white line. "The industrial nightmare," he grumbled out loud. "This is where folly leads."

Then a snatch of scripture played across his mind and would not go away, of Abraham, by faith sojourning in a strange country, looking for a city whose builder and maker is greater than man, confessing that he is a stranger and pilgrim on the earth, desiring a better land where God is called God, choosing rather to suffer affliction with the just than to enjoy the pleasures and comforts of the lost. "Let us run with patience the race that is set before us," he remembered Paul's words aloud. "Lift up the hands that hang down and the feeble knees and make straight paths for the feet. Follow peace with all men."

Chauncey did not pick up his pace. He walked at his usual gait, neither more slowly nor faster, as if he trod grass in the pasture and fields of his home. Still, slow as he was, he was again leaving the bus behind him, as he headed up hill. The solid congealed parking lot of cars was getting more irritated with itself as it sat motionless, congealed, collectively throbbing and seething as one, inching its way, when it moved at all, slower than snail. Chauncey imaged again, "A slow-motion, freeze-framed version of lemmings to sea."

The several UNITED WE STAND buses rose from among the mass of the cars, like dead pieces of drying worms carried above heads of plodding red ants, ready to sting, as they carried the worm segments on their driven, self-absorbed way. At other times, they all reminded Chauncey of the flies that got stuck fast in rows in Kildee's molasses-coated flypaper that once dangled from the summer rafters of his store. The buses were like the occasional angry caught bee, or a wasp in a spider web. They all had this in common: they were rushing to go nowhere and were mightily frustrated and mad.

The fumes came and went like mustard gas, or wisps of mace, or lingering tear gas, the remnant pockets settled in low places like the residue of riots now quieted, quelled. Chauncey's nose and eyes burned, but he kept on his way.

The bus caught up to him, and then there was the woman's face once again, sealed in its air-conditioned tomb, protected in its cocoon from the reality outside where Chauncey walked and lived and tried to breathe.

He grunted as the bus came astride. It stopped again in the clog, like miring in sand; and then again he outstripped it, passing a laundry, the U.S. flag-clad storefront of a small hardware store with a going-out-of-business sign, then by the lit fake golden glow of arches, and a caption proudly proclaiming in illuminated letters: OVER 99 BILLION SOLD. The figures ignored the defunct hardware and the irony of its U.S. flag. The sign winked its bright yellow figures at the matching, color-coordinated digital yellow of the UNITED WE STAND that flickered from the bus, now throbbing and idling noisily behind him. The bus's command-message trilled and winked back knowingly in answer to the burger sign, as the straining bus ran its frantic shrill words of uniformity against the despair of its space-lost empty black screen.

"More like a war to make the world safe for the sale of these 99 billion burgers, or the CEO megacompany Masters of Burgers," he muttered, for our Chauncey was no fool. "Cheney-Corp," he muttered to himself. To those fat merchants of war, the dealers and speculators in the wealth of the earth who own this world and its government, its converse of media and opinions and its colleges, to all those who enslave mankind and feed off its sweat and its substance, he was on the verge of hurling a great oath and curse. Instead, he then thought of all those who decried these merchants of war, that like him, they examine their own hearts and see to what extent they too were blood-guilty. He offered a prayer for all these, that they see clearly, that they quit their existence as they are and avert the curse and just judgment that most surely would otherwise fall upon them.

Still he walked faithfully on, by Arby's, and Subway,

and Hardee's, and Wendy's, past the biologically dead desert expanses of Wal-Mart parking lots, then the entrance to Mall. He called the former Sprawl-Mart and Swill-Mart when he was in a good mood, and Wal-Fart when he was not, for Chauncey understood clearly enough what these faceless megacompanies stood for and would mean. None of their wally-world smiley-faced logos had ever fooled him. He knew what was at stake. They were death to all Kildees, great and small, wherever they paved a lot, plopped down a store, and cast their shadow on the land.

There would be no saving this ruthless bland world from its own destruction. The watchman would watch in vain. Chauncey saw it as a matter of community or commodity, and in the face of commodity, community would have little chance. "Prophets or profits, take your choice," he said aloud, a habit that had grown on him; and he answered himself, knowing full well which the world had already decided to choose.

Chauncey understood that a corporation was beyond feeling and was set up for that reason. It was like a motor, a dynamo, essentially a machine like the bus with its grinding gears. Yes, the factories and businesses and colleges kidnapped people from nature, their farms, and family, and all the traditional good that these had ever represented to man.

The small green plot that shimmered at the top of a distant rise was visible to him now. At the bright red of the gates to the Mall is where he'd have jumped from the bus to start up the second hill, his last leg of the journey that would eventually lead to a way to get home.

Behind him, the bus was disgorging its insides, in its unpleasant way with loud, vulgar flapping slams of unyielding doors. He would not watch and he did not see. It was something for the eyes to avoid like acts of nature done inside anonymous stalls.

"Hate evil. Cherish good," he said aloud, and his thoughts were becoming as constant prayer.

After a few more minutes' walking, he was out of the bus's sway and orbit, away now from its sound, smell, and feel, as if escaped from a sentence of death in the desert, napalm, nerve gas, or self-immolation on a gasoline sea.

"Hinnom and Gehenna," he said aloud, voicing the strange Hebrew words for the ancient valley of refuse, that solemn dumping-ground landscape of ashes where man had made a hell of earth. He turned his back to the din, and like good Lot of old, never looked back at the cloud of dust and fumes and commotion rising below.

Time to head on home to the Fair Realm and Far Kingdom of Kildee, he thought to himself and smiled with the sweat cooling on his upper smooth-shaven lip. They can keep all their 99 billion burgers in the Land of the Jolly Green CEO.

"Hinnom and Gehenna," he repeated, then he prayed his petition for mercy to the Lord and Giver of Life, that man be saved from himself. These were his final words as he quit the scene, a kind of solemn, hopeful benediction on the troubled valley below, for he did not feel himself righteous or guiltless enough to hurl the withering curse he was most capable of.

He let his mind coast now as he crested the hill. Ahead lay the outline of an honest and genuine rooted line of bright trees. Miles beyond them flowed the silver ribbon of deep river, undammed and free, whose crossing would bring him whispers of home, and a further river, the living, familiar one that ran silently behind Kildee's store.

With his walking, he'd worked up an appetite. In his imagination, he could already taste grits and red-eye gravy, biscuits and black-strap molasses, and maybe some of Kildee's hoop cheese, newly cut and handed by Kildee's own kindly hands. "Want some saltines with this?" he could hear Kildee say.

The tree line hovered apparition-like, but solid enough to last in its sheen and glow.

As he climbed up the final hill of his deliverance, Chauncey still gave no glance at the dust cloud well behind him now, and his mind was lightened, as if freed from some heavy dread load. Spontaneously he began to break into quiet under-his breath song. It cleared away the fermenting and undigested residue of the frantic scene he had walked his way from and was about to put miles between.

It was an old song from his childhood that he hummed, a tune learned at his mother's own knee, of his going home, and of having and knowing a home. With its rhythm, good rhythm for walking, it accompanied and mirrored, supported and strengthened and lightened his steps on the way. From time to time, his fingers would find the outline of the tiny gold locket beneath his shirt. Eventually, some piece further, he'd be able to sing his song out joyous aloud to hills, clouds, and the stones. United he'd then stand with these—and with those gone before, family, neighbours, and friends.

Unlike those who had swirled chaotically around him here in this alien place, he had no desire to venture out from home, not for learning, glory, not for wealth. He had come here out of necessity to help young Clint, and now was going home. As he walked, his mind cleared into vision. There in the valley of the eighth chasm, swathed in consuming fire, arose Odysseus, twinned with Diomede. In highest tongue of war's forked flame, as if from off the funeral pyre of Theban brothers battle-slain, the two were frozen, caught. As then of old, Odysseus spake again, this time to Chauncey all alone: *Nor fondness for Telemachus my son, nor reverence of my father old, nor return of love that should have crowned Penelope with joy, could overcome my zeal to wander out again through all the world and search the ways of life beyond the boundaries ordained for man.* Odysseus spoke his torment, and then was swallowed, silenced, in the tongue of leaping flame, labouring with the wind. Unlike Odysseus, Chauncey had neither son nor father and wife left him, but still had no lust to wander or roam. His at least would not be that circle in hell.

The utility poles that Chauncey now passed became scarcer and the spaces between them drew out longer as he went. The poles were great fire-scorched cylinders of salt to his mind. He still did not look back. As he walked, the earth seemed to be growing more solid beneath his feet, and he became ever surer that what he stood for was what he would soon be standing on. He was thinking again now mostly of home as he hummed his little song.

"'Live and let live' is just the best old motto!" Cousin Kildee was heard often to say. The rhythms of Kildee's "Live and let live. . . . Live and let live" got mixed up in the rhythm of Chauncey's footsteps and the gentle tune that he hummed. It fit there quite nicely and was naturally appropriate besides, in an old song of walking toward home.

XXIV

Gilead's Balm

We have nothing to do with Aulis, nor intrigues
At Mycenae . . .— Allen Tate, "Aeneas at New York"

Chauncey was already at the door when Kildee came to open up the store. He knew he was welcome to go on in, but didn't have quite the will to enter the dark, empty room, empty indeed with its master gone. He'd been waiting outside there only a few minutes when Kildee showed on the scene, just in time, truth to tell, to allow Chauncey his accustomed whizz round at the back of the store. "One of the little pleasures of life," Chauncey had said, "not having to aim at a hole." He had his own personal view of why hunting was so popular in these parts. Just a chance to whizz in the woods. No real care to kill deer, just marking territory, that's all. As for Chauncey and Kildee, they both still felt it a bit uncivilized to have the outhouse indoors. One day Kildee had said in his wry, deadpan way, "You know, Chauncey, old friend, we do live in strange, puzzling times. Now we cook outside and shit inside." And Chauncey had agreed.

As for Chauncey's state—physical and mental—since

returning home, he said he felt like he'd been kicked in the ribs with combat boots, been dragged behind a bus for a mile, or beaten up by a prize fighter in the ring.

After the delivery of greetings and news from Clint, some personal catching up on things and some little communications about events that had occurred while Chauncey was away, Chauncey settled down to tell Kildee the story of where he had been and what he had seen.

Kildee listened amused, whiling his time with the tale while he arranged some few items on shelves, but showing no curiosity, no desire to know more than was told.

"Why are people today so hell bent on destruction?" Chauncey asked.

"Why do the Heathen rage?" was Kildee's reply. To all unanswerable questions having to do with absurd behavior, Kildee usually answered with this further question, which was in itself a kind of answer. These days, Kildee had occasion to use it often.

"I'd be thrown away in that place," Kildee had concluded with gravity, and said little more. That was all that was needed. Chauncey knew what he meant.

One thing about Kildee: people interested him mightily, and the road went both ways. And that fact was made once again singularly apparent on this day. There was a somewhat fashionable lady now with them in the store. Her presence was announced by the gentle creaking of the old pine floor as she walked about looking at the things for sale. Kildee bid her good morning in his usual open, frank way.

She came from the courthouse town of the neighbour-ing county, where she said she ran an antique and interior decorator's shop. It was a pleasant-enough, horsey-set town of some pretensions, and a place of some means. Steeplechases, polo, hunt-meets, that sort of thing. Here, at Kildee's store, she was buying some wire egg-baskets, Uncle Pete's split-oak baskets, and such. Kildee sold them as the Sprawl-Mart would its plastic pails; but she was interested in them as crafts from the folk—"folk-art" for fashionable city folks fashionably tired of machine.

She had mounded up quite a tall pyramid of them on Kildee's honest, use-polished heart-pine counter. Chauncey felt sure the lady would have bought that too, were it not nailed down. Give her this: she stroked its plane marks with the caress of genuine appreciation.

The prices of the items were modest, but she'd pur-chased so many—in fact, all that her eyes had seen—that she didn't have her checkbook or quite enough cash to cover the tally of all. Kildee, of course, had never gotten a credit card machine. She had never expected, as she admit-ted, "to find so much here," and had not come prepared.

Of Kildee, she inquired the location of the closest Automatic Teller Machine. On their best manners, neither Kildee nor Chauncey belied their inclination to laugh. But the novelty was rich for them both. An ATM in a place whose sole other building was a post office made from a one-room housetrailer set on cement blocks. And they were lucky to have that. Only an influential local congressman had been able to keep the post office for them, and with it their official, on-the-books existence as a place. The modified trailer was their final flimsy stay against official oblivion, total and complete.

The nearest ATM was over twenty miles away.

"No need to drive all the way to town and back, Ma'am," was Kildee's answer to that. "Just bring it by next time you're near, or mail me a check when you've got the time."

She took his address and was about to give him hers, so "if he'd need to, he'd know whom to call."

"Ma'am, no need of that either," he answered her then. And no need to follow that up with a single word. He operated on trust, nothing more, nothing less. And that's the same reason there was no lock on his door.

When he said this, you could tell from the slight jerk of her head and the look on her face that her world had just collided with his. It was much like Titanic and berg. It was the first time she had really looked straight at him.

Chauncey and Kildee took the eight boxes of folk-art to the sleek, shiny new car. They filled up the trunk, and back seat besides.

"Another happy customer," Chauncey summed up the deal. "Folk-art for the masses. Folk-art for each! Folk-art for all! Bet she'll remember this day."

Kildee, however, bless his heart, had no idea what Chauncey could mean. He'd found nothing extraordinary with the way he'd handled the sale. For "sale" was too big of a word for what had occurred. Or maybe too small. It was more of a trade. At issue was no copper of profit, but of trust for a stranger to be the best our Kildee could conceive.

Those around Kildee knew that was his way. Till you gave him a reason to doubt it, he looked at you, believed in you, as what you wanted to be at your best. And till you proved he was wrong, you just were.

Another way to say it, as our Chauncey finally surmised, "Kildee believed your own best view of yourself, what you wanted others to believe of you at your best, and took it as real." Some could even live up to their ideal, and Chauncey knew from experience because he counted himself as one. As he could testify, Kildee's trust was often what it took for this to be achieved. Yes, his friend was special that way.

Then, if you failed to measure up, Kildee's manners kicked into play. He had a habit of saying that manners weren't inventions of a wise man to keep the fool at a distance, but instead acted as the means to protect the fool from the consciousness of his being a fool. On the subject of manners, Kildee was one of the natural best.

The world flowed around him as a gentle stream. He sat at peace in the middle of it on one of its warm, smooth autumn rocks and turned his face to the sun.

Truly, if any man cared little for getting and spending, it was Kildee. He would never have understood, or approved if he did, the use of money to make money with. Few in these parts would. Like Chauncey, his chief economic fear was the impersonal transaction, the mechanical response that kills.

In fact, he'd often just give items away rather than sell. At this, Spurgeon Adams asked him how he'd think to stay in business giving everything away that-away. Kildee's wry answer came fast. "Volume, I reckon," he'd said. That occasioned quite a laugh around.

He ran the country store, passed down from his kin; he farmed family land and that of his wife. His sons lived right near him on land he'd given them for theirs. They ploughed and harvested together at the proper times, lending willing hands. He mechanicked when needed, to pay for shortfalls in lean times in between. They lived in a kind of luxurious poverty. Without a dime sometimes, they had plenty, and at other times, some little extra to help others out.

Lula Bess had sent a sweet potato pie to the store with Kildee today. It was just as Chauncey liked it, crusted with chopped pecans on top—pecans from the tree out back. Kildee divided the pie into fives, and each person at the store got one. They sat around the stove in their rockers eating in silence, relishing its sweetness, and doing justice to the hands that had made it, and the proprietor's hands that had just profered it to them. Lula Bess was known as a very good cook in a community of good cooks, and sweet potato pies were one of the special treats in which she excelled. Kildee's favorite was his wife's fried pies made out of dried apples from trees in their own yard and sopping up fresh cinnamoned cream; but Chauncey specially loved sweet tater pies, and it was no doubt in honor of his return that she sent it along today. She'd rightly guessed he'd be worn plumb out.

That was their way in their part of the world. Folks instinctively knew that the best gesture of solace for a neighbour who's stressed or got trouble is a plate of fried chicken, a big bowl of potato salad, or a sweet tater pie. If the trouble happened to be a real crisis, they also knew to add a coconut cake or a banana pudding too.

Chauncey broke silence at last. "Tell Lula Bess, much obliged. This pie is sure one of her best. Thank her for me. Thoughtful as usual," he said.

Kildee nodded assent and said he would, but hoped Chauncey would be able to tell her in person himself very soon, at their supper table, which would also include him. They'd all missed their friend. For Kildee, there was nothing like getting all their feet under the same table to show them and Chauncey he was home.

Now Kildee was genuinely troubled by all that was transpiring in the great self-devouring world all around. Though he didn't show or say, what Chauncey had told him of the sojourn from which he had just returned had troubled his soul, and not just for the effect it had had on his friend.

So in one of the long lulls of the day, when several were gathered in their usual chairs, he spun out his latest tale. It was quietly, magically done as a comfort to Chauncey, who had been through the fire, and the tale was so designed without telling his friend it was so. Again, as usual, what wasn't said with our Kildee was key.

As the story, one of his inspired best, ran to its conclusion, like living river to sea, the small gathering was hushed into what amounted to awe. It sometimes happened that way, but this time Kildee had outdone himself, and this all of them there knew. The story soothed and reassured. Given the moment, it was better than pulpit's benediction, as if the Creator through Kildee were indeed lifting His countenance upon them, each one and all, and granting one of them, his single lost sheep, most particularly, most especially, a much-needed peace. Chauncey knew the story was mostly for him.

From the viewpoint of an observer, it might have seemed that on this day Kildee had generally clean outdone himself in every way he possibly could. As for Kildee himself, it was just another day good to be alive and thankful for it. And now the sun was ebbing to the west over the fringe of dark cedars behind the store. The chill of night would soon come down the road like a footsore old tramp needing rest, warmth, and food.

Men said their goodbyes. Some wives or daughters had come then into this mostly man's world to claim them and some of the stray children, one by one. Our Chauncey was the last on the scene. He'd brought a mason jar of his best scuppernong wine, and he and Kildee had them a small glass in honor of Chauncey's return. They sipped without talking, savouring the taste.

"Reckon it's time to get going," Chauncey said to his friend, as Kildee's black-and-tan rubbed at the top of his duckboots. "It's good to be home."

"Well, ain't that a fact," was the solitary sentence to end this good day, here at what the great fashionable world of getting and spending would call the middle of nowhere, the flyover country, the jumping-off place, the very end of the world.

Without thinking how it might sound, town folks often casually tossed off that middle-of-nowhere sentiment; and to it, our Kildee, taking no offense, would as often cheerily reply, "Why, nowhere? It's everywhere, the centre of universe, the mid-point of all. Like the centre of that old dartboard nailed up there on the wall, it's where I always just aim to be." And Chauncey could add his own "Yes, destination, and deliverance too."

Kildee's "Well, ain't that a fact," echoed long its sonorous tones, accompanying the sweet-sour scuppernong taste on their tongues, the taste that Chauncey swore he could always tell was his soil. So here they drained their glasses, here at the rag-tag, knocked-about, jagged edge of the world. As they walked to the door, the store's old floorboards, polished with generations of feet—brogans and boots and shoes and the bare heels of children in summer and spring—spoke its own approval with reassuring voice. It was getting toward dusk now and the season's last lightning bugs were signaling in trees.

The two friends parted at the store's front door and went their separate ways, to their own hearth circles of light—Chauncey silently musing on Kildee's unquantifiably precious gift of the tale, and Kildee unconcernedly whistling himself from the scene. Above them, and blended with Kildee's jaunty tune, could be heard the plaintive cry of a redtailed hawk circling high overhead.

The sun had set where the men walked, but searching him out, Chauncey saw the great wheeling bird burnished copper by the sun, as if it had been caught by a sculptor in gold. In the sun's dying light, the bird had the colors Chauncey had only seen elsewhere on a splitting-open-with-ripeness pomegranate skin. He touched the gold locket through his shirt and took the moment all in, looking deeply and long.

XXV

Chauncey's Christmas Dream

Mid-December: rains, fogs, overcast days one after another when the sun was not seen. The earth was leaning away from light and warmth, approaching the shortest day of the year. Folks down deep in their natures understood that the drama of a great ancient struggle was going on, unfolding all around, and they could discern it only from the corner of eyes.

That was the old struggle of dark and light, of good and evil, of benevolent spirits warring with demons possessing unspeakably ugly faces, great startling eyes and horns, waging it over the very futures of men, to determine if men were to be allowed future at all. Indeed, these forces were locked in mortal, deadly combat.

Edging toward Solstice, dark was gaining on light. The sun walked timidly along the horizon and never rose high in the sky, as if keeping its head ducked low, afraid to risk showing it much above the cover of trees. It seemed powerless to help in the fray. It had no warmth on the skin and stayed pale white all the short hours of the day. At this time of year it was dangerous for a person to walk out alone, for the nether world was very close, was there to step into at almost any step.

Chauncey was now home again, but very much in this struggle too. For all his usual outward cheerfulness and good will, he sometimes battled his own demons of despair. As always, he wanted to enter into the action, do his part too in the great conflict outside. He struggled to do, but was mired in slow motion, as if trying to do in a dream, like trying to cry out from sleep for help or a warning, but not being able to get out a word. And yet sometimes words came flying at him like razorblades, and he struggling to capture and say them, struggling to say them out loud or onto the white page.

He looked at the calendar on the kitchen wall: December 13, Saint Lucia's Day, it read—a celebration of light out of dark, Saint Lucy, the patron saint of the blind. How much then was she needed today in this bleak world precariously poised on the edge of a distant war. The blind following the blind all around, and a babble of tongues, with no eyes to see. These blind seemed to be walking in mire, caught in just that same dream they shared with him. Not being able to speak, he greeted them with a wave, but they could not see. They turned their cowled backs to him. In his mind, he spoke prophecy, but he could not make them hear, could make no one understand.

In the old Julian calendar, this day was already the Solstice, the darkest day of all, but now it was mated with Saint Lucy, poised to bring light in the new calendar of faith. "Light out of darkness, *Lux ex tenebris,*" Chauncey said out loud, in the tones of a petition, of a prayer.

In some ancient lands, Lucia appeared a fresh virginal maiden in white with a live holly wreath on her head, candlelit from above. Chauncey relished the picture. Her face was the mirror of Hoyalene's own in the blush of her youth before illness took the rose from her cheek. There she was before him, as in life, in a garden of red roses, a white-stipled, old-fashioned red rosa mundi in her raven hair, as red perfect as the rose pinned on holy Mary's blue blouse, or that Dante's beloved held in her purified white hand, all flesh burned away.

Now it was Saint Lucy who sat with him at his solitary breakfast, just come to an end. Chauncey remained still for a moment, thinking, before he cleared away the breakfast things. He was thinking again of sad, patient Dante and his Beatrice, and a tear welled in his eye. It gathered and fell to the plate before him; then others followed on the red checkered cloth. Some fell on the green of his camo pants. After all these years, there it was still, that knot of grief that would not be assuaged.

Under the spell of Saint Lucy and on her day, he remembered the olden time, as in another dream, of what his granddad would say of what he'd heard tell of days deeper in the past. Men all around, on Christmas Eve, would light big fires on pasture hills, then shoot off their great blackpowder blunderbuss rifles, like miniature cannons, with extra charges of powder and cotton wadding, bearing no lead.

These accomplished two things. It told the Christ

Child where their humble place was, a little like His own Bethlehem, welcoming Him there to their homes, this time homes and no stable for Him. And it scared off the evil spirits and demons of dark crowding in on the scene, thus preparing for light, Epiphany and the star to guide, when the light won the battle, and pushed back the dark to its cold cave.

The men, young single men especially, visited around, perhaps in the back of their minds, perhaps in the front, looking for wives. They stomped about loud and raucous with cowbells and chains, firing off guns, around and under the house, until welcomed inside. The farmhouse and its family would be warm and would greet them that way, to hot bowls of spiced cider and sweet cinnamoned rum, or perhaps syllabub. Folks in these parts pronounced it silly-bub, maybe because all those who drank it, heartily spiked as it was, became silly with time. Even the soberest among them too. The visiting bands would supplement cheer in between homes with the corn-liquor jug and break into spontaneous carol and song. This loud singing and the spiritous liquors would also help drive the worst demons away. All this was done in good fun. The men sang deep and danced boisterously long on their way.

Grandpappy vaguely remembered from the way back times, hear-tell of the hearty, tall men of the forests wearing fearsome and frightening homemade masks. They'd put on antlers, and long coats, fringed deerskins, and such, in their noisy masquerade. Their fancy dress and false faces presented an awesome, weird sight. Little chaps would cling to the dresstails of mamas and big sisters, and peep out scared from behind. Even the oldsters would have to look on in a wide-eyed amaze.

"To drive the cold winter away," they would sing; and they'd shout down the years "Welcome Yule!" with holy rejoicing that the forces of dark would not win, not be allowed to prevail, praying for help in the cause. Maybe Saint Lucy was also with them too, then. Or more like, with radiant blushes, in the guise of a local maiden, she poured sillybub from the great earthen bowls, opening the eyes of particular previously blind young men, blind to her charms.

Down the centuries, Chauncey saw people dancing, heard them singing joyous, spirited songs. They brought in armloads of evergreens into their homes. Behind him, he could hear them reveling, feasting, rejoicing in the new day as it blazed them awake after a night of beseeching bonfires, to keep life alive, singing the same happiness and relief as hope reawakened in a cold sleeping land. "Tidings of comfort and joy," they sang. "Tidings of comfort and joy." True comfort. True joy.

They gave thanks, prayed for a fruitful new year, drove the demons back to their dens with loud song and dance, caroled, feasted, loved dearly their neighbours, family, and friends, and hoped for the blessing of peace, among themselves and all men. Death and rebirth were factored in all that they did.

Chauncey longed for some such ritual again. He grieved its passing as if the death of one of his close kin. It was sorely needed in these impoverished, antiseptic times, when harsh, brutal forces of darkness ruled the diminished day, and the light seemed to have given up wholly its fight. The world was only just dark, unrelievedly so, so it seemed. Everything of beauty was stripped from it. Even memories too; and what few were left would be erased, and cruelly soon. Kildee's potbellied stove, stoked to its lid with best seasoned wood, though potent in its small circle, was no adequate defender of good. All the world had grown blind, so did not know how desperately dark it had become.

Tidings of comfort and joy. . . . It was as if he could hear these people of old singing so close behind him, almost near enough to touch, so close, but yet great gulfs between.

He mused long as he sat at the supper table, the remnants of a winter's meal before him there, grease congealing grey on his plate. At last, he cleared the dishes as he thought.

Still under a mountain of quilts drifting in and out of sleep, he was thinking, was gradually, carefully forming a plan. His long winter dreams mingled and blurred with that plan.

Next day at his breakfast, it was taking its shape. He worked with it as he went about chores. He fed all the chickens, put sunflower seed, the dark shiny kind full of oil, in the feeders for his favorite red birds, thistle seed for the goldfinches in bright winter plumage, and the chicadees that were now abundant there. The scolding twitter of wrens lit the scene. He thought, all these bright feathers would have to be replacement for sun.

By the time he'd put hay in the stall with the cow, he'd

about finished his scheme. He would test it, run it by Kildee and some others at the store.

That had to wait till the following day because some repairs to the gate, some hauling off limbs, had to be done. It took most of the day. But the branches, mostly of cedar brought down in an early ice storm, he piled on a great heap at the highest point of his pasture, clearly seen from the road, and down it too a good ways. This would be his bonfire on the shortest day of the year, about a week away.

Chauncey, as he usually did when the spirit moved him, got in full swing. The next day, working alone, he built two more fifteen-foot piles, from the bushes and brush and small trees he'd been meaning to clean from a path near the road. It made the approach to his farmhouse more inviting and friendly, as he had hoped. He put his whole heart in the plan. He was opening the doors of his house to the world.

Then off to the store. He'd earned a good sit by the fire in his favorite rocker and a catching up with the scene.

Today the store was full. He had hit it just right, so at times and slowly 'round the stove, he unfolded his plan. Lyman was there, Jim-Jesse Sims, and old Caleb too. About a dozen other regulars came and went at the stove. A few hunters in camo passed in and out. They all approved, at least in theory, of his plan. Some were even enthused, particularly the young.

For Chauncey invited the whole lot there assembled, and all others that they wanted to bring, to his giant bonfire less than a week from the day, that fell at the true Solstice, when they'd have longest night to revel, without then losing much sleep. Old and young were welcome, he said, from babies to old men; "And bring the oldest and loudest guns that you own," he added, "to shoot gloom away." All but Caleb said that they'd be there; and Caleb would have been there too, but went nowhere at night. He was nearing ninety, and all understood.

But this was not all of the plan Chauncey had conceived. He'd enroll Kildee's two youngest sons, Lyman's and Caleb's young unmarried grands, Jim-Jesse's two single boys, and all of their friends, to form up a group of randy wassailers, of which he'd make a part, and would go house to house, especially where sweethearts or sweethearts-to-be might find their abode.

All this would take some doing, but he put Kildee, Lyman, and Jim-Jesse in charge. The reveling was set for the evening and night after Christmas, Saint Stephen's Day— "Second Christmas," as Caleb remembered the old folks had called it in their time. For in the long, long ago in these parts, Christmas was a matter of two weeks or more, beginning with the Solstice, and no work but the absolutely essential was done during that span. Not even sweeping of floors would be dreamed of. "You'd be sweeping out the good luck," old folks would say. And particularly, nothing, as Caleb remembered his grandpappy recalling, was done that involved circular motions or wheels. No turns of the lathe, no use of the flail, no spinning of spinning wheels, no grinding of meal at the mill, no rolling of wheel barrows, wagons, or carts.

All the world stood motionless, holding its breath in anticipation, as if frozen still, waiting, hoping, for return of the light. Caleb remembered his grandpappy speaking, as if it was just yesterday, a kind of runic rhyme: Open the door for the old year. It is the dead one's time. *Open the door for the new year, and let the new one come. Bundle your wintered joy and grief on the back of the year that's done. Open your heart for the new life, and let the new Child come.*

A hint of this no-work tradition still hung on, like fox fire or will-o-the-wisp in the dark woods, though few knew just why, and that it was tradition at all. But Chauncey had awakened the genii and like rose petals of summer dried up in a sachet and placed in a drawer, the opening up gave full a surprise and brought back the rose in full summer blow.

Of late, Chauncey was beginning to think that they'd better go back to the old, and start shaping their own world in its image, if the world was to survive. Like a struggle of wren with the eagle, it would be; but they had a great good start here with tight families, neighbours, and friends, and a good enough, stable life on rich Carolina soil. What was needed was a strengthening, some serious shoring up. He'd give it a try. Without elaborating much on the why's, except to Kildee and Lyman, Chauncey got the answer he desired. They said, "Yes, Chauncey, you've got something there. We'll sure give it a try. There's nothing to lose." His dream was working its way.

Their blessing was all that was needed. Chauncey went straight to his work. The womenfolks were brought into the plan and onto the scene. "You want anything done," Kildee advised, "get the women involved. They know how to do."

So Kildee's daughters, daughter-in-law, and Lyman's two granddaughters would help Lula Bess, Jim-Jesse's wife, and Caleb's three unmarried young granddaughters set up a plan. They'd make up a map of houses for the young men to visit and make sure they'd be plenty of hot cider waiting, and sillybub, and food.

To be done on such a short notice, they made progress that picked up some steam. The community remembered from having heard tell, that such things were done there in the distant long ago. This gave its reverend blessing and sanction, and added its energy to the doings around, for in truth the folks had never cottoned too much to the jingle bells and jingling coins of the industrial-material Santa Claus scene. And that strange, foreign elf with the pack full of Sprawl-Mart plastic seemed too devious to them. Sneaking down chimneys at night was just not their way. Why didn't he knock like a neighbour at the front door? What example for children was that? There was enough true wonder in the world all around than making this up from the material brain. With a Coca-Cola in one hand and the latest fad in toys in the other, this Santa just seemed strange, confused—yes, truly strange.

Plastic might be fine in its place, but they were starting to question if it was the wonder it had first been proclaimed.

"Why complicate life with plastic holly berries that had to be bought at a store and gathered dust and faded away?" Lula Bess had just asked. So one sunny Sunday afternoon, Kildee and his little granddaughters went to the woods and brought in fresh dark green boughs filled with explosions of red, and smelling of the deep woods.

The bonfires came off with success on the Solstice as Chauncey had planned. Their great orange arrows shot up higher than thirty feet into the dark sky. They could be seen for near miles around. It was an icy, clear still night with a black sky and a million stars. The fire's sparks rose up to them, mating their red points of light with the faraway blue gleams.

The men had some drinks as they passed jugs, jars, and bottles about in the circle of fire. Old Triggerfoot showed up for the festivities too. A friend drove him in in a shiny new red SUV. Chauncey and Kildee joked about that. He brought a dozen jars of his best.

In all, there were about fifty men present, from old men to young sons, a big happy scene. They lit up the fires about seven and burned them till well after three. A great coming together it was, to talk and share news and just to glow in the friendships, and of just being there and alive, being warm by the fire, driving cold winter away, by hearts beating stronger and warmer with each degree that the temperature fell.

The red sparks swirled and danced high behind the silhouette of men who worked hard to keep family together and body tied to soul. That was a struggle of its own, and of similar kind to the old warfare of dark and the light. It was a very cold night, but the fires were sufficiently warm.

And the conversation was good. The tone of the night was cheerful, often jaunty, and the blaze joined with the bourbon, whiskey, and mellow moonshine to light pinpricks of sparks inside. The fire lit up the trees and the woods with a soft orange glow, and made ghostly shadows that moved eerily. The familiar place was changed to a landscape Chauncey had never seen. The men as they stood and moved cast long shifting shadows on familiar things now transmuted magically.

Yes, this was a good, perfect time for all of them to catch up on the news, for some of the men had not seen one another for months. It was also a good time to look forward to the big shivaree on Second Christmas, of which some of the men there gathered had not yet heard about at all, or only a word. The men showed all the excitement it was seemly for men in these parts to show. The young singles especially thought it a good chance to start thinking of engagement rings, though of this they said or hinted none, not a word.

They wondered how their sweethearts would take a bunch of them showing up rowdy, firing guns. Most of them determined to be as loud as they could. A few drew the line with the masks. But the bravest among them had camo black grease that they used to paint their faces in their hunting, and camo wool face masks that they used for hunting disguise. One had some leftover Halloween stuff that he'd pass around, that is, till they could do better and learn about masks and make some from wood for next year's big scene. If they could only just find a single old one, to model theirs from.

Yes, but for now, they still had their own plans, and plenty of deer antlers to attach to their heads, and a few bulls' horns, plenty to provide all around. They could cavort about with deer antlers on head, acting like children, with a sanctioned excuse.

So this holiday season, big doings were afoot and anticipation was high. The bonfires burned hot and bright on this cold winter night, bright with stars, and the Solstice was passed. The demons of dark were pushed back toward their caves, the entrance to that bleak nether world.

But the struggle as yet was far from won. It would hotly go on, but on this night was a victory—most especially for one. For Chauncey, it was better than a dream.

There at the bonfire, several men suggested that on Second Christmas they all bring cowbells with their guns. "The more racket the better," they said. "If you're going to do it, you'd best do it right" was Jim-Jesse's word.

"Yes, the world does too many things half-assed enough," Lyman agreed. "Let's not add one more."

Cowbells, it would be then, because as Caleb had rightly said, that's what he'd heard tell that they used with the guns in days of old—cowbells and heavy chains.

"Hot dam," said a youngster, "This is better than Star Wars. Can I come?"

The bonds between the old and the young were forged stronger 'round the fire. The younguns behaved more like grownups and the grown turned again young.

Triggerfoot's friend, who'd travelled some, had been down to New Orleans for Mardi Gras. "I know it's the wrong season, Christmas and Epiphany, not Lent, but you know, that's what they do down there too. Masks and feasts and refreshments and visitings and parades. Joy and noise."

This conservative neighbourhood wasn't going in for that too raucous stuff, but, yes, they were Southern brothers and sisters under the skin.

The fellow continued, "Down there, they have all these clubs that put on the big show. Can't remember their names, but they make all the plans. Maybe this thing can catch on, and we'll do year after year. I'd sure like to be part."

Chauncey had one of those inspired moments and had a new name for this potential new crew. The Cowbellion de Rakin Society, he proclaimed with a smile. They'd carry their cowbells and pitchforks and hay rakes and hoes, with their old blunderbuss blackpowder rifles and guns, when they went house to home in their raucous masquerade. They'd serenade and put on a quick play, of the masked grumpy, tight-lipped old dark man beaten out by a red, round-cheeked shining new babe. They'd get the burliest strapping big fellow to strip down as much as was seemly to play part of the child.

Chauncey could even envision the homemade masks they all would wear. And they would chant,

> *Up rakes. Down tools.*
> *Don't be thinking we are fools.*
> *We're just lads from out the farm,*
> *Bringing luck, and scaring off harm.*

Chauncey said to the men: "The Cowbellion de Rakin Society, then, it is!"

"The Cowbellion de Rakin Society, huzza! The name of the Club of the Bonfire, it most surely will be," echoed all the men with hearty voices 'round the fire. And they lifted their glasses, jars, and jugs in a toast, after which Kildee's youngest led them in three spirited huzzas. For indeed, the neighbourhood around Kildee's store had their churches, but luckily no Masons, no Kiwanis, Rotary, or Optimists Club. This would be their own, of their own making, from their own traditions and soil, and no franchised chain of them, no other like it besides.

So the struggle against the powers of darkness in earnest would be waged. They'd fire off their double-charged blackpowder muzzle-loading guns, clang cowbells, clank chains, and holler and shout, to drive all the demons away. They'd rouse up the kennels, frighten the babies, and wake up the old grandmas dozing by fire. The young bucks would seek out their does. The old stags would wink at their wives and approve.

As they left each house, Chauncey would proclaim with great gusto and resolve: Glory to God in the highest and peace to all people on earth!

Then suddenly, with a start at the chime of his clock striking six in the morn, Chauncey woke up from his dream. It jerked him back to the reality around him like with a cold chain. A dream—it had seemed so real. Maybe, like Marley's famous ghost, it was a bit of undigested beef or, more like, all that rich yellow-based barbeque sauce and pork he'd eaten at Lula Bess and Kildee's last night. He reluctantly roused himself from under his quilts and put the grits and bacon on, and fried him an egg.

As in the dream, it was indeed cold December, and he knew the dark and light struggle was as real as it had been in his dream. Maybe he should and would work on just such a plan. He'd think on the scheme to have it full in its place for the very next year, if the Lord allowed him one.

He said grace over his breakfast alone. The Solstice was here, December 21st; but Lucia, bringer of light to the blind, though her time was past by a week, still sat by his side. The day was overcast and a fog had already set in. If he'd had just one such bonfire to light late this evening, he most certainly would, even if he'd do it alone.

Demons forced back to their caves, he'd light up that fire.

"I'll just talk this thing over with Kildee tomorrow at the store," he mused, "and we'll do this thing next year for sure. Till then for a bonfire, we've got Kildee's stove. But that stove's not enough to keep all them powerful forces at bay. Next year, we'll give it some help, with cowbells and guns, with masks, pitchforks, and the clanking of chains."

Chauncey thought to himself that he should have known this thing would come to him from across the line, ever since he'd noticed the feast day on December thirteen. Yesterday afternoon, when he was bringing in the hay, he saw wrens in the bramble. They held him with their chatter, as if talking to him. He remembered the legend that it was the wren that flew highest of birds because it rode on the back of an eagle on high. He'd thought to himself,

"How's that ancient old song about the wren go, after all? The one about the wren, the wren, the king of all birds, on St. Stephen's Day, got caught in the furze."

Come out from the muddle of musing now, Chauncey broke out aloud: "This wren's going to beat out the eagle, or I'll dam sure do all I can to help it to try. It's a most knowledgeable bird, wiser than owl. The eagle's a great swaggering, fierce imperial bird, all flutter, fuss, bluster, and beak."

As the echoes of his slow drawl hit the corners of his high-ceilinged kitchen, they reverberated like giant blunderbuss, muzzle-loading Christmas guns of old, celebrating light and life, their sounds spilling down fruitful and peaceful hills, in a land at peace with itself and all men.

> *Oh, the wren, oh, the wren,*
> *He's the king of all birds,*
> *But on St. Stephen's Day,*
> *He got caught in the furze;*
> *So it's up with the kettle,*
> *And it's down with the pan.*
> *Won't you give us a penny*
> *To bury the wren?*

That's the way the song went. Chauncey hummed it, as he put on his duckboots and hunting jacket and called to the hound waiting patiently at his door. Bossy to milk and chores to be done, and a war to be waged with the demons about. How could any be bored in such a world? Forces were duking it out, and high drama worked all around, like the bubbles in the kegs of sauerkraut he had set in the pantry in their great earthen crocks, a plate topped by a flat river rock to keep the kraut down, or the deep frothing on the big crocks of scuppernong mash, slowly bubbling their way into wine.

Busy all day and in high spirits, by that evening he'd piled up a head-high mound of old cedar branches and limbs. As in his dream, they had fallen during an ice storm earlier that month. Another pile of old brush that had been there since last summer, he was just about to light. A couple of wrens, however, played in and out of it, so he left it alone. No doubt they sought cover there and maybe had even built a nest.

But he lit up the newly gathered pile just at dark, and had him a giant flame with spikes of high dancing sparks, which he attended, celebrating the Solstice alone, but for the silent company of those gone before. Next year, if God willed it, he'd see that there'd be many neighbours with him besides, shoulder to shoulder, in silhouette against sparks, just as he'd seen in his dream. While he stood at his fire, the pair of wrens, quit of their scolding and chatter, nested peacefully in the warmth and shelter of the old brush pile beside, and Chauncey could see the pinpoints of orange firelight reflected deep in their eyes.

XXVI

A Mid-Winter's Tale

The sleet fell in peppering waves on the old store's tin roof. With every gust of storm, the overalled men at the potbellied stove drew a bit closer to the fire, their thumbs in their galluses. Kildee had stoked her full and had a bigger than usual supply of stovewood stacked neatly under the lean-to shed at the back door, out of the ice.

It was just after New Year's. Some sprigs of dried holly that Kildee and his granddaughters had cut from his woods still lay about prickly on the store shelves. Kildee wore a bright new flannel shirt that one of his daughters had given him for Christmas. Others who came in evidenced similar gifts from their families. The women had gone back to their washing again, for as the old custom would have it, to hang clothes on the line during New Year's would be washing someone out of the family—a sure sign of a death to come. But the clothes in this cold now froze on the line and dried through their ice.

Chauncey had delivered his usual collards and messes of turnip greens to half the community around in time for

271

their traditional New Year's Day meal. It had been a good growing year. The cold had made the neatly folded heads of the collards firm, crunchy, and almost white. The holidays were through. Folks had stopped their Christmas visiting around; and it was into that lag hollow time of the year that this big ice storm fell. The neighbourhood was now more than ever Kildee's hotbed of tranquility, and he liked it that way. Things were moving slow, with fewer chores on the farm, a time mainly of remembering the last year, the late holidays, and old times and friends and especially those like Joe-Blair Graham, who had passed from the scene; and now there wasn't much else to fill up the time but talk of the cold.

In truth, the weather was something to talk about. Back several days ago, Kildee had predicted it. He noticed how the smoke from chimneys was drifting to ground. This "fallin' weather," as he called it, predicted snow or ice storm. Yesterday he had said, "It's fixin' to storm." And storm it did. Old Caleb, whose memory was the longest in the neighbourhood, vowed this was the coldest weather he'd ever seen, or at least the coldest sustained for this length of time. "Never in my borned days," he declared, "have I seen water in the cattle troughs stay froze solid so long. It's cold enough to freeze the stink off of manure."

Chauncey replied that he'd heard tell that it was so cold in New York that Bill and Hillary Clinton had to sleep in the same bed.

"That *is* some kind of cold," Kildee declared.

It hadn't gotten above freezing during the daytime

now for over a week. The lows had stayed in the teens or lower at night now for more than ten days. The great deep river just behind the store flowed under the skim of thin ice at its edge. There indeed was frost on the rabbit's foot and the rose bush was reduced to a thorn. These were tough times for bobcats and foxes and the creatures of woods. If you encountered them closer to the dwellings of men, drawn there by want, they had a woebegone look, something wild and defeated, proud and stoic, at the same time.

But around the glowing stove sat Caleb and Lyman, our Chauncey, and when he wasn't moving back and forth to the counter or to the stack of wood at the door, our Kildee. Caleb and Lyman, who both had long memories and liked to use them, called up winters and cold snaps that stood out for them. Caleb's octogenarian experience corroborated with definitiveness Lyman's septuagenarian tales. They had some good "believe it or not" occurrences to share from lives lived in the same community among the same folks, during the same winters, close to the sleet and the cold.

Their stories and stray bits of wisdom were not lost on the rest. Other folks, like a moveable feast, came and went through the day. One hunter, who'd been on his deer stand since before dawn, hurried in so cold that when he came up to the stove, instead of putting his hands out straight, he held his arms 'round the stove, looking for all the world like he was about to embrace it, give it a big bear hug. This occasioned a few chuckles from the lads. The fellow, whose name was Spurgeon Adams, was a regular at the store, but never took much time to sit. He always seemed to be going somewhere, or getting ready to go. But even then, he took time to be sociable, in his frank, friendly way. Today, he seemed a bit out of sorts. Kildee could tell straight away, but didn't intrude. Spurgeon, however, soon matter of fact-ly gave reasons why.

"Seems it's not going to be much of a good New Year for me," he began. "I've just had to get my youngest son out of jail. He's been raising hell generally in Clay Bank again. Too much New Year's fun. I've got three grown sons. My first wanted to be a doctor, and he failed. The next wanted to be a lawyer, and he failed. My youngest wanted to be a son of a bitch, and damned if he ain't succeeding right well."

The lads took it all in stride and hoped young Spurgeon Jr. would soon straighten out. It often happened that way. It might just be a matter of wild oats to sow, but he had being sowing them now later in the season than was mete.

Then as quick as he came, Spurgeon Sr. was gone from the scene. He had a deer to gut and dress.

For those who drifted in, Kildee as usual would invite them to light. Most of them joined in—whether standing or lighting—at least for awhile, added their take on the weather, what they'd heard told, listened awhile, maybe told an anecdote or two, paid their respects, then bowed out, saying their goodbyes around, and went on their way. "Bowed" was a mite fancy, but essentially the right word, for there was a gracious, mannerly method in which to do that too, and most of them knew the courteous way. Spurgeon was the exception to that rule, but the men thought nothing of it, for they knew that was his way.

Coming and going, sojourning, it was generally a congenial crew. Most came in stamping their shoes on the old wood floor, bluff, hearty, and spirited. They shook off the sleet from their heaviest coats, knocked off ice from ball caps, and scarves, and stetsons, then warmed their backs and hands at the stove. Kildee's "Light a spell" was like a chorus throughout the day, not that he'd have to invite. All knew they were welcome at the potbellied stove.

Chauncey noted that during the whole day, only one umbrella was to be seen. And that belonged to young Sissie Lyles, who'd come in her car on her way to work in Clay Bank to drop off her great-grandpa Caleb, and covered him with it as she walked him into the store. Caleb, she knew, would spend all the day there, would have company and good entertainment besides. She brought in his dinner pail, and a bag of cold, crisp apples for all the lads. She'd pick him up after she got off of work at five.

"'Minds me of the time," was the commonest expression about the stove. Chauncey noticed this too. If it was said once, it was said a hundred times. "Yes, kindly 'minds me of the time the river froze." "Yes, 'minds me of the time it snowed fourteen inches in a day."

"Kindly 'minds me of the time my daddy had to break a foot of ice in the pond to let the cows drink," Caleb said.

And that 'minded Lyman of walking on that same ice that year and falling "arse over elbow, arse over teacup" into that same pond when a lad. "If my brother Sammy-Lee hadn't been there with the rope he was using to lead old Sukey to barn, I don't reckon I'd have something to set in this chair rocker with today."

"So, you mean Sammy-Lee saved your sorry butt," old Caleb replied. "And I hear tell Sammy-Lee did that more than once." No one else could or would have said that to Lyman, not Kildee, not Chauncey; but our Caleb through age could just pull rank and say truth as he pleased.

Caleb was often declaring that age, for all its bodily infirmities, had certain advantages. Yes, you could say just about anything you wanted and get away with it. No matter how cantankerous, or outrageous, the world would just pass it off with "That's just old Mr. Caleb, old as Methuselah, cranky and set in his ways."

Caleb continued, "Just a few weeks ago, I overheard a woman at church, on the very church grounds, call me an old fart. You know, they think 'cause I'm old and often don't answer, or ignore them, that I'm stone deaf. Wouldn't it surprise them to know what all I hear. I don't miss much."

"Why did she call you that, Mr. Caleb?" Chauncey inquired, for he figured the answer would be choice or might even lead to a tale.

"Seems I'd grumbled some comment loud enough to hear, about the church council's taking up whether we ought to bring our annual August homecoming dinner-on-the-grounds inside. 'Flies and heat. Flies and heat,' a council member whined. Now, I ask, what in Sam Hill would dinner-on-the-grounds be called if they held it scrooched up in that little air-conditioned pigeon hole of a parish hall room? Dinner in a jail cell? I've seen thieves and criminals with more free space than that. And with all of the food our folks bring? Where'd they put it, I'd like to know. You couldn't get all the cakes and pies alone in that room. Next thing you know, they'll be cutting back on the food and calling it lunch. What's wrong with sawbucks and boards spread over with bright cotton cloths out under the big old oaks in the yard? Why nothing, of course, but these young folks nowadays are afraid if they sweat, they will die. Next thing you know, they'll be wanting the food catered in."

"Little slices of quiches, most likely, and melon balls on a toothpick," Chauncey agreed. They both knew that scene, and avoided it whenever they could.

Caleb confessed he had to brag a little on his grand-daughters and daughters-in-law. He heard them talk and they usually held to the old honest ways. One of his grand-daughters had laughed about the woman who'd spoken ugly of Caleb on the church grounds.

"Well y'all know Mrs. Swift," she declared. "This year she tried to get the ladies altar guild to electrify the candles in the Advent wreath. Too much trouble to light candles and clean up wax behind. We didn't say no, but just didn't do it." So not all the young liked this modern way.

Caleb's "young" was, of course, relative. He'd have con-sidered Chauncey and Kildee young too.

"Speaking of lazy, old or young, kindly 'minds me of Big Biscuit Jeter," Kildee contributed, "who said the reason he didn't work was that his Doc had said if he sweated, he'd die. Maybe a lot of folks these days have been to that same old medicine man. Bet you'd have to stand in a line all day to get to see *him*."

"It does get a mite hot for August homecoming," Lyman ventured carefully, for the sake of a mild needling to create some little tension there at the stove. As Lyman well knew, it didn't take a whole lot sometimes to set Caleb off, and it didn't take long.

"Not as hot as the perdition most of this sorry world's headed to," was Caleb's definitive answer; and all there at the stove let that one go.

Truth is, they all agreed with Caleb on that account, both of dinner and the softness of the comfort-seeking "young." Dinner on the grounds was an institution around these parts, older and much more important than Kildee's store. What was a fly or the heat next to that?

A winter gust brought them from August back to January, and the lull which followed was an opportune time for Chauncey to bring up his ideas for a rekindling of the old holiday customs, planning for the next year to come. Lyman contributed some more memories of the season passed down to him, which Chauncey knew he could use in his plans. They were like gold coins of buried treasure that moles had scattered down their runnels and now reclaimed by the buryer one by one.

Caleb and Lyman—in fact, all round the stove— thought such a Christmas and New Year's rekindling would be good. "Why sure, we'll just have to do it!" Kildee's son declared. His ballcap and back covered with sleet, he'd come in to the store from the pasture, in time to hear all Chauncey had said. His voice had a surprising degree of enthusiasm that caused his father to glance up at him. He was a tall, strongly built lad, sober and slow moving, and was not accustomed to show eagerness, even if eager he was. So they all pledged Chauncey their help. Lyman too, as he said, "If spared by my Maker above." Lyman continued, "Another good enough reason to stay alive for another sweet year. I'd like to see all these doings 'fore I go, and I'd like to help what little I could."

"Mr. Lyman, you've helped us already," Chauncey replied, "by just being here and remembering what of the old ways you've heard tell."

Then Chauncey let all of this rest. He knew how to do with his folks. Not be too eager. Not give them too much to chew on at one time. They eased into things. He'd planted the seed, now covered it with soil, and he'd wait for the warming spring sun.

About the time that this little wave of the day-long river of conversation ended, the old wooden store building shook on its timbers from another gust of the storm. It was like a white-sailed galleon tossed at sea, or some great Noah's Ark. Ice pellets fell clattering down the stovepipe and caused a crackle and spew. The sky was dark as lead outside and it made the inside murkier than usual. The buckets and pails and baskets hanging from nails on the rafters cast shadows and loomed above them like ghosts. The hundred-watt bulb that hung naked on its cord from the store ceiling flickered a time or two, making the shadows dance on the wall.

"No doubt the storm'll soon put our electricity out. It usually does," Kildee predicted, but this time the light burned on, and the conversation turned to the honored guest at the stove, a man who'd sat quietly by in the shadows, listening intently, and not interrupting Caleb and Lyman with a word. He'd been there all day. He sat with Kildee's big black and white cat on his lap.

That guest was none other than Triggerfoot Tinsley himself, in the flesh, old legendary Trig from his farm on the edge of their county seat town. Everybody 'round the stove knew Triggerfoot or knew about him, having heard tell of the scrapes he'd been in, and was glad he'd come to weather out the storm with them.

Four days ago, Chauncey drove in to Clay Bank to Triggerfoot's farm. He and Kildee had been keeping up with the weather and they knew how drafty and cold Trig's old rundown, shackelty farmhouse could be. A fire in the fireplace, lots of quilts, yes, he could make do; but this would just be the greatest best excuse to get him to while away time with the lads.

Too, Chauncey had heard tell that over the holidays Triggerfoot had been traipsing about, sampling his corn whiskey more than he'd ought. And they wouldn't mind swapping some supplies for a gallon or two for themselves.

It was the best holiday cheer money couldn't buy.

So Chauncey drove his old pickup on his mission of mercy (manifold mercies, you might say). He found Triggerfoot draggly, but helped him feed and water Queen Beulah enough in her barn for a week, saw to the other live-stock, and brought him on back to the store. And Triggerfoot admitted he was kindly glad because he said the wind was blowing hard and cold enough to freeze whitecaps in his slop jar, and bite the bark from his trees.

Kildee, Chauncey, and Lyman took their turns taking Trig to their homes. Triggerfoot was an easy and unde-manding guest. He didn't ask for a thing and was no trou-ble at all, requiring of his hosts what he gave to his own visitor-guests in return. On him, it was told that he once showed an overnight visiting couple their room with "Thar's the bed. Here's the pot. If y'all need anything else, just say what it is and I'll teach you how to get along with-out." And the story was probably true. It fit simple old unassuming Triggerfoot to a T. Knowing him, you could never take that as ill-mannered or rude. He lived just that way himself and was being sincere.

Though he'd been sitting out of the limelight at the edge of the circle, Triggerfoot, as was his usual observant way, was taking all the scene in. Like Mr. Caleb, nothing got by him. He enjoyed being there by the fire in the ring.

When Chauncey had gone to get him those four days before, he'd just come off of a more serious than usual tear, one of his "high lonesomes" as folks around these parts called a big drinking spree. "For the last two days," he told Chauncey, "I been three-thirds drunk."

And as Chauncey knew, with a whiskey-proof gizzard like Triggerfoot's, it took a lot of corn liquor to get him that way, and, yes, this was another good reason to bring Trig into the company of friends. The winter and holidays were hard on some. So, in a sense, by the stove, Triggerfoot was drying himself out. But not teetotally so. At the right moments, he passed 'round the bright mason jar. As usual, it had been capped with a peach in it, to give it just that right taste and that welcome cheery color of red on a cold winter's day.

Next year, things would be different, Chauncey vowed, if his plans kicked into high gear, as he had no doubt they would. No need for anyone to be at the mercy of loneliness during the holidays.

One such jug-passing was perfect introduction for a tale, and Triggerfoot rose to the scene. "'Minds me of the time," he began.

It was a typical Triggerfoot vintage tale, two-hundred proof. The men laughed till one of them said he hurt, and more than one had to wipe tears from their eyes. One old fellow feared he'd wet his Depends.

Old Caleb and Lyman particularly enjoyed Triggerfoot. They both declared that never in their borned days had they heard such a tale as this one today. They gave it their highest praise. Even though younger, Triggerfoot's ideas seemed yet older than theirs—more like their own pas', as they said, and full of the truth. His take on the world made him seem older still than them.

At the end of Triggerfoot's story, the lights flickered again, but still did not go out. The fire popped, sputtered, then crackled and spewed. "Calling the snow," old Caleb said. As those around the stove knew, it was this sound that predicted snow coming on soon.

"Biscuit weather," old Lyman declared. "Mark my word. There's fixin' to be snow on the ground before this week is through."

Triggerfoot passed his mason jar, the sleet clattered and pelted; the stove, like their cheeks, glowed red. The hounds, asleep, lay at or on the men's feet. They stretched and yawned and took up their positions again, sometimes attentively eyeing Kildee's bevy of cats that had their own special little realms in which they furtively moved in the store. Folks came and went; it darkened further outside, sleet peppered heavier, lights flickered again, the wind spoke in the gutters—the voices of all those gone before in this little place—and the gallused men at the stove were at peace with themselves, each other, and, at least for a time, with the great hurrying, feverishly getting-and-spending world outside their own.

In that other realm, even windshield farmers, as Triggerfoot called them, were becoming fewer and further between. No kind of farming nowadays was much getting done. Seems the world was trying to get shed of their kind.

"When the food stops appearing in supermarket bins, people are fixin' to know," Kildee declared. "They won't care till then; but that day they will know, and remember it well." He'd often said that folks nowadays thought that instead of from the earth, vegetables came from tin cans and the store, and meat from neat little shrink-wrapped packages instead of hogs and steers.

"As long as I got Beulah to plough, we won't go hungry 'round here," Triggerfoot gave his promise that all there assembled knew was sincere. He didn't need windshield or gasoline to plough. As for seed, like Chauncey, he saved them from each year to year, the tried and true best for this climate and place. If all the world went to the bad, he'd not jog-trot blindly along.

"And I've a roof for us all," Kildee joined in, as he returned to the stove from the counter, "as long as the tin decides it still wants to be tin, and no more precious metal besides in somebody's bank."

In truth, a realtor from the city had just approached him before Christmas speculating to buy up tracts of land. Chauncey had seen his car with the realty ad on its door, and the news had already gotten around the neighbourhood. But Kildee turned down his several offers, courteous yet firm. So, God willing, the tin, as long as he lived at least, would stay tin and not turn into silver for a "bedroom community" of Deer Fields, Red Fox Run Acres, or Plantation Estates.

"And I've wood for the stove as long as trees grow," Kildee further affirmed, as he minded the blaze and put another piece of stovewood in the stove. The resounding clank of the heavy stove door made an exclamation point and gave dramatic finality to his words.

Kildee paused, then declared, "Food, shelter, and a fire in the cold. Any much more might be tempting our Lord."

All this was a genuine comfort to Chauncey, who better than most 'round the stove was witness to the extreme precipice that the feverish world had edged up to. It seemed to him that the slightest push of a finger could just send it plummeting over. Like meat not properly cured, yes, the world had gone to the bad. What spoilage and waste, what a shame, a matter for tears.

It was getting on in the day. In a short while, there would come, like a lace curtain drawn at a window, that transient moment of dusk that the old people called early candle-lighting time.

In the store's dark corner sat Joe-Blair Graham's empty stool, with the King Edward cigar box and his shards of glass. Triggerfoot passed his mason jar one last time for the day, and they drank to the memory of Joe-Blair. The jar sparkled in the light of the naked bulb, as Chauncey took him a good sip. Then quiet fell on them like a blessing. The calm let their memories reign, their recollections hold sway.

Now with this fellowship of the known and loved world around him like a warm old quilt, Chauncey felt doubly at peace. He thought to himself, "Food, shelter, and warmth, and friends, family, and neighbours besides."

He breathed a deep sigh, exhaling the breath that emptied out all the stale air and tensions inside; and, with half consciousness of comings and goings, jovial greetings and hearty good-byes, and thoughts of plans for another year, in the full solace of the corn and wood's heat, he fell partly to doze, while the sleet kept on pelting outside.

Envoi

CHAUNCEY'S SPRING SONG
FOR AN OLD HOUSE

My candle burns beneath its crystal bell.
It makes the shadows dance
And flower white
Against a darkened wall:
Silverbell and serviceberry blossoms,
Sprays and drifts.

CHAUNCEY'S EVENSONG

Old Master's got a lantern burning
As the glow dies in the west,
And the sound of frogs chir-RO-ping
Tells of the coming spring.
My footsteps echo on the creek's old bridge
Coming home. Coming home.
The gaited rhythm of my stride,
Coming home.

Notes

In "Our Green Island Home," the core narrative about the great flood of 1863, with a few genealogical changes, comes from an unpublished letter by Lula Bess Henderson Whitney to her kinsman Caldwell Sims, dated August 1939, and provided by Ronnie Abrams, himself a descendant.

"The Road" owes its inspiration to a short essay by Louise Huscusson Stewart of Robbinsville, North Carolina.

In "When Shall the Swan," Triggerfoot adapts an ancient Celtic folktale, about the struggle for Irish independence, to his own cause and purposes. The First Scots Presbyterian Church of Charleston, South Carolina, is the source for the bell story. Its twin towers have been silent since its bells were given to the Confederate cause in the war for Southern independence. See Thomas Moore for the Irish treatment.

In "September Gale," the outline of the flat-boating tale comes from an interview by Caldwell Sims with

Richard (nicknamed "Dick Look-Up") Jones of the Jim Gilliam Plantation, Union County, South Carolina, on August 9, 1937.

The image of the university as a trough in "United We Stand" comes from Flannery O'Connor in her letter to Betty Boyd, in which she describes her college years as having her "noodle" filled with "Lord knows what at the Columbia trough." (p. 884)

In "Chauncey's Christmas Dream," an actual Cowbellion de Rakin Society was founded in Mobile, Alabama, in 1830, its purpose being to celebrate the holiday season with masked processionals with cowbells and hoes, rakes, and chains—on New Year's Day, ending with calling on lady friends and being served cakes and wine. This tradition developed into an exclusive social society with the years.

The actual traditions of shooting guns to bring in Christmas and the noisy two weeks of visits of masked revelers that accompanied the holiday in early nineteenth-century South Carolina, took place in the actual setting of this novel, and can be found described in my *A Carolina Dutch Fork Calendar* (1988), pp. 37-45. These customs came from Germany's Swarzwald with the early settlers to Lexington and Newberry County, South Carolina.

Lucia is a fourth-century Italian saint. Her feast day is particularly festive in Sweden, where her wreath contains seven lit candles, worn on the head of a maiden dressed in white, a kind of anima figure, to be sure.